MURDER À LA MODE

BOOK 16 OF THE MAGGIE NEWBERRY MYSTERIES

SUSAN KIERNAN-LEWIS

SAN MARCO PRESS

Parlez-Vous Murder?
Crime and Croissants
Accent on Murder
A Bad Éclair Day
Croak, Monsieur!
Death du Jour
Murder Très Gauche
Wined and Died
A French Country Christmas

The Irish End Games
Free Falling
Going Gone
Heading Home
Blind Sided
Rising Tides
Cold Comfort
Never Never
Wit's End
Dead On
White Out
Black Out
End Game

The Mia Kazmaroff Mysteries
Reckless
Shameless
Breathless
Heartless
Clueless
Ruthless

Ella Out of Time

Swept Away
Carried Away
Stolen Away

The French Women's Diet

1

Everybody knows smoking can kill you.

Maggie squinted through the French doors to the terrace where her best friend Grace stood with the glowing tip of her cigarette visible in the darkness. Maggie let out a huff of annoyance and slipped on her channel-quilted jacket and stepped outside. Instantly the cold January weather sliced through her and she shivered.

Not only will smoking kill you, she thought peevishly as she hurried over to Grace, *but it will freeze off all your important bits in the process.*

Grace huddled in a long black cashmere coat, a curl of cigarette smoke lazily looping over her head. Even in the dark, even with a cigarette held to her lips, Grace was stunningly beautiful. The absolute image of her namesake Grace Kelly, she fit the role perfectly in manner and style.

"Don't you worry about sending a bad message to Zouzou?" Maggie asked as she leaned against the stone wall of the *potager* next to Grace. "You told me you'd quit."

Grace exhaled a smoke ring and turned to Maggie.

"Everything in time, darling," she said. "Besides, Zouzou's seen me do much worse than this."

"Well, that's not much of an argument," Maggie said, rubbing her arms through her jacket. "What did you want to tell me? It's freezing out here."

Grace tossed down her cigarette and ground it out with the toe of her Jimmy Choo boot. Then she picked up the butt.

Maggie was tempted to tell her not to bother. Her husband Laurent also smoked, and although she had recently ramped up her efforts to nag him into quitting, the evidence of his bad habit was littered throughout the garden.

Grace tucked the cigarette butt into her coat pocket and looped her arm through Maggie's.

"Walk with me," she said. "I don't want Cheryl to be tempted to join us."

Cheryl Barker was an old college friend of Grace's who was staying at Grace's bed and breakfast. Maggie and Laurent were hosting a dinner for the contestants of the upcoming *patisserie* competition in which Cheryl was one of the contestants.

"Oh?" Maggie said mildly. "Keeping secrets from your old college chum?"

"Don't be jealous, darling. We weren't even that close in college. When's dinner?"

Maggie pushed back the sleeve of her jacket to look at her watch. "We've got thirty minutes. But Laurent will want me inside mingling with people before then."

Laurent happily handled all culinary chores for their family, especially any and all formal dinner parties like tonight's, so much so that Maggie had been surprised when he hired the village baker and his wife to help with tonight's dinner. Maggie was sure it had more to do with Laurent helping out the baker Antoine that Laurent actually needed any help.

Six months ago Cheryl Barker had contacted Grace about a pastry competition that a professional contact of hers was putting together in order to launch his new culinary lifestyle magazine. Grace had suggested that the somewhat remote but extremely picturesque village of Saint-Buvard where both she and Maggie lived would be the perfect venue. After much research it was finally decided to have the competition in nearby Aix-en-Provence, but the contestants would stay in Saint-Buvard, divided between *Dormir*, Grace's *gîte*, and Domaine Saint-Buvard, Maggie and Laurent's large country house.

The three other contestants besides Cheryl, were Marie-France Babin of *Le Coucou Paris*, Geoff Fitzgerald from London, and Helga Richter from *La Pomme* in Bonn.

Cheryl had driven to Domaine Saint-Buvard with Grace, Grace's fifteen-year-old daughter Zouzou, and Danielle Alexandre, who lived with Grace and helped her run the bed and breakfast.

Grace's small grandson Philippe had been shipped off to Atlanta to visit his grandfather, Grace's ex-husband Windsor, for two weeks. If not for that, Maggie knew Grace could not have managed any of this. Philippe was a dear little boy but at five he was also rambunctious and full of mischief.

The German pastry chef Helga Richter had arrived at Domaine Saint-Buvard earlier in the day, then claimed exhaustion and retired to her room. Maggie still hadn't seen her emerge.

Marie-France, along with Geoff and his wife, Debbie, were expected any moment. They were staying at *Dormir*.

"Okay," Maggie said. "What's up?"

"You're not going to believe this."

"Not until you tell me."

"Cheryl seems to think I live a charmed life."

"Why is that a problem?"

"She told Zouzou if she really wanted to go to *l'Academie de Patisserie* she's welcome to come to Paris and stay with her."

L'Academie de Patisserie was the premier *patisserie* school in Paris and the place Zouzou had her heart set on attending when she graduated from school in three years.

"Did she run this by you first?" Maggie asked.

Grace made a face. "She doesn't have kids of her own."

"I don't think that's much of an excuse. She honestly didn't think to ask you?"

"I think it's because Z looks so mature, you know? She looks more like nineteen than fifteen."

"What did Zouzou say?"

"What do you think she said? She's over the moon. So I get to play the bad guy *again*, if I pull the plug on this."

"*If*? You're not seriously thinking of letting her go to Paris, are you?"

"No, I didn't mean *if*. I have to say no. I know I do. But she's been on cloud nine all week."

"This so-called friend of yours has put you in a bad spot."

"It's not her fault."

Maggie could see Laurent through the French doors standing in the dining room, his hands on his hips. He was a big man and six foot four, unusual for a Frenchman. He stood now in his kitchen facing away from the garden. Maggie knew he would be directing four children, their own three plus Zouzou, to help create tonight's meal—from setting the table to passing the *aperitifs* and *hors d'oevres*.

A tall gawky woman appeared beside Laurent and Maggie watched as he directed their adopted son Luc to pour her a glass of wine.

"I need to go inside," Maggie said. "I think the German pastry chef is finally awake."

Grace turned to look inside the house. "What is she like?"

"I have no idea. Abrupt. Curt. German."

"Are you sorry I got you into this?"

Maggie turned to her friend and smiled.

"No, it's fun. I'm just surprised at how much Laurent has gotten into it."

"Zouzou has been delirious with excitement for weeks," Grace said, as she tried to pick her daughter out among the group of people moving about the dining room.

"I think the other guests have arrived," Maggie said. "I need to go in and do the hostess thing."

"Zouzou tells me Luc is looking at schools in the States," Grace said.

Maggie stopped. "Is that all she said he said?"

Luc would graduate from high school in four months. Maggie had been working with him to send out college applications and had been surprised and dismayed to see his interest in going to school abroad.

"Well, that and all the excitement over his Napa internship. Well done, Luc," Grace said. "I imagine Laurent is very proud?"

"I suppose," Maggie said, biting her lip.

"Darling, an internship at one of the most prestigious vineyards in Napa doesn't automatically mean he'll want to go to school out there."

"It won't help," Maggie said.

"Have you mentioned to him how you feel?"

"Would that be fair? I don't want to hold him back. I just don't want him to leave."

Grace laughed and stood up. "They all leave, darling, didn't you know?"

"I'm not sure I did," Maggie said as the two turned and made their way back to the house.

2

L aurent stood in the doorway to his kitchen and counted the trays of *gougères*—crackers with *tapenade* and miniature tomato tarts.

His kitchen was painted a pale ochre yellow. The floors were terra cotta that matched the kitchen backsplash. The kitchen was Laurent's space and it was designed for utilitarian use. The look was clean, airy, and masculine.

The window over the sink faced the front drive and—when it wasn't in the middle of January or when the dreaded *mistral* wasn't tormenting the front topiary—tended to bring in a ray of Mediterranean sunlight to infuse the kitchen.

He turned to Luc who was leaning against one of the kitchen walls and craning his neck to watch the guests in the dining room.

"Take the tarts out," Laurent said to him before looking over at Zouzou who stood ready with the platter of *gougères*.

"Follow Luc," he said to her. "If they take a *gougère*, hand them a cocktail napkin. *Comprends-tu?*"

She nodded, her face serious. Both Luc and Zouzou were

passionate about the business of French food and wine—making it, cooking it, serving it. As far as they were concerned, dinner parties like tonight were a glittering manifestation of all the good things they worked toward to make and present exemplary French food.

One day Luc would be a *vigneron* and follow in Laurent's footsteps, going even further with the family vineyard than Laurent had done. Zouzou would take her passion for pastries and baking and find a position somewhere in a hotel or restaurant that allowed her to bake to her heart's content.

Laurent glanced at his son Jemmy and daughter Mila. Those two were a bit more of a conundrum. At thirteen Jemmy had shown only a mild interest in the vineyard, certainly not to the extent he'd need were he to make a career of it. And Mila—his dreamy and quixotic daughter—had shown no real interest in anything yet.

"What shall I do, Papa?" Mila asked him now.

He bit his lip to refrain from saying *just look beautiful*. He'd never believed that women were only good for decoration or just to please the eye. But his feelings for his daughter were so protective—a feeling he'd never experienced to this degree—that a part of him wanted to wall her up in a tower and keep her safe and untouched from life and, of course, men.

"Can you mingle and see that everyone has what they need?" he said with a smile.

"*Oui, Papa*," Mila said and hopped off the barstool. She followed Luc and Zouzou into the dining room.

Laurent glanced out the kitchen window to see Jemmy directing the parking of another guest. Like the other cars, it was a rental from Aix, which he could see from the plates. He watched a tall man unfold his legs out of the car and pat his jacket as though thinking he should tip Jemmy. Laurent snorted.

An American or a Brit.

The man settled for patting Jemmy on the head before making his way to the front door.

Since Laurent knew that two other contestants—Marie-France and Cheryl Barker—were currently in his living room drinking the wine harvested from grapes from his fields and eating *gougères*, and the other contestant was half of a couple, he assumed that this new arrival was the competition organizer Bertrand Glenn, the one sponsoring the *patisserie* contest.

Laurent's past had been one largely lived in the shadows. Being able to size up someone on the fly had been essential to his livelihood—not to mention his survival. Even now, years later, his instincts rarely failed him.

"Everything on schedule?" Maggie said breathlessly as she appeared in the doorway.

He watched her scan the kitchen counters, her cheeks flushed from the cold outside, her eyes bright. Even after thirteen years of marriage, her beauty and vivaciousness still surprised and enchanted him. He smiled.

"*Bien sûr,*" he said.

She reached over to take a quick sip from his glass of Campari and soda on the counter before turning to go back to mingling with their guests.

The man Laurent guessed to be Bertrand Glenn appeared from around the corner of the foyer, his coat still on. He locked eyes with Laurent and Laurent felt a sudden chill in spite of the man's large and somewhat rubbery smile.

"Welcome," Laurent said, looking past him to see Jemmy ready to take his coat.

"Quite a place you have here," Bertrand said, wriggling out of his coat and extending a hand to shake hands with Laurent.

Laurent was never sure what to say when people said that. It was only the truth but it always seemed like they expected him to thank them for noticing.

Bertrand turned to make his way into the living room, effectively ending any further need to continue conversing with Laurent.

Which was just fine with Laurent.

3

For such a small dinner party, things looked pretty chaotic. That's what Maggie was thinking as she surveyed their guests, all of whom had congregated in the living room over drinks and nibbles. Luc, Zouzou and Mila moved among them like ghosts, collecting wadded up napkins, brushing crumbs into catchers and refreshing drinks.

When she and Grace came in from outside, Grace went straight to her friend Cheryl, a long-legged California blonde in her early forties.

Danielle, a beloved family friend and Grace's business partner, sat at one end of the couch in the living room talking with Helga Richter and a petite dark-haired woman who Maggie guessed was Marie-France Babin.

"Maggie," Grace said, "I want to formally introduce my college gal pal, Cheryl Barker. Cheryl, this is the famous Maggie Newberry Dernier."

"Oh, my God," Cheryl said dramatically holding her hand out to Maggie. "I have heard so much about you!"

Maggie shook her hand but before she could say anything,

Cheryl jumped up, nearly knocking over her drink on the coffee table and rushed past her.

"Bertrand! You're here!" she squealed as she embraced the tall man.

Maggie smiled and held out her hand to Bertrand who took it eagerly.

"Mister Glenn," she said. "Welcome."

"Mrs. Dernier," he said, his eyes disappearing into crinkles of mirth as he smiled. "Thank you so much for having us all. This is so generous of you."

"Please call me Maggie. Come sit down. Luc?"

Luc was at her side with a tray of wine glasses.

Maggie took a filled wine glass and then turned to Marie-France on the sofa.

"I'm sorry I wasn't here when you came," Maggie said. "I'm delighted to meet you, Madame Babin."

"This is a wonderful old *mas*," Marie-France said looking around the living room.

The downstairs of Domaine Saint-Buvard was four very large rooms plus the kitchen. The living room was forty feet square and anchored by a massive fireplace on one wall, with French doors on the adjacent wall that led to the garden.

A worn but regal Oriental rug stretched from the kitchen to the French doors. Over the years Maggie and Grace had scoured nearby *brocantes* and flea markets to find the four heavy chairs in damask and cotton fabrics of blue, rose and ochre beside the large couch that faced the fireplace.

The chair pillows, which Maggie had found in Lyons, were braided and fringed with colorful tassels. Every side table and the massive walnut coffee table held at least one vase of roses, petunias or peonies from the Aix flower market.

"The *mas* was in my husband's family," Maggie said to Marie-France. "We believe it's well over two hundred years old.

"Americans always think that's old," Helga scoffed from where she sat next to Danielle.

Maggie turned to her. "That's true," she said. "We are a young country."

Something about the way she said it must have stung Helga because the woman curled her lip but buried the sneer in her drink.

"Please, sit down," Maggie said to Bertrand. "I'm sure dinner won't be long." She turned back to Marie-France. "I thought you came with Mr. and Mrs. Fitzgerald?"

"I did," Marie-France said. "Your charming daughter is giving them a tour of the house."

"I'm here, Mom," Mila said as she entered the room with a barrel-chested man and a mousey looking woman with light brown hair. "They wanted to see the house."

"So American," Helga said.

What the hell is her deal?

Maggie forced herself not to react to her. After fourteen years living as an expat in France she had run across anti-American sentiment before. It wasn't pleasant but it was never personal.

"You have a beautiful home," Debbie Fitzgerald said, glancing at Maggie and then down at her hands.

"Thank you," Maggie said. "You must be Mrs. Fitzgerald. Won't you come sit and have a drink?"

"Debbie, please," the woman said and shook Maggie's hand. Debbie's hand was damp.

"And I'm Geoff," the man beside her said. "No need to stand on ceremony. What did this place set you back? If you don't mind my asking?"

"Geoff!" his wife said in horror.

"What? It's a perfectly civilized question."

"We inherited it," Maggie said smoothly. "Can I get you a drink?"

. . .

By the time Jemmy came into the living room to announce that dinner was ready, it was well past eight o'clock and Bertrand was already drunk.

Maggie always worried when a guest became inebriated with children around. She wondered if Laurent would mind if she sent the children upstairs. Zouzou could bunk in for the night with Mila.

Even Cheryl looked like she should have held back on the last couple of cocktails. When she stood up from the couch, she wobbled and made a quick grab for Luc as he was collecting empty wine glasses.

"Oh, darling," she gushed, not releasing him once she was steady on her feet, "you must work out or something. Are you sure you're only eighteen?"

Luc blushed and glanced at Maggie who smiled woodenly at her guest. She stepped over to them and nodded at Luc toward the kitchen while she peeled Cheryl's hand from his arm.

"We should go in," Maggie said with a smile. "I think Bertrand wants to say a few words before the first course."

Cheryl allowed herself to be steered to the dining room but Maggie felt her stiffness under her hand. When she caught Grace's eye, Maggie could see she wasn't happy about her friend's condition.

It was going to be a long night.

4

The farm table in the dining room had been set for an elegant dinner for ten complete with crystal goblets, silverware, and matching china on a stark white linen tablecloth.

Laurent directed everyone to their seats, shaking hands with anyone he hadn't formally met yet. Over his shoulder Maggie saw that Antoine and Sybil from the village *boulangerie* had arrived. Antoine was a large man with a big belly and a nearly always serious expression on his face. His wife Sybil was slim as if she regularly eschewed the products of their shop and smiled only on command. Maggie had long ago stopped trying to decipher the differences in other people's marriages, why they worked. If they did.

She didn't know the baker and his wife very well beyond the fact that they were essentially employees of Laurent's. After twelve years with no bakery—an embarrassment for any self-respecting village in France—Laurent had bought a vacant space in Saint-Buvard which had been used as a bakery years before and hired Antoine and wife to run it.

That had been nearly three years ago and the venture had

worked out well for everyone. The couple's teenage daughter Mireille also helped out in the bakery.

Bertrand sat down heavily in his seat and immediately flapped out his napkin.

"I can't tell you how grateful I am to you, Madame and Monsieur Dernier," he said loudly. "This is a memorable kickoff to what I hope will be an annual event and one that might well change the lives of everyone at this table."

Maggie she was pleased to notice that, drunk or not, Bertrand seemed in decent possession of himself.

The children had already had their dinners and as soon as everyone was seated quickly retired to their rooms.

Laurent poured the champagne for the first toast of the night and Bertrand got clumsily to his feet, his champagne flute in hand.

"To our amazing contestants," he said, nodding to each one around the table. Maggie noticed that Helga didn't bother looking at him but just drank her champagne.

"Zouzou will be in this contest one of these years," Danielle whispered proudly to Geoff's wife Debbie who sat on her left.

"It is not an annual event," Helga snorted, giving Danielle a condescending look.

Maggie felt a blaze of indignation but before she could respond to Helga, Debbie said to Danielle, "You must be very proud of her. Is she your granddaughter?"

Danielle smiled. "Yes," she said. "In fact, she is."

That wasn't technically true, at least not in the biological sense but certainly in all the ways that mattered. Danielle had been the grandmother-defacto to all of the children except Luc since the beginning.

Antoine and Sybil entered the room holding trays of the first course which consisted of shallow bowls of mussels steamed in white wine.

Geoff sat on the other side of Danielle. "So, at the risk of being called out again," she said to him with a twinkle in her eye, "what exactly is this contest for which we are all gathered tonight?"

"It's none other than *the* new and definitive contest in order to determine the best pastry chef in all of Europe," Geoff said.

"Except the UK isn't in Europe," Debbie said with a smile.

Geoff rolled his eyes. "Fine. Whatever."

"I see," Danielle said, taking a bowl of mussels from the tray Sybil held out for her. "And why?"

"Oh, that is a very good question!" Bertrand said from the head of the table.

All heads turned in his direction.

"Madame Alexandre, is it?" he said to Danielle.

Maggie was impressed that Bertrand had bothered to remember Danielle's name. Her opinion of him nudged up a bit.

"We are gathered here tonight," he said, watching his wine glass as Laurent poured the wine for the first course, "to get to know each other before the big competition tomorrow. A competition unlike any undertaken anywhere."

He took a swig of his drink and smacked his lips.

"It is an international affair to be sure," he continued. "Sponsored by LUSH Magazine and heralding the best pastry chef in the world—which will be discovered the day after tomorrow. We have three world-renowned judges coming in and twenty thousand euros as the cash prize."

"Goodness," Danielle said.

Maggie glanced around the table. Helga still didn't seem interested in what was being said and Maggie wondered how good her English was. Everyone else seemed raptly attentive.

Grace and Cheryl sat beside each other and managed to spend a good deal of their time whispering to each other behind their hands.

Maggie felt a pain start up in her jaw like she was clenching it too tightly.

Marie-France sat next to Bertrand. She must have tired of his monopolizing the spotlight because she tapped her water glass with her knife and waited for everyone to be quiet.

"To better answer your question, Madame Alexander," she said to Danielle, "I should mention that while it is true LUSH is sponsoring the winning purse and the contest, as well as paying for each of us to come to the south of France in January, the magazine itself does not yet exist. Is that not so, Bertrand?"

Bertrand gave Marie-France an annoyed look.

"What Madame Babin means to say," he said, "is that this contest will be the making of LUSH. Our inaugural issue, anchored by the best of the best in the world of pastry."

Geoff turned to Danielle and said under his breath.

"The main question is who is launching whom? Is LUSH launching the contest or vice versa?"

"Did you say something down there, Geoff?" Bertrand asked.

"Nothing, old man," Geoff said, turning to the large dish of *ratatouille* that Antoine now held before him.

"I should think not," Bertrand said icily.

Maggie glanced at the two men and wondered how well they knew each other before tonight. They were both British and both in the food industry. It stood to reason they might not be strangers.

She made eye contact with Laurent from down the long table. As usual, he was impossible to read.

On the other hand, she could probably guess as to his thoughts.

5

Thirty minutes into the dinner and Maggie was already kicking herself for planning a scavenger hunt for afterwards. Grace had suggested it weeks ago and then become extremely insistent about it. Now that Maggie had met Cheryl, she had a fairly good idea of who had really been driving the idea.

Cheryl had gone from hissing whispers that only Grace could hear to making loud and snarky comments on just about everyone else's conversation at the table.

Maggie already knew that Cheryl was unmarried and had no children. But that didn't stop her from advising Grace in a loud voice about everything from Zouzou's schooling to her fashion choices.

"You always were the best dressed girl at Ole Miss," Cheryl said to Grace. "And in the South, that's saying something. Why do you allow the child to wear those hideous leggings? She's a pretty girl but I hardly recognize her as yours."

It annoyed Maggie to hear Cheryl talking about Zouzou and she worried that the girl might come downstairs and hear.

"So, Maggie, I understand your oldest is going to school

overseas?" Cheryl asked.

"Well," Maggie said. "That's still up in the air."

"You did a semester in Germany, didn't you, Cheryl?" Grace asked.

"In high school," Cheryl said, tapping her nails against the base of her wine glass. "One semester. Ghastly. No offense, Helga."

"Where in Germany?" Laurent asked.

Cheryl turned her body to face Laurent as she answered. Maggie noticed she was playing with the rim of her wine glass as she spoke.

"Heidelberg. Ever been there?"

"Of course he's been there," Helga said disdainfully. "Europe is very small."

Maggie couldn't help but notice that Cheryl gave Helga a scorching look before turning away.

"You speak a little German, don't you?" Bertrand asked Cheryl.

"Me?" Cheryl said. "God, no." She smiled at Helga. "Such a harsh language. Always sounds like you're being arrested or asking for identity papers."

"That's in the north," Helga said defensively. "In the south we have a strongly melodic cadence. German is the language of the angels."

Marie-France laughed and then looked around the table.

"Oh, sorry. I thought that was a joke."

"I speak it a little," Debbie said. "I spent a summer there once."

"Hardly worth mentioning," her husband said dismissively.

God, this guy is a tool! I wonder how many foreign languages he speaks?

"Americans and the English don't bother to learn any language but their own," Helga said. "So arrogant."

"Your English is very good," Maggie forced herself to say

to her.

"Everyone should speak English," Geoff said. "It's the international language of business after all."

"Except it isn't," Helga said. "I have it on good authority that the job at *Eatz2* required their staff to be able to communicate beyond English grunts."

Maggie frowned. She'd never heard of *Eatz2* but from the look on Geoff's face, he was familiar with it.

"*Eatz2* is an English establishment." Geoff said. "What the hell language would the staff talk? You're so full of shite."

"Ach. Another charming English expression, I believe," Helga said drinking the rest of her wine and waving to Laurent for a refill.

"I do not even know why you invited that woman," Marie-France said in a loud whisper to Bertrand who worriedly glanced down the table at Helga. "She cannot even converse civilly at a dinner table."

"Well, we want to have a well-rounded competition, don't we?" Bertrand said in a low voice, trying to shush the French woman.

"With a *German* pastry chef?" Marie-France said in astonishment. "Does the world really need more gingerbread men?"

"I can hear you, Marie-France," Helga called from the other end of the table.

"And I don't care, Frau Richter," Marie-France said.

"Hear, hear!" Geoff said, his face red as he glared at Helga.

"This competition will be wonderful for everyone's career," Bertrand said loudly. "The public relations, the increased social media—"

"The twenty thousand euros," Geoff said.

Bertrand shot him a look of frustration.

Maggie looked at her watch. Just one more course and then dessert and coffee. She wondered if she could ask everyone to come back for dessert *after* the scavenger hunt. It was already getting late. At this rate it would be midnight before they served the *clafoutis*.

She tried to catch Laurent's eye but he had his hands full directing Antoine and Sybil who appeared to be willing but less than skilled as servers.

Maggie felt a flash of annoyance. What had he been thinking? More of his charity projects, she thought as she watched Antoine drop the serving spoon from the *ratatouille* onto the dining room rug.

But what had *she* been thinking to plan a scavenger hunt after dinner? She must have been out of her mind.

Helga was standing now at the table and pointing a finger at Bertrand.

"As if anything *you* have to say can be trusted!"

Whoa! Where did that come from?

The rest of the table conversation came to an abrupt stop as everyone turned to see what was happening between Bertrand and Helga.

Bertrand blushed but responded to the table's attention with an embarrassed shrug.

"Everyone has an opinion," he said and then laughed nervously.

"You should have had a contest for the naming of your magazine," Cheryl said as she reached for the wine bottle on the table. "The name's idiotic."

"No, it's not," Bertrand said clearly hurt.

"She has a point," Marie-France said. "LUSH is grossly contrived. Like you are trying too hard."

"That's not true," Bertrand said. "It's in the vein of *le weekend* or *le blue jeans*. It's hip. You really must learn to think outside the proverbial tart pan."

"Oh, because I'm so renowned for being traditional?" Marie-France said sharply. "Wouldn't that be more *Geoff's* area of expertise?"

"Hey, hold on now," Geoff said as if suddenly waking up. "That's not on. What did you mean by that?"

"It's pretty clear what she meant," Cheryl said with a laugh. "The British are hardly known for their food."

"That was decades ago!" Geoff said with agitation. "Everyone knows that was decades ago."

"If you say so," Marie-France said with a conspiratorial smile at Cheryl.

"Well, the proof will be in the pudding," Geoff said, sticking his chin out aggressively.

"Another imbecilic British saying," Helga said, reseating herself.

"She's only teasing, Geoff," Debbie said softly.

"That's right," Bertrand said loudly. "We're all friends here."

"Oh, now *that's* not at all true," Cheryl said to giggles from Grace.

The sound of a dish hitting the hard terrazzo floor in the kitchen made Maggie jump. Danielle knocked over her water glass at the sound.

Zouzou popped her head out of the kitchen doorway. Maggie hadn't noticed her come downstairs.

"*Oncle* Laurent?" she said in a panicked voice.

Laurent got up and went to the kitchen.

"I have only been sitting here waiting for a cup of coffee for fifteen minutes," Helga said loudly to Sybil who was standing with her back to the wall holding a coffee carafe. "Any time now, *fräulein,* or must I get up and serve myself?"

Sybil's face whitened when she realized Helga was talking to her and she quickly stepped toward the German. Her foot caught in a fold in the rug and she pitched forward, narrowly missing Danielle's head with the coffee pot, which she then then dropped on the table in front of Helga, splashing the woman with the hot coffee.

Helga screeched and shot to her feet. Maggie could see that most of the damage was to the table, not Helga.

The woman slapped Sybil soundly across the face.

Sybil gasped and shot out a hand to steady herself against the dining room wall. Maggie was between them in seconds.

"How dare you!" Maggie said to Helga.

"*Das ist mir scheissegal*," Helga said to Maggie, her lip curled, her eyes on Sybil.

"It is okay, Madame Dernier," Sybil said, her hand on her reddened cheek.

Maggie was so frustrated she wanted to shake Helga. That this insufferable woman felt she could come into *her* home and assault people was beyond endurable!

A part of her wanted to tell Helga there would be no dessert for her but she knew that sounded idiotic.

"Sit down, Frau Richter," Maggie said instead before turning to Sybil. "Sybil, are you okay?"

"Yes, I'm fine," Sybil said as she gathered up the coffee pot and hurried out of the room. "But that *boche* should watch her step," she muttered under her breath but loud enough to be heard.

"Did you hear that?" Helga said indignantly.

"All right," Maggie said quickly. "Enough."

At that moment Laurent came from the kitchen. He'd missed all of it.

"Okay," Maggie said turning to everyone at the table, "if we're all finished with our dinners, I suggest we move on to the next part of the evening."

Zouzou appeared in the dining room doorway with a large tray of *crème brûlée* ramekins. Maggie knew she'd been planning to serve the cherry *clafoutis* so that must have accounted for the loud crash earlier.

"Just put them on the table, Zouzou," Maggie said. "And go to bed. We'll serve ourselves after the scavenger hunt."

6

During the last month, Maggie had searched the Internet for details on how to plan and conduct a scavenger hunt. Grace and then Bertrand had explained to Maggie via a series of emails, that the point of the scavenger hunt was to place the pastry chefs in a playfully competitive arena.

Maggie decided if they were lucky, they could have the whole thing over and done with and be sitting down to their custards and coffees after only an hour.

While everyone got up to find their coats and gloves, Maggie found a moment to connect with Laurent in the kitchen.

"It's a disaster," she said.

He said nothing as he moved dirty dishes from the sink to the dishwasher.

"I can't believe Grace talked me into this," Maggie said as she took one last swig from her wine glass. "I can't talk you into coming?"

He gave her a look and what could *almost* be interpreted as a smile.

"Can I help clean up?" a voice behind them said.

Maggie looked around to see Debbie standing in the doorway of the kitchen already rolling up her sleeves.

"Oh, no," Maggie said. "That's not necessary. Besides, you'll miss the scavenger hunt."

"Exactly!" Debbie said as she stepped into the kitchen.

Laurent handed her a dishtowel.

Maggie had to admit with Debbie in the kitchen it was one less person to worry about out in the vineyard on a freezing cold dark night.

Laurent leaned over and kissed Maggie.

"Go and enjoy your hunt," he said. "We will have the kitchen spotless and the coffee hot when you return."

She gave one last longing look at the kitchen where Debbie was asking Laurent where the glasses were kept.

All women fall in love with Laurent. You'd think I'd be used to it by now.

Maggie stepped back into the dining room where Danielle stood with her coat on. Maggie went to her.

"You don't have to do the scavenger hunt," Maggie said.

"I know, *chérie*," Danielle said. "But I am tired. It is late for an old lady."

Maggie tucked Danielle's arm in hers to walk her to the front door.

"I guess it was pretty wild tonight, huh?" Maggie said.

"It always is, *chérie*," Danielle said with a tired smile. "As long as I can go home to my own bed, it is always very amusing." She turned to Grace who disengaged from Cheryl to join them. "You and Madame Barker will have no trouble getting home tonight?"

"We'll go home with Geoff and Debbie," Grace said. "They've got plenty of room in their car."

"Is it weird I didn't see those two say a single word to each other all night?" Maggie asked.

The three stepped outside and closed the front door behind them shutting out the sounds of conversation in the living room. Maggie shivered. She hadn't grabbed her coat.

"They *are* a weird couple," Grace said. "But Cheryl said they've been married for donkey's years so maybe that's all it is. And before you say anything, darling, I know you don't like her."

Maggie's mouth fell open. "I never said that!"

"You didn't have to."

Maggie shrugged. "It's just that I would have thought that being childless gave her very little right to give advice on child rearing."

"Do you mean like *I* do?" Danielle said.

"That's different," Maggie said. "You're wise. And you love all the kids. To Cheryl, they're just a problem to solve."

"That's not true at all," Grace said with a frown.

"At least it's Paris," Maggie said. "That's only a three-hour train ride from here. Luc wants to go six time zones away from us."

"I am sure that is not his motivation, *chérie*," Danielle said pointedly to Maggie.

"Does his motivation matter when the result is the same?" Maggie said.

"I am surprised at you," Danielle said and then looked at Grace too. "Both of you. Luc and Zouzou are well-grounded children who respect and honor their parents. Is that not enough?"

"Of course it is," Grace said but then looked at Maggie and they grinned and shook their heads.

"I do not know very much about raising children," Danielle said tiredly as she slipped into the driver seat before turning to address them again. "But I do know that to keep them you need to let them go."

Maggie leaned into the car and kissed Danielle on the cheek.

"What would we do without you, Danielle?" she said and felt the tension in her shoulders ease for the first time in days.

7

S tanding on the outside terrace, Maggie addressed the gathered group. She knew she should make Grace do this but she was the one who'd researched the rules. Besides, Grace was busy acting like an obnoxious fourteen-year-old with her BFF Cheryl as they giggled at the back of the gathering.

Grace wore her favorite black cashmere coat and looked nearly invisible in the night. Cheryl wore a bright red Tyrolean jacket that shouted her presence even in the dark.

"Okay," Maggie said. "This is basically a classic team-building exercise where we break off into teams of two—"

"I do not want to be paired with anyone," Helga said loudly.

Of course you don't, Maggie thought, feeling a headache coming on.

"No problem," she said. Team building would likely be lost on her anyway. "You can do it on your own. Everyone else—"

"I am not teaming up with anyone either," Marie-France said.

"Sort of defeats the purpose of team building," Maggie said between gritted teeth, "if nobody wants to work in a team."

"Chefs are notoriously independent creatures," Bertrand said with a laugh.

"Fine," Maggie said. "Everyone on their own then."

"Except me and Grace!" Cheryl said. "We want to do it together."

"Lovely," Maggie said. "So. Here's a map showing which section of the vineyard to stick to. I've made it a fairly small area. And there are three items to be found."

Originally there'd been five but Maggie had just made the executive decision to cut the number. The sooner this night was over the better.

She waved the map and pointed to a drawing on it. "You will be looking in *this* section of the vineyard and using the flashlights I handed out in order that you don't trip and kill yourselves. You are looking for a basket of plastic grapes, a set of pastry tools—including piping tips, bags, spatulas, and so on —and a triple cake tier stand."

"Is that a triple cake, darling?" Grace called out. "Or a triple cake stand?"

Cheryl giggled.

"It's whatever you find," Maggie said. "When you locate one of these items, photograph it with your phone and leave it exactly where you found it for the next person to find. If the item is moved from where I placed it, the last person who photographed it—and we can tell because of the time stamp— will be disqualified."

"Is that fair?" Geoff asked peevishly.

"Don't move the items and you have nothing to worry about."

They're worse than children!

"What does the winner get?" Marie-France asked, rubbing her hands together, a cloud of vapor coming from her lips.

"The same thing we all get," Helga said. "The chance to go back inside where it is warm."

Bertrand laughed noisily at the joke but he was the only one who did.

"The winner takes home a hundred euros," Maggie said and glanced at Bertrand who nodded.

"Right, so off you go," Maggie said, looking at her watch. "Win or lose, we convene back here in the garden in forty-five minutes."

"I will freeze my arse off in forty-five minutes," Geoff grumbled as he snapped on his flashlight and plunged down the garden path toward the vineyard.

"This whole thing is ridiculous," Marie-France said as she turned on her flashlight and followed.

Helga pushed past Maggie, nearly knocking her over on the way down the broad flagstone steps of the terrace. What with the Sybil incident at dinner, Maggie was seriously thinking of asking the woman to leave Domaine St-Buvard in the morning.

When Grace had originally approached her about hosting a welcome dinner for the contestants, Maggie had seen it as a way to boost her recently flagging newsletter subscription rate.

After tonight she wasn't at sure another ten thousand subscribers was worth it.

Grace and Cheryl headed off, arm in arm.

"See you on the other side, darling," Grace called to Maggie over her shoulder.

Maggie watched them go and shook her head.

"Except for those two, they basically all hate each other," she said more to herself than anyone.

"Oh, no," Bertrand said, snapping his light on and off nervously. "They're just animated. Chefs have big personalities."

Maggie turned to regard him. He seemed totally sober now.

"Is everything ready for tomorrow?" she asked.

He nodded. "I just got the last text from the third and final judge who has checked into the Hôtel Dauphin in Aix. My photographer was delayed but promises he'll be here tomorrow so we're good to go."

"I'm going to need you to find alternative arrangements for Helga," Maggie said impulsively.

"Mrs. Dernier," Bertrand said with a groan. "Really? It's just two more nights."

"I don't want her around my kids," Maggie said.

And I don't want her around me.

"How about if I get her to apologize to the maid?"

"She's not a maid. She's someone from the village who was doing us a favor," Maggie said.

Laurent was paying them. But still.

"Let's talk about it later," he said expansively, offering his arm to Maggie. "Meanwhile, shall we monitor the results of our labors?"

I just want this over with, Maggie thought, taking his arm and stepping down the steps and into the dark vineyard.

An hour later, Maggie burrowed deeper into her coat as she walked through the staked, depleted stalks and vines of their vineyard. Domaine Saint-Buvard was forty hectares of neatly groomed grape vines cut into fourths by a tractor road and a one-lane country road that led to the village.

Maggie stamped her feet to keep warm. She understood calls of nature. She lived with three males, so of course she did. And she respected that a night spent drinking water and wine nonstop often resulted in people getting "caught short."

Should she have made everyone go to the toilet before they started? Like she used to do with the children when they were small?

The bushes next to her rustled and she turned to see

Bertrand emerge from the center of them, his face scratched and flushed.

"No problems?" she asked and wished she hadn't.

"Sorry about that," he said. "Sometimes French food is a little richer than I can handle. The spirit is willing, eh? But the IBS is infernal."

Dear God I'm sorry I asked.

She glanced at her watch. They'd only been out in the field twenty minutes and already she was freezing.

She could actually see ice crystals forming on the vine stakes jammed into the ground to indicate where the grape vines would be in the spring. With every step she took, Maggie heard the crunch that heralded the light crust of ice common in this part of France at this time of year.

The occasional crisscrossing of flashlight beams was visible and Maggie could pick out Grace's distinctive bell-like laugh rising up and over the dark skeleton-like rows of desiccated vine stocks.

"I should have told them to text me their photos," she said, looking at her phone. "I have no idea if anyone's finding anything."

"Next time, you should send them out with flasks," Bertrand said, blowing on his hands. "That would be jolly helpful."

"What kind of team-building exercise is this if nobody wants to work together?"

"Oh, well, it's just fun for what it is."

"No, Bertrand, it's really cold and this has turned into one more way to pit each individual against the other. And isn't that what the pastry contest is all about?"

"Have I thanked you yet for your involvement in helping to make this happen?" Bertrand said. "My social media maven back in Brussels is estimating we'll get no fewer than a hundred thousand hits from our very first e-issue."

Maggie turned away. "Yeah, that's great," she said.

They walked in silence for a little longer.

"How exactly did you choose these particular chefs for the contest?" she asked, trying to distract herself from the cold.

"Ah! That is a fascinating story. I'm outlining the main points of it for the feature story I'm writing for the first issue. It's a real human interest story."

"How so?"

"You know: adversity, heartbreak. All the good stuff that makes a good winner-take-all story."

"So do you know who'll win tomorrow?"

"What? No. How would I? It's not *rigged*, Mrs. Dernier," he said, flustered. "Have you never watched *The Voice* or *American Idol*?"

"I have done," Maggie admitted, squinting in the dark to see if she could pick out any more flashlight beams or tell if any searchers were nearby.

"It's like that. We chose competitors who had interesting backgrounds to begin with."

"You mean sad or challenging backgrounds."

"Precisely. So if they win, it's gratifying for everyone."

"Except for the losers."

"Well, of course, except for the losers," he laughed, looking at Maggie in surprise. "Nothing is fun for the losers."

"Any guesses about tomorrow?"

He stopped walking and looked as if he were giving the question serious thought.

"Helga is strong," he said. "But Marie-France is competing for the honor of all France. And Cheryl is an American so she won't quit."

"So you're saying you think Geoff will lose?"

"Just between you and me? Absolutely. Geoff has been on a downward spiral since the late nineties. I'm pretty sure this contest won't slow that trajectory."

Ouch. That was cold. But honestly, from what Maggie had seen, probably accurate. Still, she hated to think of the mean German or snotty Cheryl winning over a pastry chef from France. In fact, truth be told, something felt wrong about even making Marie-France compete for the honor of best pastry chef in the world.

Maggie stepped on a branch that snapped loudly under her foot. Bertrand grabbed her arm and for a moment she thought he didn't realize she'd only stepped on a stick.

And then she realized why he grabbed her.

A sound had erupted as if triggered by the stick snap. It was a piercing sound that hung in the cold night air.

Desperate and horror-filled.

A woman's scream.

8

T he screaming grew louder until it abruptly stopped but by then Maggie had zeroed in on which quadrant of the field it was coming from. She raced through the vineyard, heading to a clearing where she thought she'd heard the source of the scream.

When she entered the clearing, her flashlight beam caught the sight of a woman kneeling on the ground, her flashlight lying uselessly beside her.

A body in front of her.

Maggie pushed past Geoff and Marie-France who stood by the first line of fir trees, Bertrand was right behind her. Grace and Cheryl appeared opposite the clearing.

"Nobody move!" Maggie called, pushing Bertrand away with one hand and hurrying on to where she could now tell was Sybil kneeling in the grass, shaking with sobs, her head bowed.

"What happened? Maggie said as she reached her.

Sybil only sobbed louder.

Maggie stared at the body beside Sybil. Helga's eyes were

open but unseeing. There was absolutely no doubt she was dead.

Maggie felt a wave of panic begin to rock her and she took in a long breath.

"Grace," she called. "Go back to the house and tell Laurent..." Maggie licked her lips and eased herself to a kneeling position beside Helga. She reached for the dead woman's throat to find a pulse—knowing she wouldn't find one.

"Tell him what?" Grace said, her voice wavering with hysteria.

There was no pulse.

"Never mind," Maggie said pulling out her cellphone and dialing 999. "Everybody just stay where you are."

She quickly reported the death to the police dispatcher and gave her location and then called Laurent.

"Helga's been killed," she said breathily into the phone.

"*Comment?*"

"Helga. The German. She's dead."

"Have you called the police?"

"Yes. But I think we should all stay here until they come."

"I am not staying here!" Marie-France called out. "I am freezing!"

Maggie stood up.

"I will make a list of everyone and where they were and exactly how helpful they were when we discovered the body so think on that," she said heatedly. "Everyone needs to stay put and don't come any closer to the body."

It was bad enough that she and Sybil had compromised the crime scene. The least she could do was keep everyone else from damaging it further. She turned to Sybil.

"Sybil?" Maggie said. "Why are you out here?"

Sybil turned to look at Maggie but before she could answer, her eyes rolled up into her head and she slumped backwards into the grass.

The next twenty minutes felt like hours to Maggie. As much as she knew Laurent needed to stay away from the murder site, she desperately wished he was with her.

The six people milling about the perimeter of the crime scene were alternately hysterical and downright invasive. Twice Maggie had to wave both Geoff and Bertrand away from the body.

"What part of *this is a crime scene* is difficult for you to understand?" she finally snapped at Geoff who was leaning over her to get a better look at Helga.

"I just wanted to make sure she was truly dead," he huffed and walked away.

Sybil sat with her back against a nearby grape bush and rocked her knees. Maggie thought she could hear her moaning. She'd been able to get nothing out of her as to why she was in the vineyard tonight—*and why she'd been found crouching over the dead German.*

Finally Maggie heard the sirens. The village of Saint-Buvard didn't have a police force and so she knew the police would be coming from Aix—twenty miles away.

She stood up and faced the group.

"All right, everyone. The cops are nearly here. I know we all want to get back to the house and get warm and I appreciate your patience."

"Bugger this!" Bertrand said, turning on his heel and heading back toward the house. "I can talk to the cops with a hot drink in my hand."

"He has a point," Cheryl said turning to follow him.

Maggie caught Grace's eye and saw she had been about to follow her friend but Maggie's glare stopped her.

Maggie considered that both Bertrand and Cheryl's behavior was probably less about guilt and more that they were just both incredibly self-absorbed. She hoped their refusal to remain at the scene of the crime didn't complicate the murder investigation.

She craned her neck to see where the two were but they had disappeared into the dark.

The fact that they'd left meant they could destroy evidence, throw away the murder weapon—if one of them had it—and generally make solving the case that more complicated.

She went over to where Sybil continued to rock and moan.

There was no sense in asking her again what happened. The police would be here soon. But one thing Maggie knew, seven eyewitnesses had seen Sybil leaning over the dead body of the person who'd slapped her just an hour earlier.

Which was not at all good.

9

E ven from the distance of where they all stood Maggie could see the reflection of the flashing lights of the police cars lining up at the main house.

With only seconds before the police would be there, Maggie turned and looked around the body to see if there was any clue as to why Helga might be in this part of the vineyard instead of the one on the map.

She had tried to limit the scavenger hunt to a relatively small area. But where Sybil and Helga had been found was well outside that area.

Maggie frowned and tried to think *why* Helga would go outside the area of the map that Maggie had given her. Did she get lost? Had she even looked at the map?

Geoff walked over to her.

"Please," Maggie said sharply. "Stand back. It's bad enough that Sybil and I've contaminated the crime scene. Do you really want the police to have to find reasons why *you* didn't kill Helga? Because once your footprints are here, that's what they'll have to do."

Geoff backed off but he cleared his throat.

"I may have been in this area earlier," he said in a low voice.

Maggie snapped her head up. She could hear the sounds of police radios and muted conversation as the police approached closer and closer.

"What are you talking about? You think you were over here?"

"Aye, well, my footprints might be around here, is all I'm saying."

Maggie stared at him in the dim light but couldn't get a good read on his face.

"Did you see Helga?" she asked.

"What? No!" he said. "I'm just saying this clearing looks familiar. *Of course* I didn't see her." He went to stand next to Marie-France who lit up a cigarette.

For the love of all that is sane, Maggie thought in growing irritation.

"Please don't smoke," she said. "It can contaminate the crime scene."

"I do not see how," Marie-France said with a frown, continuing to smoke.

"Can I go back, darling?" Grace said. "The police are nearly here."

Maggie continued to look around the body. She realized that she'd been so distracted by the dead woman's open eyes that she hadn't realized that there appeared to be something in Helga's mouth.

"Stand away from the body, Madame!" an imperious female voice barked, startling Maggie to the point that she took an unintentional step toward the body and then dropped one knee onto the ground next to it.

"Have these people been walking all over the crime scene?" the woman said loudly as she strode over to Maggie. "Get up, Madame!"

Maggie struggled to her feet, embarrassed and angry at herself for falling over, nearly onto the body.

"I was just trying to—"

She felt a hard hand wrap around her upper arm and pull her away from the body. Instantly, a policeman in uniform was at her side.

"Take these people back to the house," the woman said to him before turning to the body.

Maggie pulled her arm away from the policeman and turned to look at the detective. It was highly unusual to have a female detective in these parts. While Maggie was heartened to see that gender equality was alive and well, her heart sank at the woman's unfriendly demeanor.

"I'm Maggie Dernier," Maggie said to the detective, who was in the process of putting nylon footies over her shoes.

"Yes, I know," the detective said. "The American. Gaston! Get these people away from here immediately."

"I'm also the one who owns this vineyard," Maggie said, flustered.

The detective turned slowly to study Maggie. She was taller than Maggie but probably a good ten years younger. Whereas Maggie was dark-haired, the detective was blonde with long hair tied back in a single ponytail. She wore a short-waisted leather jacket and leather gloves.

"I know who you are," the detective said with a curl of her lip.

Maggie watched as her group hurried back toward the warmth of the house. The policeman the detective had called Gaston—now joined by three others—was helping Sybil to her feet.

"Well, you're one up on me," Maggie said tartly. She had done her best to preserve the crime scene and frankly if this woman hadn't shrieked at her, she would've been fine.

"My name is Detective Inspector Margaux LaBelle. Now if

you don't mind I will get on with my investigation of this death in your vineyard."

"I have no intention of impeding anything you need to do to investigate this death," Maggie heard herself saying and wondered why she didn't just turn and join the others.

"Who found the body?" Detective LaBelle asked as she moved to the other side of Helga.

Maggie rubbed her hands down her slacks.

"We all did," she said, hedging.

The detective glanced up. "You were all out taking a group walk together? In the cold? In January?"

"We were having a scavenger hunt," Maggie said.

LaBelle snorted. "All of you? Correct me if I am wrong, Madame, but aren't scavenger hunts usually done solo? How does one do it as a group?"

"We all heard Sybil's screams and came running," Maggie said. "As far as I could tell, we all got to the clearing at the same time."

"Who is Sybil? Is she the one who found the body?"

Maggie licked her lips. She knew very well how easy it would be for the detective to pin this murder on the first vaguely available suspect. Promotion rates and raises in the Aix-en-Provence police department were no different from any other police department in the world. They depended on solved cases.

"You'll have to ask her," Maggie said.

LaBelle leaned over the body and gently touched Helga's mouth. Maggie squinted to try to see what it was that was in the German's mouth.

"So your determination not to *impede my investigation*," LaBelle said, sitting on her heels, "does not coincide with your desire to protect your friend. Good to know. Go inside, Madame. I will be at the house shortly to take your statement."

And with that, Maggie was dismissed.

10

Whenn Maggie returned to the house, she saw that Laurent had several carafes of coffee on the counter along with a few bottles of brandy.

A team of forensic techs were checking their equipment before setting out for the vineyard while Bertrand and his group drank coffee and talked in low voices in the dining room.

Maggie went immediately into the kitchen where Laurent brought her into his arms and gave her a long hug. Past him, she could see Sybil sitting in the living room with Antoine, his arms around her, her head on his shoulder.

"Did you meet the detective?" Maggie asked Laurent.

Laurent shrugged. "Not formally."

"Do you know her?"

He shook his head. "Just let her do her job," he said.

"Of course." She pulled away from him and heard a trill of laughter from upstairs. "The kids are still awake?"

He shrugged again. "It is hard to sleep with police sirens in your front drive. I told Luc to keep them upstairs."

Maggie turned to see Grace sitting in a corner of the dining room with Cheryl. Geoff and Debbie sat opposite them and Bertrand and Marie-France next to them. They were all drinking wine and brandy.

"Who do you think did this?" Maggie asked softly.

"You are thinking it is one of our guests?" Laurent said.

Maggie turned to look at him. "Don't you? Who else would it be? It doesn't make sense that some murderer was wandering our vineyard in the dead of the night—in January—looking to kill some obnoxious German."

"I suppose not."

Maggie took in a sharp breath and dropped her voice.

"I found Sybil leaning over her."

"*Je sais*," he said. *I know.*

"I hope our guests aren't jumping to any conclusions," Maggie said, biting her lip. "Or *mentioning* those conclusions to the detective before she completes her investigation."

"The slap was ill-timed for poor Sybil," Laurent said, leaning past Maggie to pour them both a glass of wine.

"So you think she did it too?" Maggie whispered hoarsely, stealing a look at Sybil and Antoine in the other room.

"Perhaps we should wait for the detective."

"You know she won't tell us anything," Maggie said. "The police never do. What was Sybil doing out there in the first place?"

"I do not know, *chérie*."

Maggie left Laurent in the kitchen and took her wineglass into the living room to talk to Sybil but she was stopped by a young policeman.

"No talking among yourselves," he said severely.

Maggie blinked in surprise and looked at Antoine and Sybil.

"Who said?" she asked.

"Detective LaBelle."

"But I just want to—"

"Not until after all statements are taken."

"But what about the group in the dining room?" Maggie asked.

He glanced at the whispering group in the dining room and shifted uncomfortably.

"I was only told to isolate Madame Pelletier."

"I see." Maggie turned to go into the dining room. She found a seat next to Marie-France.

"You're just in time, Mrs. Dernier," Bertrand said. "We're about to take a vote on whether or not to go ahead with the contest tomorrow."

"You can't be serious," Maggie said.

"I assure you we are," Cheryl said tartly. "As Bertrand said, the ad money's been spent and we're all here—the judges and the photographer too. There's no reason why not."

Maggie glanced at Grace to see how she was digesting this hard-hearted attitude of her dear friend, but Grace was studiously examining her nails.

"Well, you don't need *my* vote," Maggie said.

"It is not as if Helga was even really a part of the competition," Marie-France said.

"How do you figure that?" Geoff said, frowning. "She's the head pastry chef at *La Pomme* in Bonn."

"She *was*, you mean," Cheryl said pointedly.

"Okay, but the point is," Geoff continued, "she was a viable competitor. Her name lent gravitas and credibility to the contest." He turned to Bertrand. "You know it did."

"Yes, well," Bertrand said running his hands through his hair in agitation. "But she's gone. So do we go on without her or not?"

"I vote absolutely yes," Cheryl said.

"Yes," Geoff said.

"Of course," Marie-France said. "But are we now a contestant short?"

"I have an idea about that," Bertrand said smiling, his eyes going for the first time all night to Grace.

11

The night was interminably long.

Since being questioned in the comfort of their living room was preferable to being questioned at police headquarters in Aix, everyone readily agreed to the all-night interrogations.

Detective LaBelle came into the house an hour after she'd arrived at the crime scene. Through the French doors, Maggie had watched the police bring crime scene tape, lights and metal detectors into their vineyard.

The forensic techs spent nearly the whole night outside although they came in often for hot coffee and the sandwiches that Laurent provided.

Maggie gave the detective the use of her den at the back of the house for her interviews. The first person Detective LaBelle spoke to was Sybil, first alone and then with her husband Antoine.

Maggie appreciated that LaBelle spoke to Sybil first. The poor woman was disintegrating by the hour and the late night wasn't helping. Laurent couldn't get her to eat anything and by the time Antoine led her from the house just before dawn, he was half carrying her to the car.

"How are we ever going to be in any condition to compete?" Marie-France said to Bertrand. "I need my rest!"

"I've already thought of that," he said, wagging his hands to calm her down. "I've texted the photographer to have him meet us at the contest venue to take pictures of the kitchens and each of the chefs by their ovens. This will just be for publicity's sake. We'll do the actual competition on Sunday."

"But what about the banquet?" Cheryl said.

"We'll have the banquet immediately following the contest," Bertrand said. "I've already informed the judges what has happened and they are amenable to giving their judgements within an hour of the competition."

"After all," Debbie said, looking around the room, "the Iron Chef competitions are all decided during the space of one television hour. Shouldn't be too difficult to determine who the winner is."

"Sometimes you talk like such an idiot," Geoff said peevishly to his wife.

Maggie saw Debbie blush darkly and she felt instantly sorry for her.

"Debbie's right," she said. "You're either the winner or you're not. This isn't the Pulitzer being decided."

With frayed tempers and exhaustion levels high for everyone, that might not have been the most sensitive thing she could have said. But Maggie was so tired she didn't care.

When the door to her office opened and Sybil and Antoine emerged, she stood up but Laurent met the couple at the door. He spoke in a low murmured voice to them both.

"As I said," LaBelle said as she followed them to the door, "please do not discuss the case with anyone." She watched them hurry through the door and then turned to Laurent.

"Monsieur Dernier," she said. "I will talk to you now."

Laurent arched an eyebrow at her. "That would be a waste of your time," he said.

"Why don't you let me decide that?"

"I never left the house. Surely Antoine told you that he and Madame Fitzgerald and I were in the house during the scavenger hunt?"

LaBelle blushed and turned on her heel, spotting Maggie watching her. She reddened even darker and pointed a finger at her.

"You. Madame Dernier," she said. "I will take your statement now."

Maggie glanced at Laurent who had already turned back to the kitchen. As she watched LaBelle's angry, stiff back move toward the den, Maggie realized with unease that this woman clearly had at least one secondary agenda she was working in addition to the murder case.

12

By the time the police left, everyone was dead on their feet. Because Maggie was the first of their group questioned after Sybil, she felt she should stay up to keep her guests company. Laurent quickly put that idea to bed.

Maggie didn't argue with him. She was exhausted.

They didn't have enough space to offer everyone a room for the night but since Bertrand had come from Aix, she overheard Laurent telling him he could have the couch.

Because LaBelle didn't want anyone discussing their answers to the questions the detective asked them, Maggie was forbidden to connect with any of her guests in any case. She gave Grace a sad, apologetic smile and went up to bed.

It was the scent of bacon frying that aroused Maggie the next morning. Surprised that she'd slept so late—it was nearly nine —she dressed quickly and hurried downstairs.

Bertrand was drinking coffee in the dining room. Laurent was outside with the dogs. Maggie tried to remember if she felt him come to bed last night.

"Aunt Maggie!" Zouzou said as Maggie came downstairs. "Have you heard the news?"

Maggie frowned. Zouzou was a little too excited to be referring to the death in the vineyard last night.

"There's news?" Maggie asked as she stepped into the kitchen and reached for the coffee pot.

"Mom said I can be in the pastry competition tomorrow!"

Maggie stopped pouring and turned to look at Bertrand who was getting up from the dining room table.

"It's totally brill, don't you think?" he said, nodding at Zouzou. "We need another contestant and Zoe here is a pastry chef."

"Zouzou," Maggie corrected him. She turned to Zouzou. "Your mother said it was okay?"

Bertrand laughed. "We're not talking pole dancing," he said. "It's a great opportunity for a kid with the kind of innate talent I've seen in her."

Maggie's mind flashed back to Zouzou in the kitchen yesterday piping custard into an éclair.

"The audience will eat it up!" Bertrand said. "Young girl. Half French, half American."

"Zouzou is fully American," Maggie said.

"It doesn't matter. She looks like a Frenchie. And with that name! Ooh la la! Half of showbiz is smoke and mirrors anyway."

What was Grace thinking? Putting Zouzou—with no formal pastry training!—up against seasoned professionals like this?

Suddenly the realization came to Maggie that twenty thousand euros or not, Bertrand's contest was nothing but an overblown marketing sham.

"And you want to do this?" she asked Zouzou.

"Do I ever!"

But there was a slight tic under Zouzou's eye when she said it. She looked excited, Maggie had to admit. But manically so.

Not too far underneath her excitement was the very real fear of making a fool of herself.

"Well, I must be off!" Bertrand said. "Now, you're coming to the photoshoot, right, darling?" he said to Zouzou who nodded energetically. "That's the girl!"

He drained his coffee and grabbed up his jacket from the couch.

"You do put on a hell of a dinner party, Mrs. Dernier," he said teasingly to Maggie. "I'll give you that." He strode to the front door where he passed Laurent coming in. "Thanks for the use of the couch, Squire," he said and then was gone.

"Did you hear?" Maggie asked Laurent as he came in, his arms full of kindling.

"About Zouzou?" he said. "*Oui.*"

"*Oncle* Laurent thinks I could win," Zouzou said breathlessly.

"But that's not why you're doing it, right?" Maggie said. The last thing she wanted was for Zouzou to get hurt. If worse came to worst, she could lose her confidence and walk away from pastry-making—something she *loved*—for good.

"Why else would she do it?" Laurent asked as he stacked the wood in the fireplace. "Where are the boys?"

"They went to see the murder site," Zouzou said. "Is that okay?"

Laurent continued to stack logs. "The *flic* will shoo them off if it's not."

"Is Mila still asleep?" Maggie asked, moving back to the kitchen and her now cold mug of coffee.

"Can I wake her?" Zouzou said. "I'm dying to tell her my news!"

"Sure," Maggie said. She waited until Zouzou was gone before coming into the living room where Laurent was stuffing twigs and sticks under the logs.

"When did everything shut down last night?" she asked.

"The police left at five o'clock."

Maggie sat down on the couch. "I can't believe this happened. Poor Sybil. She looked like she was falling apart."

Laurent dusted off his hands and turned to her. "What did the detective ask you?"

Maggie knew her husband and she knew he was asking for a reason.

"She doesn't suspect me," she said.

Laurent waited patiently.

"She asked where I was and what time I was in the clearing and how well I knew..." Maggie looked at Laurent unhappily, "...Sybil."

Laurent nodded grimly.

"She's their main suspect, isn't she?" Maggie asked. "*She* found the body. *She* had an altercation with Helga just beforehand."

"It does not look good."

"Do you have any idea why Sybil was in the vineyard?"

"Antoine called this morning," he said. "He said Zouzou wanted to watch a movie with Luc but needed her mother's permission."

Maggie frowned. "Zouzou asked Sybil to find Grace to see if she could watch the movie?"

"I do not think Zouzou expected Sybil to go looking for her mother."

"But she did."

"Apparently."

"Let's keep this under our hats," Maggie said. When Laurent frowned, she translated. "I'm saying let's don't mention to Zouzou that the reason Sybil was in the vineyard was because of her."

Laurent sat down next to Maggie.

"The detective did know a few things about your background," Maggie said, watching his face.

For several years before he met Maggie, Laurent had made his living as a con man in the south of France. He'd long ago given up that life but the police memories—and those of his victims—could be long.

"What things?"

"She wasn't specific. She also made a cryptic comment along the lines of how suspicious it was that so many homicides happen around us."

"Well, on that point she is of course right."

"Why did she want to question you?"

"I do not know."

"And you're sure you don't know her?"

"*Non.* But I know the type. She will try to wrap this case up quickly."

"With Sybil on the hot seat." Maggie said unhappily. But the thought kept coming back to her:

If it wasn't Sybil, then who killed Helga?

Two hours later, Maggie was dressed and ready to take Zouzou to Aix for the photoshoot at the contest venue kitchens.

Zouzou had taken much longer than usual to dress and at one point had ended up in tears before Maggie loaned her a cashmere sweater from her own closet.

Laurent stopped her in the driveway as she and Zouzou got into the car for the drive to Aix.

"You will have time to hit Bechards on the way home?" he asked.

Bechards was the ultimate *patisserie.* Located in Aix its windows of premium baked delicacies looked more like an elegant jewelry store than a bakery, complete with artistic spot on its amazing products which were arranged on glass shelves in the display windows.

"Of course," Maggie said although there was no place to

park near Bechards which meant she would have to hoof it to the famous *patisserie* from the main parking garage at the end of the Cours Mirabeau.

Suddenly Laurent frowned and dug out his cellphone which must have been vibrating in his pocket. He glanced at the screen and held up a finger for Maggie to wait. Then he turned away and took the call.

Maggie wondered if it was LaBelle calling Laurent and then quickly dismissed the idea. There was no way LaBelle would be calling a *civilian* to apprise them of details of an investigation. And yes, Maggie had seen that flicker of interest in LaBelle's eyes when she looked at Laurent that told Maggie that either LaBelle knew him or knew *of* him.

"Is everything okay, Aunt Maggie?" Zouzou asked from the passenger's seat. "Is this about the woman who was killed last night?"

Maggie put a hand on the teen's knee. Zouzou jumped at the physical contact.

"You didn't have coffee this morning, did you?" Maggie asked.

Zouzou shook her head. "*Oncle* Laurent made me cocoa."

"Today is just to take pictures," Maggie said. "And you already met everyone last night."

"I know but last night I didn't know I'd be competing against them."

"I don't suppose there's any way you cannot get too obsessed with trying to win?"

She wanted to add that winning would be extremely unlikely but held her tongue.

"I know I'm lucky just to be competing with these people," Zouzou said slowly. "I don't really think I can win."

"It'll still look good on your résumé," Maggie said.

Zouzou's eyes widened. "I didn't think of that!"

Maggie turned to see Laurent coming back to the car.

"Aunt Maggie?" Zouzou asked tentatively.

"Yes, sweetie?"

"Madame Pelletier isn't going to get in trouble, is she?"

Before Maggie could answer, Laurent was back, his face grim.

"Is everything all right?" she asked, knowing by his face that that was the last thing anything was.

"That was Antoine," he said. "The police have arrested Sybil for Frau Richter's death."

13

That afternoon was interminable.

After Laurent's announcement about Sybil being arrested—really not such a bombshell given everything they already knew—Zouzou had cried on and off during the entire twenty-mile drive to Aix. Maggie was glad she was there to talk to her and try to dissuade her from any thoughts that she was to blame for Sybil being in the vineyard at the time that she was—which was tricky to say the least.

"But it was me who sent her there!" Zouzou said, chewing on a nail as they drove into Aix. "If I hadn't done that—"

"Zouzou, I know this is difficult for you to understand but it was Madame Pelletier's idea to go into the vineyard. You did not send her there. And secondly, whatever happened in the vineyard—whether Madame Pelletier killed Frau Richter or not—has nothing to do with you. Stop blaming yourself. *Adults* made this happen. From beginning to end."

Maggie wasn't sure how much Zouzou was truly believing what she said but she'd at least stopped crying by the time they pulled into the parking lot.

Bertrand had said the photo shoot would take one hour and

Maggie was going to hold him to that. Not only did she have a live crime scene back at Domaine Saint-Buvard but Zouzou didn't need to be reminded by seeing the other chefs that she was involved—even peripherally—in the fact that the competition was down one chef.

The contest venue was large and airy with open shelving that lined the walls, stocked with jars of briny olives as well as crocks of fig and plum jams.

Two large freezers stood side by side. Four baking workstations were positioned equidistant from each other, each with a food processor, a nest of ceramic bowls and a set of brand-new baking tools in identical racks on the counters.

Everyone was there and in high spirits except possibly Debbie who just looked tired.

The photographer, a cute young man named Buzz, positioned each of the contestants by their workstations, giving special attention to Zouzou. That seemed to make her more nervous but at least helped jolt her out of her moodiness.

Maggie stepped away from the activity to call Laurent.

"What did you tell Antoine?" she asked when she reached him.

"What *would* I tell him?"

"I hope you told him that we'll get to the bottom of this," Maggie said, trying to keep her voice down.

Cheryl glanced over at her. When they locked eyes, the American pastry chef smiled icily and turned away.

"Surely that is the job for the police," Laurent said to Maggie.

"Laurent, you know as well as I do that the cops will go for the path of least resistance. They took one look at the woman who got slapped *and* who discovered the body and didn't see any reason to look any further."

Laurent was quiet.

"Can we at least get her out on bail?"

"Antoine said they are not allowing that."

"Laurent, we need to do something!"

"And what if it becomes apparent that Sybil killed the German?"

Maggie let out a long breath. "Of course, that's possible. But at least then we'll know we tried everything first."

"*D'accord.*"

"*D'accord* what? *D'accord* you'll investigate this with me? Or *d'accord* that's how things go?"

Laurent laughed.

"Yes, *chérie*. We will get to the bottom of this together."

14

That night was a somber one at Domaine Saint-Buvard.

Every time Maggie called Grace she was pushed off with texted excuses of how busy they were at *Dormir* and that Grace would see Maggie at the competition.

Perhaps it was the handsome young photographer's attentions but Zouzou seemed in much better spirits that night. She and Mila looked through Zouzou's favorite cookbooks for the chocolate *gâteau* that each contestant was to prepare for the competition the next day. The cake was a basic chocolate cake and one Zouzou had made many times before.

After dinner, as Maggie listened to the two girls talking in the living room, she wondered if Mila was feeling a surge of interest in baking. Mila loved to watch her father cook but had not really shown the kind of passionate interest—as Zouzou had—to suggest she might be interested in it as a life's work.

Between putting the dinner on and working with Jemmy on a school project he had due on Monday, Maggie and Laurent had little time to discuss any sort of plan going forward on their newfound commitment to investigate the German woman's murder.

Probably just as well, Maggie thought. Right now, they had enough on their plates with the competition. Once that was over, they could focus on the case.

Thinking of that, Maggie tried one more time to get a hold of Grace. She sent her a text message.

<When is everyone leaving after the competition? How long is Cheryl staying?>

Maggie watched the bubbles of Grace's reply form on her phone before giving up and going into the kitchen where Jemmy and Luc were doing the dishes.

"I'm sorry you can't come tomorrow," Maggie said to Luc as she picked up a dish towel. "Zouzou could really use the support."

Luc glanced at Maggie and ducked his head. His cheeks reddened.

"Zouzou will be fine," he said. "She has you and Laurent. And Mila." He turned to Jemmy. "You are not going?"

Jemmy shrugged. "I have my science project to work on."

Maggie saw what Luc was doing. He was reminding Maggie that he wasn't the only one not going.

"What's your girlfriend's name again?" she asked.

Luc blushed darker. "She's not my girlfriend. But it's Anna."

Not your girlfriend but important enough to blow off a major family event, Maggie thought.

A peal of laughter from the living room made all three of them look in that direction.

"Zouzou will be fine," Luc said again.

As Maggie left the kitchen, she saw a text message had come through on her phone from Grace.

<Geoff & wife leave the day after the contest. Cheryl will stay on a bit. MF hoping to move in with you @ DSB since you now have room. I said it would be ok?>

Maggie felt a flush of annoyance. She knew Grace wouldn't normally be this insensitive. It was truly a reflection of the company she was currently keeping.

The next day Laurent drove all except Jemmy and Luc into Aix. Zouzou was much less excited this morning, Maggie noted. In fact she looked nearly ill and spoke little on the drive in to Aix. Mila chatted happily, unaware that Zouzou had fallen silent.

It angered Maggie that Grace wasn't the one to be with Zouzou this morning, although truthfully, Zouzou probably got more helpful advice from Laurent. Grace loved Zouzou but only Laurent—or possibly Danielle—truly understood Zouzou's passion for baking and how much it meant to her.

"Grace texted me last night that they all intend to get there a little early," Maggie said to Laurent.

"We will get there in plenty of time," he said, glancing in the rearview mirror at Zouzou.

Unable to engage Zouzou, Mila had put her headphones on and was listening to music. Maggie turned in her seat toward Laurent.

"It bugs me that Luc didn't come today," she said.

"*Je sais.*" *I know.*

"I see it as him taking one more step away from us."

"He is just a man in love," Laurent said.

Maggie frowned. "He said she wasn't his girlfriend."

"I believe that is the problem."

Maggie narrowed her eyes at him. "What do you know?"

"Less and less every day," he said with a smile.

"Don't be flip, Laurent. Luc is virtually a child."

"Tell yourself that if it helps."

Deciding that talking to Laurent about Luc was not helping her mood, Maggie turned to focus on the highway, and pushed thoughts of Luc and Zouzou away at least temporarily. She reminded herself that Sybil's daughter Mireille must be terrified at what was happening to her family.

"I wish we thought to ask Mireille to come today," she said.

Laurent raised an eyebrow but said nothing.

"Are they letting Antoine see Sybil?"

"It has only been a day."

Maggie turned to see that Zouzou had put her headphones on too and was looking a little less nervous. Maggie turned back to Laurent.

"Drop me off at the police station," she said. "I can walk to the contest venue from there. It's not far."

He frowned. "They will not let you see her."

"I'm sure you're right," Maggie said. "But I can at least try."

15

This wasn't Maggie's first visit to the Aix-en-Provence police station. When Roger Bedard ran the place a few years ago, she'd become quite familiar with it—and with some of the people who worked there.

When she walked into the lobby after Laurent dropped her off, she was disheartened to see she didn't recognize anyone.

She went to the front desk which was separated by a glass partition from the waiting area. The sergeant seated at the desk, a handsome but portly young man, looked up as she approached.

"I need to see Detective LaBelle. My name is Maggie Newberry Dernier."

He turned and looked at the screen on his computer. He picked up the phone and spoke softly before hanging up. Then without a word he nodded to the waiting room and turned back to whatever he'd been working on before Maggie had interrupted him.

The waiting area was bare bones with plastic chairs and a map of Aix on one wall that looked very old and a few plaques and awards that the station had achieved for various civic achievements. There was no one else in the room, which didn't surprise Maggie. Aix was a popular tourist destination but not so much in January.

She didn't have to wait long.

The door beside the glass partition swung open and Detective LaBelle appeared. She held a folder in one hand.

Maggie got to her feet.

"*Bonjour*, Detective LaBelle. I was hoping you could update me on the murder investigation."

"Don't be ridiculous," LaBelle said, her face slowly morphing into a sneer. "You are not family or her counsel."

"Well, the murder did happen on my property," Maggie said, knowing that would count for precisely nothing. "Can you at least tell me if you're through examining our vineyard?"

"Do you see police there?"

"Why, yes. There were police there when we left this morning."

"Then that answers your question."

Maggie wondered why the woman even bothered to come out and see her if she was just going to stonewall her.

Perhaps she'd been hoping that Maggie might be accompanied by her husband?

"I'd like to be able to see Madame Pelletier," Maggie said, knowing before she spoke what the answer would be.

"*Non.*"

"Is there anything I can do or say that might get you to change your mind?"

"Are you trying to bribe me?"

Maggie was torn between laughing in the woman's face and blurting out *Are you joking?* But she was pretty sure either reaction would get her immediately detained. And she had a pastry competition to attend.

"I'm merely asking if there is a process that might allow me to see Madame Pelletier."

Like bringing my husband with me next time.

"You are wasting my time," LaBelle said and turned on her heel and disappeared back inside the door next to the glass partition.

Maggie stood gaping at the closed door and wondered what it was—besides seeing Laurent—that LaBelle would have thought would *not* waste her time? Had she hoped that *Maggie* had information?

But that flew directly in the face of Maggie's main theory—more believable than ever now—that the police had their culprit and were not open to learning any new evidence that might contradict that.

16

The space for the contest on the day of the competition was festooned with banners announcing the launch of the magazine LUSH and the virtual crowning of the world's best *patisserie* chef. Sounds of laughter and conversation filtered through a double-doored entrance which led into the same large space Maggie and Zouzou had visited yesterday. The four workstations were in position with stools perched beside them, a small refrigerator, and a set of double ovens.

Because Zouzou was tall for her age, Maggie was glad to see that she was not disadvantaged by the double ovens. She would be able to slide her cake pans in and out of the ovens as easily as the others.

Bertrand had done some local advertising for the event and Maggie was pleased to see that most of the seats in the audience section were filled.

Each of the contestants was standing at their workstations. Laurent stood with Zouzou, his head bent, talking to her in a low voice.

Maggie scanned the room until she found Grace who

waved to her from the first row in the viewers section. Danielle sat beside her and Mila beside Danielle. Maggie hurried over and kissed Danielle in greeting.

"Z looks nervous," Grace said as Maggie sat down. "I thought she'd be over the moon about this."

"She will be fine, *chérie*," Danielle said, patting Grace's hand. "And maybe not at this very moment, but afterward, she will be very happy she did this."

Maggie had to admit that Danielle was probably right about that.

"Marie-France is the one who looks green around the gills," Grace said.

Maggie turned to see with surprise that it was true. The French *station chef* at *Le Coucou* and easily the most acclaimed of the four pastry chefs, Marie-France looked downright ill.

"Maybe she doesn't do well with tests," Maggie said.

"She would not have gotten where she is today," Danielle said, "if she was not comfortable with competitions."

"Good point. Lord, Geoff looks drunk," Maggie said.

Geoff was red in the face and rubbing his ears repetitively.

"I can personally attest," Grace said, "to the fact that the man isn't drunk. Just clinically annoying. And from what his wife said last night at dinner, he has a lot more riding on this contest than the others do."

"Oh?" Maggie looked at her.

Grace glanced around to see if anyone was listening and then leaned in close to Maggie.

"She said they're inches from declaring bankruptcy."

"I'm sorry to hear that," Maggie said, looking back at Geoff who now didn't look so much drunk as just very nervous.

"Plus there was some connection about a job and Helga," Grace said. "But we were interrupted before Debbie could tell me the details."

"Do you think any of these people knew each other before this week?" Maggie asked.

"I don't know, darling. Cheryl might know."

Maggie searched the crowd until she spotted Debbie sitting next to Bertrand. She held a paper cup of coffee in her hand and stared out over the contestants' heads, a glazed look on her face. Maggie reminded herself that this was a free trip to the south of France for her and Geoff. While granted it was in the middle of winter, it was still cost-free.

Laurent kissed Zouzou on the cheek and left her and took his seat on the other side of Mila. Grace leaned over and touched his knee.

"Is she all right, Laurent?"

"She is fine."

"What did you tell her?" Danielle asked. "She looks much steadier than when she came in."

"I told her she has made this *gateau* hundreds of times," he said. "And to just imagine she is at *Dormir* making it for Sunday lunch."

"Oh, well done, Laurent," Grace said with a broad smile.

They settled in to wait and watched as Bertrand stood up to approach the dais and the microphone. He appeared to have dropped a note card because he returned to his seat and the audience, thinking the competition was about to start, relaxed again.

"What's all this about Marie-France wanting to come to Domaine Saint-Buvard?" Maggie asked Grace.

"Oh, darling, you don't mind, do you? Now that Helga's gone you have the room and I'm at my wit's end. They all think I'm there to wait on them."

"Well, you do run a bed and breakfast," Maggie reminded her.

"Please, darling? I'll owe you forever. Geoff and Debbie are enough to deal with."

"I take it that means Cheryl is no problem?"

Grace arched an eyebrow.

"She makes her own bed and gets her own coffee," she said. "That's more than I can say for any guest I've had in the last two years."

Maggie turned to look at Cheryl to see that she appeared to be handling the anticipation of the competition with nonchalance and poise. She was busy sorting through her ingredients, checking them off a list as if this was just any other day of baking in her own kitchen.

"Fine, Marie-France can come," Maggie said to Grace. "I'll talk to her after the competition."

"If the poor woman can survive until then," Danielle said pointedly making both Maggie and Grace look at the French woman who was leaning on her cook station and sweating heavily.

Bertrand came to the front of the room where a microphone had been set up. He was smiling broadly and Maggie imagined he might be the only one in the room except for Laurent not eaten up with nerves at the moment.

"Good morning, everyone," he said. "Thank you for coming. This is the first of many future annual *Patisserie* Challenges for the inaugural issue of LUSH magazine, a magazine dedicated to exemplifying the good life through good food and wine. Whether you are a housewife in Freiburg or a copy typist in Cincinnati, LUSH was created to bring the best of the world's culinary achievements into your home."

Several audience members began to cough and fidget and Marie-France had already sat down on her stool and was resting her head in her hands.

"Allow me to introduce our judges!" Bertrand said. "From *Sherry's* in London we have Maddy Simpson, a master baker in her own right. From Paris and *LeJute* there is Vero LaButte, a connoisseur of all that is delicious in French cuisine. And finally there is Jason Dempsy, the editor of *Savor Magazine* and someone who definitely knows a good chocolate cake when he sees one!"

Expecting a laugh but getting none, Bertrand seemed unperturbed.

"And finally," he continued, "our competitors who will each be baking a classic *gateau* using identical ingredients and equipment. To my right, the station chef at *Le Coucou Paris*, the incomparable Marie-France Babin!"

There was a smattering of applause but Marie-France didn't look up.

"She really does not look well," Maggie whispered to Grace and Danielle.

"And from across the pond, the former station chef of *Darby's*, the creative and always genial Geoffrey Fitzgerald."

There was no applause at all and Geoff snorted and shook his head in disgust.

"From further across the greater pond all the way to America," Bertrand continued, "we have Cheryl Barker who recently competed on the Food Network channel's show 'Titanium Chef' and is currently wowing international guests at the Soho chain of hotels in Paris with her much imitated, never equaled desserts."

Grace clapped and one or two others in the audience.

"Lastly, we have a junior chef—half French and half American. Please welcome Aix-en-Provence's own Mademoiselle Zoe Dernier!"

"He got her name wrong," Grace said. "*Both* her names wrong!"

The audience favored Zouzou with more applause than they'd allowed Cheryl but she looked too nervous to notice, let alone that Bertrand had gotten her name wrong.

"All right, Bakers!" Bertrand said. "Remember, once the

clock starts, you must mix, bake and plate your cake for our three judges before the timer goes off. Are you ready?"

The four contestants simply stared at Bertrand who didn't seem at all concerned by their lack of response.

"For the purse of twenty thousand euros and the title of best *patisserie* chef in all of Europe," Bertrand said loudly, "Bakers, start your ovens!"

17

From beginning to end, the whole contest was just over two hours—with half that time accounted for the cakes baking in the ovens.

Geoff dropped half his cake pans and a beaker of cream had to be replaced when that too skidded to the floor. Cheryl worked silently and smoothly as did Zouzou, who never lifted her head but sifted flour, broke and whisked eggs, and poured her batter into her prepared pans with singular focus and determination.

Marie-France on the other hand appeared stymied by the workings of her refrigerator. She opened it several times as if unsure if she'd taken the cream out and wasted a good ten minutes looking for the quarter pound of softened butter that sat in plain view on her countertop.

In many ways the entire spectacle looked like a sort of ballet to Maggie. Zouzou and Cheryl moved in smooth graceful movements, practiced and sure as they ultimately slid their cake pans into their ovens and set the timers on their separate counters.

Geoff was slower—and much noisier—but Maggie knew it

didn't matter how messy, clumsy or loud you were—the proof
was always in the perfect presentation and taste of the
finished product. Nothing about how you got to that point
mattered.

By the time he slid his cake pans into his oven, closed the
door and slumped with relief into the chair next to the oven
where he, like Cheryl and Zouzou would watch his cake
through the window, it was clear that Marie-France was in
trouble.

She waved to Bertrand to come over to her and when he
refused—saying he didn't want to get her disqualified by
speaking with her—she slurred out in a loud croak that her
oven wasn't working.

"God, is she drunk?" Maggie asked Grace in a hoarse
whisper.

"If she's drinking she's doing it secretly," Grace said. "I never
saw it."

"*Secretly* is the main way most drunks do it," Danielle noted,
frowning at Marie-France as Bertrand scurried over to her.

Maggie realized that as much as Danielle would prefer for
Zouzou to win, of course the honor of France rested on Marie-
France's shoulders. Losing to Zouzou was one thing but losing
because she had attempted to compete drunk was completely
unacceptable.

Bertrand examined Marie-France's oven and then reached
out to dramatically turn it on.

It was a devastating moment and as soon as he did it the
entire audience gasped. The oven had not been preheating.
There was no way Marie-France would be able to bake her cake
—still not even mixed—in time.

"I don't believe this," Danielle said numbly. "She's
disqualified."

As soon as Marie-France saw that her oven had not been
on, drunk or not, she realized the truth too. A distressed wail

emitted from her followed by her grabbing her stomach and bolting for the toilets.

"Surely they'll allow for illness," Maggie said.

Laurent snorted, which told her how likely that was.

"Marie-France is out of the competition," Grace said in a disbelieving voice. "It's just the three of them now."

Bertrand followed Marie-France but he wasn't gone long before he returned to the small stage and once more took the microphone.

"Unfortunately," he said breathlessly, "due to illness, Madame Babin will not be able to finish the competition and has conceded her position."

A hush swept the small audience even though it had been apparent for a good forty minutes that Marie-France would have to drop out.

Maggie tried to catch Zouzou's eye but the girl was focused only on her cake in the oven. Maggie wasn't a baker but she did know that there was more magic than science to baking cakes. In her experience baking a cake for *less* time than the recipe called for could often be the key to producing a perfectly light and moist cake.

Or an unmitigated disaster.

All of it came down, not so much to the oven timer, but to the baker's eye. After years of pulling ruined cakes and perfectly fabulous cakes from various ovens at various altitudes, only an intuitively experienced baker stood the best chance of judging the exact moment when a cake was done.

"This is so nerve-racking," Grace said, repeatedly rubbing her hands along her slacks.

It occurred to Maggie that she didn't know whether Grace was rooting for Cheryl or Zouzou. She had to admit that in the long run winning wouldn't matter that much to Zouzou—who had many more challenges to be won in her life. But for Cheryl, this might be an important contest. Now that Maggie thought of it, she didn't remember whether Cheryl was currently employed anywhere.

Geoff stood up and mopped the sweat on his neck with an already drenched hand towel. He ran his hand through his hair and knelt in front of his oven. He turned his head to look at Cheryl. It was obvious to everyone that he was closely monitoring her. Cheryl sat relaxed and nonchalant in her chair, a Mona Lisa smile on her lips, her eyes alternately on the audience or her nails.

When Zouzou stood up and opened the oven door to pull her cake out, Maggie saw Cheryl smile knowingly.

She thinks she's bringing it out too soon, Maggie thought with dismay.

Zouzou carefully set the cake on the counter and used a toothpick to insert in the middle. Her face showed no hint to what that told her. She simply turned to the ceramic bowl of ganache she'd prepared and began to stir it, readying it to be draped over the cake.

Maggie looked at Cheryl who had now pulled out her cellphone and appeared to be scrolling through her social media feed.

Maggie had to admit, she had nerves of ice.

Suddenly, Cheryl stood and opened her own oven door and looked inside before pulling out her cake.

Geoff took his cake out at nearly the same time.

Maggie glanced at the clock. The contestants had less than five minutes to unmold, glaze and slice their cakes onto three plates before the judges would appear.

Now that it was nearly over, Maggie could see that Zouzou's hands were shaking. She dropped the outer rim of her cake pan and set the cake on a stand. Then she picked up the pitcher of ganache and poised it over the cake ready to pour. Laurent cleared his throat and she stopped. She didn't look at him. Her eyes never left the ganache pitcher. But she didn't pour the chocolate either.

Maggie could almost hear the seconds tick by as Zouzou stood holding the pitcher over the cake but not pouring. Meanwhile, both Cheryl and Geoff had unmolded their cakes and draped them with thick layers of ganache.

One minute left.

"I don't think I can take this," Grace said, biting her lip and ending any doubt Maggie might have had as far as who she was rooting for.

Soft cursing came from Geoff's workstation. His cake had been too hot when he poured the ganache on top so that when he tried to cut the slices for the judges, the pieces crumbled.

Maggie saw him trying to use his fingers to push the cake pieces back together onto the plate until turning back to his cake to cut another wedge.

That one was every bit as messy.

"Thirty seconds," intoned Bertrand.

Zouzou took in a long breath and finally poured the ganache over her cake. Then she set the pitcher down and picked up her cake knife which she used to cut three pieces of cake for the judges. She transferred them smoothly to three white plates.

Even from where she sat, Maggie could see there wasn't a dot of chocolate—cake or ganache—to mar the presentation on Zouzou's plates. Each one of the cake slices looked pretty enough to photograph.

"Time!" Bertrand called as Zouzou stepped back and set down the serving trowel. Then and only then did she look at Laurent. Maggie saw him nod nearly imperceptibly.

When Maggie dragged her attention back to Cheryl and Geoff's cake slices, she saw that they too had managed to get all their slices onto plates in time. But while Cheryl's cake slices were tidy and symmetrical, like Zouzou's, Geoff's looked downright sloppy.

Maggie slipped her hand into Laurent's and squeezed it.

A young man wearing a starched shirt, tie and apron approached the tables and carefully brought each of the nine cake slices to the front table and set up blank placards in front of each set of three that would later identify which cakes were whose.

Maggie couldn't help following Zouzou's cake slices all the way to the front. Just in case there was any question later, she would know which ones were hers.

When the judges entered the room—to applause from the small audience—Bertrand formally introduced them again and said there would be time for meeting them and photographs after the judging.

Geoff, Zouzou and Cheryl came to stand in front of the judges' table. Zouzou clasped her hands behind her and Maggie watched her as the girl rocked from foot to foot.

The first cake slices were set in front of each of the judges. Maggie had been so busy keeping track of Zouzou's cake slices that she didn't know who these first slices elonged to.

But by the expression of pride she saw on Cheryl's face, she guessed they were hers.

After a brief history by Bertrand of the *gateau au chocolate avec ganache* and how cakes would feature prominently in each issue of LUSH magazine, each of the judges addressed their first cake slice. One picked up his cake dish and actually turned it around to see it from every angle. Then he picked up his fork and carefully, dramatically cut into the cake slice. The fork went to his mouth where it hesitated. He wrinkled his nose and then turned to say something to one of the other judges who also picked up his fork. He sniffed his fork too.

Now Cheryl was much less sure of herself. Her body

language was stiff and bent forward as if she wanted to run up to the dais and see what it was that they were smelling.

The second judge slipped his forkful into his mouth.

And then promptly spat it out onto his plate.

"*Dégoûtant!*" he declared loudly. *Disgusting.*

The third judge lifted her cake plate up and then replaced it, shaking her head. All the judges turned to Bertrand who was looking at them in bewilderment.

"Do you want us to judge this cake?" one of the judges said, "or does the contestant want to withdraw?"

"What's the matter with it?" Bertrand asked in bewilderment as Cheryl stormed the dais. She picked up one of the cake plates and held it to her nose. And then blinked and set it back down. She turned and looked at Bertrand.

"My ingredients have been tampered with," she said.

"Now, now, Cheryl—" Bertrand started to say.

"No! Smell it! Someone put garlic in my butter!"

The judges talked among themselves. "What is she saying?"

"No one put garlic in your butter!" Bertrand said, trying to keep the edge out of his voice and putting his hand over the microphone. He turned to the audience. "It is difficult to lose even at this level of competition." He turned to Cheryl and said with a hint of steel in his voice, "Nobody likes to lose but let's be a good sport about it, eh?"

Maggie saw the effort it took for Cheryl to get herself under control. She went back to stand in line between Geoff and Zouzou.

Grace leaned over to Maggie and Danielle.

"Is it possible someone tampered with Cheryl's ingredients?" she whispered hoarsely.

The offending cake slices were taken away and the next three pieces set before the judges.

This was now a two-contestant contest.

The first judge made a face as he studied the cake slice in front of him that Maggie knew to be Geoff's.

"Food is not just about taste," he said solemnly, looking at Zouzou as he spoke. "Appearances are important too."

Something flinched in Geoff's cheek but he held his chin high.

Then judge turned to his score card and jotted down a number. The other two judges also remarked on how untidy the presentation of the cake slices were, going so far as to comment that they were even worse than the "garlic cake."

But they nodded as they tasted their slices and they busily scribbled their scores down on their cards.

The last three cake slices were Zouzou's. Because she'd waited before pouring on the ganache, her cake slices were beautiful, intact and glossy. The judges still sniffed the cake slices to be sure there was no issue with them, and then tasted the cakes. More nods. One of the judges even ate two more bites and Maggie overheard him remark to one of the other judges that it was "perfectly moist."

Then they put down their pens and handed in their cards to Bertrand who passed them on to the manager of the Aix-en-Provence catering company, a Madame Denoit who would serve as an independent accountant for the event. She quickly counted up the score and handed the cards back to Bertrand.

Maggie would swear that Bertrand's face whitened when he looked at the score card but he straightened his shoulders and turned to face the audience and the three contestants.

"Considering the unfortunate diminishment in contestants," he said, a line of sweat beginning to roll down his jaw, "it almost doesn't make sense to announce the runner-up." He laughed but the audience was French and uninterested in his ironic attempt at humor.

Get to it, Maggie silently urged him.

"In any case," Bertrand said with a sigh, "the runner-up to

the inaugural *patisserie* competition for the best..." He licked his lips as if deciding about whether or not to truly name it under the circumstances but then forged on. "...for the best *patisserie* chef on or off the continent...drum roll!" He looked around the room but if he'd hoped for a smile from anyone he was disappointed.

"Ladies and Gentlemen," he intoned, "I give you Geoffrey Fitzgerald!"

18

For a moment nobody said anything and then Laurent began to applaud very slowly. Geoff was the runner-up. Which meant...

Zouzou had won!

Because of the way he had phrased it, the contestants looked at Bertrand in confusion.

"Zouzou!" Danielle called. "You won, *chérie*! You won!"

Zouzou turned, her mouth open, to gape at the audience. Laurent was on his feet and striding toward her and she launched herself into his arms.

Maggie turned to hug Danielle and Mila before turning to Grace who was staring at the scene and shaking her head. There was a smile on her lips.

Within seconds, Zouzou was hugging Danielle, Mila and Grace and Maggie.

"I don't understand what happened!" Zouzou said as Mila hugged her.

"I have eaten your chocolate *gâteau*," Laurent said. "It is *not* a surprise."

"Should I thank the judges?"

"It might be a nice thing to do," Laurent said holding out his hand to accompany her.

Maggie watched the judges gather up their belongings as if about to make a quick exit which didn't surprise her. They weren't even trying to pretend the contest was credible.

Maggie stood up in time to see Cheryl roughly throwing her things into her bag.

"She's making a scene," Maggie said to Grace. "You'd better skip the banquet and take her home."

"She's upset," Grace said to Maggie, her voice with an edge to it.

"It's a stupid contest," Maggie said back to her. "Nobody died. Oh, wait! In fact, somebody did."

Grace's face reddened but before she could respond, Debbie came over to them.

"Geoff and I have decided to stay in town tonight," she said. "I don't want him driving those curving village roads after drinking."

"Of course," Grace said. "Whatever you want to do."

"I just can't believe it," Debbie said. "And Geoff definitely can't believe it."

"Does anybody know how Marie-France is?" Maggie asked.

Debbie looked at her text messages. "Somebody drove her to the infirmary. And Bertrand is heading out to go see her. I asked him to text us when he knows what her status is."

"What terribly bad timing," Danielle said.

Maggie wondered.

Was it bad timing? Or was it deliberate?

"Bertrand should cancel the banquet," Maggie said suddenly. "Nobody's in the mood for it and Zouzou's too young to drink."

"Well, it's true nobody's in the mood," Debbie said. "But the judges are here and both Cheryl and Geoff know that they can schmooze and pretend to laugh it off. They'll get some points for that. You really won't allow Zouzou to stay for it?"

Grace hesitated but it was Maggie who spoke up.

"Zouzou has had her big night. I'm sure Laurent will want her to end it on a high note. After all, we're all very proud of her but I'd hate for her feelings to get hurt once alcohol starts loosening tongues of the losers."

"You might have a point there," Debbie said and turned to glance at Geoff who was talking to Cheryl. He was red in the face and punctuating his words with harsh jabs with his index finger.

"I will get a ride home with Laurent and the girls," Danielle said to Grace. "Stay for the banquet, *chérie*. I'm sure Madame Barker will want to talk."

"Yes, good idea," Grace said, gathering up her things. As Zouzou and Laurent came back from speaking with the judges, a smile played across her face. "Imagine," she said softly, nearly to herself. "Z beat out all of them."

As Laurent began to usher Zouzou, Mila and Danielle toward the exit, Maggie tugged at his sleeve.

"Laurent...." She began to say.

"You want to stay for the dinner," he said.

Maggie knew she shouldn't be surprised at his ability to read her mind but she always was.

"It's just that everyone's staying for it and with Geoff crying in his bourbon it would be a perfect time to ask a few pointed questions about last night."

Laurent nodded at Mila and Zouzou.

"Go to the car with *Mamère*," he said to them. "I will be there in a moment." He turned back to Maggie.

"You were not allowed to see Sybil at the police station?"

"Just as you said," Maggie said. "But I'm telling you there is something about that detective, Laurent. Something I can't put my finger on. Are you sure you don't know her?"

"*Non*," he said. "But perhaps you should be careful."

"What do you mean?"

For a minute, she didn't think he was going to answer. Then he leaned over and kissed her.

"People with secrets often do things they're ashamed of later," he said.

Now *that* was mysterious, Maggie thought. *Is he talking about himself or the detective?*

"I'll be careful," she said. "About tonight?"

Geoff stormed up to the open bar that was just being set up at the front of the room, Debbie trailing behind him.

"At the rate Monsieur Fitzgerald is looking for a drink and a place to cry into it, as you put it, you will not need all night," Laurent said. "I will take Danielle and the girls home and return to pick you up in two hours."

19

The banquet was to be held in the adjoining room where everyone was ushered after the winners were announced. The room was much larger and held twenty tables, indicating that Bertrand had expected a much bigger crowd.

A six by three foot poster of the cover of LUSH magazine was set in the center of the room.

Maggie stepped into the room and found a place to sit. As she looked around she saw all three of the judges shaking Bertrand's hand and then leaving, presumably to find a better meal at one of the local restaurants in Aix.

So much for schmoozing, Maggie thought as she watched Cheryl slump into a chair at her table. Grace sat next to her, her concerned eyes on her friend.

"Can you believe he had the nerve to tell me to be a good sport?" Cheryl said to Grace. "I mean first I get rancid ingredients making it impossible for me to compete—"

"Was it rancid?" Maggie asked. "I thought it was emulsified butter."

Cheryl glared at her. "Well, when it's emulsified with *garlic* and you're making a *cake*, I'd say the effect is the same."

Trying to temper whatever ugliness Cheryl seemed intent on creating, Grace turned to Cheryl.

"I agree it seems quite deliberate when you consider the butter had to be hand-melded with the crushed garlic."

A portly woman from the audience who had eaten all the bread on the table waved her butter knife at Grace.

"Except emulsified garlic and butter is a common combination in France," she said. "It's not like it was rat poison and butter."

Her husband laughed loudly. "That is very good, *chérie*," he said to her. "Excellent point."

Cheryl gave both of them withering looks.

Bertrand was across the room talking with the waitstaff as they served the first course: oysters on the half shell. He'd obviously not yet gone to check on Marie-France.

Maggie saw Geoff and Debbie sitting at a table not far from them. Geoff was drinking heavily and the plate of oysters that had been set in front of him sat untouched.

It occurred to Maggie that her plan to get information out of Geoff—specifically how well he'd known Helga and where he was exactly the night she was killed—might have a major flaw in it.

Twice Maggie saw Geoff slap his wife's hand away from his arm as she attempted to get him to lower his voice.

Maggie excused herself and walked over to Debbie and Geoff's table. Debbie looked at her as she approached with an expression of relief and shame.

"Hey, you two," Maggie said as she sat down. "Quite a night, huh?"

"You've got a bloody nerve," Geoff snarled and promptly knocked over his drink.

"Excuse me?" Maggie felt a sudden tension flit through her.

"Geoff, *don't*," Debbie said in a pleading voice. "None of this is Maggie's fault."

"It's everybody's fault!" Geoff said loudly, waving his arm to encompass the room. "My last chance! Bugger everyone!"

He stood up, knocking over his chair in the process and wavered uncertainly on his feet for a moment.

"Geoff, *please*," Debbie said, putting a hand out to him which he slapped away.

"Get off me, woman," he said before turning and lurching off in the direction of the restrooms.

"I am so, so sorry," Debbie said as she watched him go, her eyes filled with tears. "This isn't like him."

"Well, he's disappointed," Maggie said as she watched Geoff bump into one of the servers before staggering into the hall that led to the toilets. "It's understandable."

As Maggie watched him go, one thing was certain: he was in no condition to be questioned.

"He's had a terrible year," Debbie said. "What with the job falling through, this was the last straw. And the worst of it was he was up against Helga for it."

Maggie's antennae began to tingle.

"Oh, yes?" she said, leaning toward Debbie. "Helga got the job he wanted?"

"More than *wanted*. He was counting on it. We both were."

"Did he know Helga? I mean before the competition?"

Debbie shook her head. "He knew *of* her, of course. It's a small world, the *brigade de cuisine* of *patisserie*. He might have bumped into her at a conference or something but, well, you met her. She wasn't very friendly."

Maggie nodded. No, Helga wasn't very friendly.

And neither really was Geoff.

So was the job competition really their only intersection point except for the LUSH contest?

"When did Geoff hear about not getting the job?" Maggie asked.

Debbie frowned and glanced in the direction that Geoff had gone.

"At *Eatz2*? He heard about it a few days ago," she said.

Just before Helga was brutally murdered in my vineyard.

"Which is why he was counting all the more on this contest," Debbie said. "Honestly, I think he thought he had it in the bag."

"Really? Even against Marie-France? I understand she's very big as far as *patisserie* chefs go."

"It would have been a major feather in his crown to have gone up against her—well, technically he *did* go up against her —and won."

Maggie thought about the contest and how it had all gone down. Marie-France—the only real competition now that Helga was out of the picture—had been sidelined making it essentially a two-person contest.

Three if you counted Zouzou but had anyone really seen her as a viable contender?

The thought came to Maggie and she was shocked that she hadn't thought of it before. Were Marie-France's illness and Cheryl's wrong ingredients deliberate? And if so, who else could have done it except for Geoff?

"Not to mention," Debbie said, finishing off her drink. "We really need the money. I mean really."

Maggie was shocked to hear Debbie talk about their financial woes. Most self-respecting Frenchmen would rather take a dive off a cliff rather than talk about money and she'd never met anyone French who might allude to possible financial hardship.

"I'm sorry to hear that," Maggie said, uncomfortably.

"Well, it's his own fault," Debbie said bitterly. "No one was forcing him to visit the racetracks—"

"Are you talking about *me*?!" Geoff bellowed.

He had come up from behind them and Maggie had been so intent on hearing Debbie that she hadn't noticed him.

Debbie's face went white and she stood up, one hand reached out to her husband but never connected. Geoff recoiled from the suggestion of her touch and curled his lip.

"How dare you, you stupid cow!" he shouted at Debbie.

Maggie watched her shoulders cave as if the force of his words were hammers pounding away at her. She looked around desperately and spotted Bertrand. She waved frantically for him.

"I'm sorry, darling," Debbie said to Geoff. She grabbed her purse and held it to her chest as if for protection.

"You're sitting here on your fat arse telling the world our personal business!"

"Hey, knock it off, Geoff," Maggie said. "There's no need for that."

"And you!" he said, whirling around on her. "Don't you tell me what there's no need for! Don't you dare—"

"I say, old man, steady on!" Bertrand said as he hurried over to the table.

"I'll steady on *you*, you bastard!" Geoff snarled. "Is this how you run your competitions? What a ruddy dog's dinner!"

"I think you need to call it a night, old chap," Bertrand said, flushing, "You're representing the United Kingdom—"

"Oh, sod the United Kingdom!" Geoff said. "Sod it and you and your whole bloody magazine!"

Geoff turned and stumbled away from the table, lurching towards the exit.

"I don't need any of you," Geoff shouted over his shoulder. "By God, I'll see you all pay for this humiliation!"

20

Maggie wasn't sure what Geoff was threatening to make them all pay for. He was angry at her and Debbie and Bertrand—who he seemed to think had let him down. Did Geoff think because he was friends with Bertrand it meant he'd automatically win? Surely he knew the judges were independent agents only doing the contest so their various restaurants would get line credits in Bertrand's magazine?

And of course for whatever financial inducements Bertrand had promised them..

"I'd better go," Debbie said. "I'm sorry about this, Bertie. He's upset."

"So's Marie-France," Bertrand said indignantly, "and you don't see *her* making a scene!"

Maggie wanted to mention that that was probably because Marie-France was currently in the hospital hooked up to IV fluids but she didn't say anything. The fact that both Geoff and Cheryl had lost—to an amateur baker and a teenager at that— combined with the fact that none of the judges had bothered to stick around, revealed this whole enterprise for the charade it had always been.

As Debbie hurried off after her husband,

"I feel sorry for the old girl," Bertrand said. "She's a sweet kid and deserves way better. You know she basically married him to get rid of a nightmare maiden name?"

Maggie looked at him in amusement in spite of herself.

"Seriously? How bad?" she said.

"Humper." Geoff made a face.

"You're making that up," Maggie said with a laugh.

"I swear I'm not!" Geoff laughed.

Maggie shook her head, not believing for a minute that Debbie really married just to get rid of an unfortunate last name.

Out of the corner of her eye Maggie noticed that Grace and Cheryl were walking toward the toilets. Cheryl seemed to have calmed down.

"What did you think of the night?" she asked Bertrand as they walked back to their table.

"Bloody marvelous!" he said, smiling expansively and shaking hands with the couple from Maggie's table who appeared to be just leaving.

When a brand new heretofore undiscovered talent is revealed to the world? Geoff and Cheryl—and even Marie-France—they're on notice, wouldn't you say? They've had their moment in the sun. Time for the new ones to shine."

Maggie wanted to point out that while Marie-France and Cheryl were not in the zenith of their careers—neither were they exactly washed up yet. But if Bertrand wanted to put that kind of happy spin on the event, she wasn't going to talk him out of it.

"Even so, it still must have been a shock, Zouzou winning," Maggie pressed.

"I admit it was unexpected but obviously she was the better of the three—at least today."

"What do you mean?"

Bertrand cupped the back of his neck with his hand, clearly flustered.

"Well, of course this contest doesn't suggest categorically that Zoe is the best *patisserie* chef in the country. That would be ridiculous. Let's face it, Marie-France is the station chef at *Le Coucou*."

"But that's exactly how you set up the contest. That the winner would be acknowledged as the best."

"Yes, well, for dramatic purposes, of course. But nobody really thinks a fourteen-year old American beat out Marie-France Babin."

Oh, so now she's American?

"Except she did," Maggie said.

"She did today," he stressed.

"Is there something special about today that might make it a singular exception to Zouzou winning again?" Maggie asked.

"What? No. Except of course that both Cheryl and Marie-France had their hands tied so to speak."

Maggie took a bite of her main course, an over-salted *coq au vin*. Looking around the room she saw several people crowded around the bar but all in all, the group had thinned considerably.

"How do you think the mix-up happened with Cheryl's butter?" she asked. "Who was in charge of that?"

"Well, ultimately of course I'm responsible," he said with a sigh. "The buck stops with me and all that."

"But you didn't personally put the butter on her counter?"

"No, that was handled by the catering staff. I've spoken to the manager and she's promised heads will roll."

"Little late to help Cheryl."

Bertrand threw up his hands. "It was a screw-up! Cheryl

will have other opportunities to show how wonderful she is and frankly, just between you and me, I don't think it did her any harm to be taken down a peg."

One of the caterers came over to ask Bertrand how much more of the *foie gras* he should put out. Bertrand panicked and jumped up.

"Bloody hell! I told them to stop serving that before the first course!"

After Bertrand left the table his phone rang. Without thinking Maggie picked it up and watched it go to voicemail. Then she opened up his email and searched for Helga's name

She found an email sent to Helga a week ago where Bertrand asked if she would please consider bowing out of the contest. He would pay her for her inconvenience.

<It was all a big mistake I'm horrified about but I'll need to rescind my invitation to you to the competition.>

Maggie was shocked. Bertrand wanted Helga *not* to come? Why? She found Helga's reply on top of Bertrand's email.

<You invited me so I am coming.>

Holding her breath and glancing furtively around the room in case Bertrand was headed back to the table, Maggie quickly scrolled to the top of Helga's email to see Bertrand's reply.

<I'm willing to pay you half the prize money for your trouble. I'm asking you as a professional to stay away or frankly deal with the consequences.>

21

G race and Cheryl left as soon as they came back from the toilets and Bertrand only came back to the table long enough to scoop up his phone and disappear again.

Maggie texted Laurent to see if he could come get her early and he texted back that he was just pulling up outside.

The weather had turned even colder and Maggie hadn't dressed for it. As soon as she got in the car she was shivering. Laurent automatically turned up the car's heater.

"I found out a few interesting things," she said.

"I am eager to hear them all," he said with a dead pan expression.

"It turns out that *Geoff* has a motive for killing Helga."

"Yes?"

"Did you know that the winning purse was twenty thousand euros?"

"But that motive would work for Cheryl and Marie-France, too," he said. "*N'est-ce pas?*"

"Yes but *they* don't sound like thugs are going to come to

their house and break their kneecaps if they don't come up with some money fast. Geoff's in a bad way debt-wise."

"He told you this?" Laurent frowned. It was inconceivable—even if falling down drunk—that a Frenchman might reveal something so personal as his finances.

"Debbie told me when Geoff was in the toilet."

Laurent shook his head at the thought of Geoff's wife's lack of discretion.

"Did you find out where he was when Frau Richter was killed?" he asked.

"I didn't get a chance to ask him tonight," Maggie admitted. "He was pretty wasted by the time the first course came out."

"Was he alone in the vineyard?"

"They all were except for Cheryl."

"And Bertrand."

"Yes, which reminds me of another very interesting tidbit I discovered tonight. It seems that after Bertrand invited Helga to come and compete, he tried to uninvite her."

Laurent frowned. "How do you know this?"

"I looked at his emails on his phone when he left the table."

"You looked at his phone? Surely that is a crime?" Laurent said.

"Is it really *you* asking me that? The point is Bertrand was offering Helga *half* the prize money if she didn't come to France and compete. Why would Bertrand be so desperate for Helga not to compete? Once I find out his reason, I'll have a motive for his eliminating her."

"It does not sound like a motive. It sounds like he didn't want her to compete and offered her money to stay home."

"Half the winning purse?" Maggie said incredulously. "Plus his email sounded vaguely threatening, like *stay away or else*."

Maggie gazed out the car window into the dark. She shivered just looking at all the ice hanging from the streetlamps.

"I wish we could get some information from Detective LaBelle about the DNA at the scene," she said.

"Antoine said the police found Sybil's DNA on the body."

"Yes, well they would have since she was trying to give her chest compressions."

"And then there is the unfortunate fact that Sybil was heard to threaten Helga."

"Who told the cops that?"

"Everyone who was at the dinner table, I imagine," Laurent said.

"You're not saying you think Sybil really did it?" Maggie asked.

"I am saying we do not know who really did it."

Maggie was silent for a moment. The day had been a long one. Her eyelids grew heavy.

"How's Antoine doing?" she asked through a yawn.

"Not good. But he must be brave for Mireille of course."

"I'll stop by and see her tomorrow," she said, leaning her head back and closing her eyes, the gentle hum and rocking of the car lulling her.

"I still can't believe Zouzou won," she murmured. "I mean, Marie-France is the friggin' station chef at *Le Coucou* in *Paris*."

"*Je sais, chérie*," Laurent said. "As proud of Zouzou as I am, it is still very odd."

22

The next morning, Maggie woke up late and the house was quiet except for the sound of the two dogs, Buddy and Izzy, as they looked up from their dog beds on the floor in her bedroom.

Since it was a Sunday, she assumed Laurent had let her sleep late. She pulled on jeans and a sweatshirt and came downstairs to find that the coffee was still hot. Normally Laurent would put on a major Sunday lunch here at Domaine Saint-Buvard. But because of the contest and extra houseguests they'd opted to skip it this week.

She settled onto a kitchen chair and looked at the note Laurent had left her. He'd taken everyone to the village church in Saint-Buvard and would drop Danielle and Zouzou off at *Dormir* afterwards.

It was unusual to have the house to herself and Maggie wasn't sure she really liked it. But as a member of a big and active family she knew not to waste it either.

She sat down at the dining room table with a spiral note-book, her coffee and one of the *chouquettes* that Laurent had set out on a tray in the kitchen.

While it was true she didn't know for sure if Sybil was innocent, one thing she did know was that the police wouldn't be trying to look in all directions to solve this murder. Case completion rates in any police department meant raises and promotions.

They would take the easiest way there.

She wrote down *Did Sybil do it?* Then she jotted down three words: *motive, opportunity and means.* She tapped the end of her pen against the table. Sybil definitely had motive and opportunity. She'd been slapped by the victim not an hour earlier and she was found leaning over Helga's body. That left means.

How was Helga killed?

Maggie tried to remember what the body had looked like to her. There was very little blood but it could have been hidden by Helga's outerwear. She remembered seeing something in Helga's mouth.

Was it a message from the killer?

If so, it was a message that had been delivered only to the police because Maggie had been afraid to touch the body for fear of contaminating the crime scene worse than she already had and so hadn't been able to determine what it was in Helga's mouth

She looked at the sentence *Did Sybil do it?* and wrote underneath that *Who else?* Underneath that she wrote the name *Cheryl* and then drew a line through it. She admonished herself for thinking of Cheryl when the woman had an alibi—she'd been with Grace the whole time.

I must not let personal animosities cloud my objectivity.

Next there was Marie-France. As with Geoff, she too had been alone in the vineyard. Maggie jotted down their names. Everyone else was paired up.

She studied Marie-France and Geoff's names. She would need to talk to them both to see if either of them had anything in the way of motive. She'd already discovered that Geoff's gambling debts made him desperate to win the contest but honestly in spite of what she'd said to Laurent last night—she'd been tired and had downed at least four glasses of wine—unless Geoff was thinking of bumping off both Cheryl and Marie-France too, his desperation to win the contest wasn't much in the way of a motive for killing Helga.

So if he's the killer, there must be some other reason than what I can see.

She frowned as she studied the words on the page of her notebook. She never did find out if Geoff had known Helga before the contest. It seemed likely since the pool of professional *patisserie* chefs in the world wasn't that big.

She looked back at her suspects list. Since she was revising her list from the night before she should probably let Bertrand off the hook too since she'd been with him the whole time, so he'd had no opportunity.

Right, she thought looking at her notebook.

Marie-France and Geoff.

It was at least a place to start.

An hour later, after receiving a text from Laurent saying he had a pork roast for today's lunch but had spent too much time visiting at *Dormir* and could Maggie run to the village bakery for bread? Maggie was in the car headed for Saint-Buvard.

Truth be told, she was glad of the outing and the fact that she was going to the *boulangerie* in the village gave her a chance to check in on Mireille and Antoine.

The bakery was small, wedged tightly between a defunct shoe repair shop and a *tabac*. It was doing a brisk business even on Sunday or, as Maggie reminded herself, perhaps because it was Sunday. Most of the villagers would have their midday Sunday lunches—none of which could be complete without bread. And because it was Sunday, there would need to be pastries too. Nothing too extravagant, perhaps just croissants or a *tart au framboises* or brioche,

Maggie stepped into the bakery and got in line behind four people. Tall glass cases at the front of the shop were filled with *croissants, tartes au fraises, brioche,* and *pain au chocolat.* Wicker baskets were set by the cash register displaying three different kinds of bread: the traditional baguette, *pain de campagne,* and *pain de mie.*

It was amazing to Maggie that the village had survived nearly a decade without a bakery when Antoine seemed to bake enough to serve a city the size of Arles with few to no leftovers.

The scent of yeast and toasted nuts came to Maggie as she waited in line. She could also pick out cinnamon, ginger and even cardamom. Antoine had a middle eastern background and his cinnamon cardamom glazed rolls were very popular.

Maggie spoke with everyone in the line. Being the only American in the village didn't necessarily give her prestige but it certainly made her well-known. That and the fact that Laurent was a prominent area landowner and a friend of the monastery gave her near celebrity status.

After greeting everyone, Maggie focused on Antoine who was busy waiting on customers, wrapping up bread purchases, and moving back and forth along the front counter.

There wasn't a time that Maggie came into the bakery that she didn't remember the time she had literally fought for her life in that backroom with a deranged killer and walked away alive but with an arm broken in two places. She knew that Grace often got her bread in Saint-Buvard and that she—pregnant with Zouzou at the time—had been hurt even worse than Maggie during that terrible altercation.

A sudden crash broke Maggie out of her thoughts and she looked up to see Mireille, Antoine and Sybil's daughter, cowering behind her father, a look of guilt and fear on her face.

"You stupid girl!" Antoine barked. "Are you trying to make my life even harder?"

Maggie felt her cheeks flush and she pushed to the head of the line. She knew Antoine was under terrible strain but taking it out on poor Mireille was just not on.

She also knew that her presence would likely force Antoine to get a grip of himself. Laurent was basically Antoine's boss if not benefactor.

"Is everything okay?" Maggie asked, giving Mireille a smile.

Antoine looked at Maggie, his nostrils flaring and she watched him trying to control his anger.

"I'm sorry, Papa," Mireille said.

He waved her words away angrily.

"Get a broom," he said to his daughter. She hurried to the backroom.

"I'm surprised you're even open today, Monsieur Pelletier," Maggie said. She was aware of stares from the shop's customers. Two customers had already left the bakery. She smiled apologetically at the first person in line and then spoke to Antoine.

"I'm sure everyone would understand if you closed early," she said in a low voice.

"Is that an order, Madame Dernier?" Antoine said, his lip curling in resentment.

What is his problem?

Maggie quickly reminded herself of what his problem was: his wife was sitting in jail on a murder charge.

Just as Maggie was about to assure him that she only wanted him to take care of himself, he turned and picked up a wet rag and flung it in the direction of the backroom.

Stunned, Maggie heard a ceramic bowl break and Mireille yelp.

"How long does it take to find a broom, you stupid girl! Get out here and wait on people! I'll do it myself!"

He turned and stomped into the back room. Mireille quickly appeared, her eyes red and downcast. She went to the counter and spoke, not raising her eyes.

"May I help you?"

Maggie stepped away from the counter to let the next person in line give her order. She turned to look at the person behind her in line, Madame Boudoir who had been the village mail carrier, retired now five years.

"Antoine has a temper," Madame Boudoir said, one eye on the entrance to the back room where Antoine had gone. "Everyone knows this."

23

"Well, *I* never knew it!" Maggie said to Laurent thirty minutes later as she moved about the kitchen helping him put together lunch. "You should have seen him, Laurent. It was deplorable."

"I have heard something to this effect," Laurent admitted.

Maggie was buttering the casserole dish for the au gratin potatoes. She stopped and turned to look at him. She glanced toward the living room where the children were playing a board game. She dropped her voice.

"You knew?"

"*Chérie*, where are the onions?"

Maggie looked around and found them in a bowl on the counter. She handed them to him.

Laurent and the children had already been back at Domaine St-Buvard by the time Maggie arrived home from the village *boulangerie*.

"And that doesn't worry you?" she asked him as she took a seat on one of the kitchen bar stools.

"Why would it worry me?"

"Well, think about it. Helga slapped Antoine's wife and Antoine has a bad temper. What would *you* do in a situation like that?"

"Are you saying I have a bad temper, *chérie*?"

"I'm saying you might be able to understand how somebody like Antoine could be capable of committing murder after seeing his wife attacked."

Laurent frowned.

"So you think Antoine left the house, went out to find the German, killed her and came back with an armful of firewood? Hand me the cheese, please, *chérie*."

Maggie reached for the large wedge of swiss cheese on the counter and then froze in mid-stretch.

"Antoine left the house?" she asked. "He doesn't have an alibi?"

"He was gone for no more than twenty minutes."

"Laurent, that is plenty of time to find Helga and do the deed!"

Laurent made a frustrated huffing sound.

"What point is there in clearing Sybil," he said, "if you are going to then blame her husband?"

"The point, Laurent is that the person who did this crime, needs to pay for it. No matter who it is. Did you tell Detective LaBelle that Antoine was with you the whole time?"

"Of course."

"Did you forget he went out for firewood?"

Laurent clenched his jaw.

"What I forgot is how relentless you can be," he said.

"Antoine might be letting his wife take the rap for a crime he committed," Maggie said.

"Who are you talking about?" Luc said as he came into the kitchen.

"No one," Laurent and Maggie said at the same time.

Luc rolled his eyes and picked up a plate of ham slices and cornichons from the counter.

"Is this for us before lunch?" he asked already on his way back into the living room with the plate.

Maggie turned back to Laurent but he held up a hand.

"Enough," he said. "Not while the children are in the house." He turned back to his saucepan on the stove and gave it a stir.

Maggie knew Laurent was right. All three of the kids knew Mireille and she would hate for them to think that they suspected either of Mireille's parents of doing this terrible thing.

She heard her phone ringing and hopped off the barstool to dig it out from inside her purse. Bertrand's name appeared on the screen.

"Hey, Bertrand," she said, moving toward her den on the other side of the living room. "How's Marie-France?"

"She is completely fine. I picked her up after the banquet last night and she spent the night in Aix at the Hôtel Dauphin. But I think she was hoping to move in with you for the remainder of her stay."

"Grace told me," Maggie said. "That's fine. How much longer does she intend to stay, do you know?"

"I don't know. She's still a little shaky on her pins. A holiday is just the ticket for her."

"If she's up for it," Maggie said, "why don't you bring her over this evening? Can you run by *Dormir* first and get her things?"

"It's precisely the reason I'm calling," Bertrand said jovially. "I say that was quite a party last night, wasn't it? I rang Geoff this morning and Debbie said he's sick as a dog."

"I'm sorry to hear that."

"Well, after how the contest went down he wasn't going to

be very good company for anyone. He should probably take the time to enjoy this stretch as a bit of a holiday himself. I get the impression things aren't financially quite as they could be with old Geoff. Oh, well. Must toddle. Is Zouzou there by chance?"

Maggie frowned. "No, she's at *Dormir*. Why?"

"No reason. Just hoping to get a couple spontaneous photos of the big winner, is all. I'll see her at *Dormir*. Cheers!" He disconnected.

Maggie sat in her office chair holding the phone, the sounds of the television in the other room much too loud. Laurent would make the children turn it off in a bit. They had a rule about daytime TV and certainly never on Sunday.

So everybody knew how broke Geoff was? Doesn't that make him desperate?

Maggie sighed. It might. But that didn't necessarily make him a murderer.

As she emerged from her office she saw that Mila was setting the table and Jemmy was in the kitchen with his father who was just setting down his cellphone.

"Who called?" Maggie asked.

"That was Detective LaBelle," Laurent said. "Jemmy, give the *au gratin* a stir and then go feed the dogs."

"Detective LaBelle?" Maggie's pulse sped up. "Why was she calling? Has something happened?"

"Not that I know of, *chérie*," Laurent said tossing down the dishtowel he normally kept slung over one shoulder. "She only called to say that we may visit Sybil now if we wished."

Maggie's eyes widened.

"You're kidding. How did you get her to agree to that?"

"I am as surprised as you are, *chérie*," he said, arching an eyebrow at her.

"Really," she said, her mind racing with the possibility of a scenario whereby a normally intractable homicide detective might call them on a Sunday to allow them to visit her prime suspect.

Correction. Not them. *Laurent.*

And as far as his being surprised about it, Maggie didn't believe that for a minute.

24

The next morning by the time Maggie had driven to Aix, dropped the children off at school and parked at the Aix-en-Provence police station off Cours des Minimes, the weather had worsened. The weak winter sun had disappeared entirely behind a thick band of grey clouds hunched over the horizon of the town and the air was cold and miserable.

Maggie sat in the sterile waiting room of the police station. Her appointment to see Sybil was for ten, and she'd already been waiting an hour. She'd asked the sergeant at the intake desk behind the bulletproof partition if they'd forgotten about her. Her query wasn't received well and she decided it would probably not in her best interests to ask again.

When an email came in on her cellphone, she read it with a frown. It was from a travel sponsor who was pulling out of advertising in her newsletter for the foreseeable future.

Maggie had begun the newsletter five years earlier when an expat blog she'd written had gotten some attention with the other expats in the area. That had grown into a comfortable business of local vendors and artisans using her newsletter to reach new customers in the UK and even the US.

In the last few months, however, her subscription rates had started dropping. She wasn't sure what to attribute that to beyond just natural attrition. Plus, January was a terrible time of the year to be advertising vacations in the south of France. While it was true that the planning of those trips might happen in January under thick duvets and in front of fireplaces, that didn't help the artisans who advertised in Maggie's newsletter looking for revenue in January.

"Madame Dernier?"

Maggie looked up and saw Detective LaBelle standing in the doorway scowling at her. Maggie got to her feet ready to shake hands when the detective waved away her attempt.

"Where is your husband?"

LaBelle had been expecting to see Laurent.

Maggie had told Laurent that but he had business at the monastery this morning and was uninterested in playing games with the detective.

"He was unable to come this morning," Maggie said. "But I am looking forward to seeing Madame Pelletier and am so very grateful to you for that opportunity."

LaBelle snorted, proving that not just French men can perfectly execute the expression, then turned and led Maggie down the hall. At the end of the hall she handed Maggie off to a guard and without a word disappeared again.

Maggie entered a communal room furnished with couches and laminate dining tables and where Sybil was waiting for her. There was no one else in the room and the guard simply closed the door behind Maggie and left them alone.

Maggie's first impulse was to hug Sybil but she didn't really know her that well and the woman was French. There were probably few instances where Sybil would welcome that kind of physical attention.

"Oh, Madame Dernier, thank you for coming."

They shook hands and Maggie sat on the couch where Sybil retook her seat.

"Please just call me Maggie. How are you doing?"

Tears came to Sybil's eyes. "It is not that terrible," she said unconvincingly. "It is just the fear of not knowing what will happen to me."

"I saw Antoine and Mireille yesterday," Maggie said. "They're bearing up."

Sybil nodded and Maggie couldn't tell if her words really had much of a comforting effect.

"I know this is a terrible time for you," Maggie said, "but Laurent and I want to help if we can."

"That is good of you, Madame Dernier."

"*Maggie*, please. Look, Sybil, I don't know how much time we have so could I ask you some questions about that night?"

Sybil looked briefly defensive but finally nodded.

"I need to ask you what you were doing in the vineyard," Maggie said. "I thought you were supposed to be in the house cleaning up with Laurent and Antoine."

Sybil groaned. "How I wish now I had!"

Maggie glanced up at the large clock on the wall. "So why were you there?"

"It is hard to explain."

Maggie felt a flair of impatience.

"If you're trying to protect Zouzou, for God's sake's, stop. Just tell me why you were there."

"I went to find her mother for her."

"Did Zouzou ask you to find her mother?"

"*Non*, Madame Dernier."

"Okay, so then why did you—"

"I have a daughter myself," Sybil said softly. "I know how important these things are to the young."

Maggie studied her for a moment. Of course Sybil was aware that Mireille lived in a repressive home with Antoine. Was she trying to create some sort of balance? Giving Zouzou the freedom she was unable to give her own daughter? It was a reach.

"It's just that it looks bad—you going out into the vineyard after what happened between you and Frau Richter," Maggie said.

"*Je sais.*" *I know*.

"Okay, so you found Madame Van Sant and gave her the message."

"I did. And then I was afraid that Antoine...that I would be missed and so I started to run the rest of the way back to the house. I got a little turned around. And then I heard a noise."

"Not a voice?"

Sybil appeared to be thinking.

"*Non.* A noise. Grunts, rustling in the bushes."

Like maybe a struggle? Maggie wondered.

"When I emerged through a line of bushes, I fell over something in the dark."

"Did you not bring a flashlight with you?"

"Yes, but the battery was dying."

"Okay. Please continue."

"I saw it was her. The German. On the ground." A sick look came over Sybil's face. "When I knelt by her I could see...I thought I saw that she was dead."

"Then what happened?"

"I immediately gave her the kiss of life. But she had something in her mouth. I had to pull it out first."

Maggie's senses perked up. So she'd been right about that. Except she'd seen it in Helga's mouth herself.

"You removed it?"

"I did but then I put it back. I became afraid that I was touching too many things."

"What was it?" Maggie asked.

"It was a toy of a little bird."

Maggie tilted her head to one side.

"Like a stuffed animal?" she asked.

"*Oui.* A child's toy perhaps."

The killer must have put it there.

"Anything else?"

"No," Sybil said. "Oh, except for the stone."

Maggie frowned. There were drystone walls on one side of the vineyard but it was not generally a rocky area. The actual planting area was meticulously free of stones.

"It looked to me like a worry stone," Sybil said. "Do you know what that is?"

Maggie shook her head.

"It's about the size of an egg. Gypsies often make them to sell. I was looking right at it when I was doing the chest compressions. It had a design on it."

"Do you think you could recreate the design?"

"I don't know," Sybil said doubtfully. "But I'm sure the police found it. It was not hidden."

The guard appeared and Sybil stood up.

"Is there anything you need?" Maggie asked.

Sybil shook head. "Just...if you see Mireille, tell her I did not do this. Tell her I love her."

"I will," Maggie said, wondering why Sybil needed *her* to tell her daughter this. Was Antoine not coming to visit her?

"Be strong, Sybil," Maggie said as the guard escorted the woman out of the room.

As she left the police station, Maggie shivered in the cold air and tried to process her visit with Sybil. How odd was it that this so-called worry stone would be next to Helga's body? Was it a coincidence or was it something left by the murderer? Laurent typically combed every inch of his vineyard before and after the harvest. Not that he inventoried every rock and pebble, but it felt unlikely that such a thing should be there.

As Maggie got in her car for the drive back to Domaine Saint-Buvard, it occurred to her that it was possible that village teenagers might use their vineyard as a romantic rendezvous point.

Except there were plenty of other, more comfortable and more private venues than a cold vineyard.

So how did a worry stone get in their vineyard?

25

That afternoon Maggie didn't get a chance to debrief with Laurent about her visit with Sybil. Jemmy had a minor crisis with his science project which was still not finished, and Luc had a flat tire in Les Granettes on his way back from his not-girlfriend Anna's house.

Maggie still didn't know the details of Luc's relationship with the girl but it was near the top of her list to find out. She was surprised that Laurent didn't appear more concerned or even interested. But first, there was a new guest at Domaine Saint-Buvard that needed to be dealt with.

As soon as Maggie stepped across the threshold of her home, she smelled coffee brewing and something baking in the oven. She'd just spoken on the phone with Laurent who was at the monastery until dinner time so she knew he couldn't be the cause of the heavenly scent.

"Hello!" she called as she shed her car coat and briefly greeted the two dogs who ran to her, jumping up and licking her face.

"Mom!" Mila called out. "We have company!"

Maggie stepped into the hall where she saw Marie-France

sitting on one of the barstools, a *noisette* coffee in front of her on the kitchen counter.

"*Bonjour*, Maggie," Marie-France said with a smile. "Mila and I have been having a lovely visit."

Mila was just pulling a pan of *Madeleines* out of the oven. She and Zouzou had made the batter a week ago and frozen it.

"*Bonjour*, Marie-France," Maggie said. "I'm so glad to have you. Mmm, that coffee smells good."

"I'm just pouring you some, Mom," Mila said as Maggie sat down next to Marie-France.

"I hope you're feeling better," Maggie said to the French woman.

Instantly Marie-France scowled and Maggie was sorry she mentioned it.

"First I was ill—disastrously so," Marie-France said. "And now Geoff is sick. Did you hear? Sick in bed."

"I did hear that," Maggie said.

"I asked Mademoiselle Mila if some virus was going around but she is unaware of anything," Marie-France said.

Mila placed a demitasse in front of Maggie and a plate of the still-warm butter cookies.

Maggie sipped her coffee. The last time she'd seen Marie-France, the French woman was accusing the world of poisoning her. Maggie was glad to see she didn't seem to be going down that road any longer.

"Your Mila is a good little baker," Marie-France said, turning her attention back to Mila who was washing her hands at the sink.

"I told her it was Zouzou who made the batter for the *Madeleines*," Mila said. "I'm just her helper."

"Well, they are very good regardless of who made them," Maggie said, smiling at her daughter and hoping to defuse any possible rant on Marie-France's part. Surely she didn't blame *Zouzou* for her getting sick that day?

"I told her that mere skill would not be enough if she hoped to succeed in the world of *patisserie* making," Marie-France said.

"Who?" Maggie asked. "You told Zouzou that?"

Marie-France sniffed and lifted her demitasse cup to her pursed lips.

"I was only giving the child a little friendly advice," she said in a very unfriendly tone.

~

Dinner that night was *poulet de Provençal*, a family favorite. Laurent got home in time to direct the main efforts of both Luc and Jemmy in marinating and sautéing the chicken.

Maggie was grateful that Marie-France had decided to take a nap before dinner which allowed Maggie to work in her office on a few last-minute news items that had come in on festival events happening in the area next month.

Advertising a village festival was never a direct line to any monetary benefit for anyone, but it was good public relations for whatever little village was putting on the festival, and it added important local color and specificity to Maggie's newsletter as well as to the other vendors and artisans she advertised.

When Maggie finally emerged from her office for dinner, Marie-France was up and observing the dinner preparations with a large balloon glass of red wine.

As usual, Laurent was directing the dinner prep. He stood in the kitchen which opened up onto the dining room and directed the activity while the tantalizing scents of cooking onions and garlic and *herbes de Provence* emanated from the kitchen.

"Everyone, sit!" Laurent called. "Luc, the dogs."

"Already fed," Luc replied.

"My, such a bustling family," Marie-France said, smiling at Luc and then at Laurent. "Your older son favors you strongly physically. The younger boy looks more like your wife."

"You will sit here," Laurent said to Marie-France, pointing to her chair, his face unreadable.

Maggie glanced at Luc to see how Marie-France's words were affecting him. But she knew that as far as Luc knew he was not related to Laurent.

Maggie and Laurent, of course, knew differently.

"Smells amazing," Maggie said, taking her seat as Luc filled her wine glass.

"Laurent put extra rosemary in it," Luc said.

"Why does your son call you by your first name?" Marie-France asked, pushing her wine glass toward Luc to have it refilled.

Luc glanced at Laurent to see how he would respond. Maggie knew that Laurent usually didn't bother answering if he didn't care for the question.

"He believes he is too old to call me *Papa*," Laurent said. "Jemmy, get the *courgettes* and bring them in."

Luc's face brightened at Laurent's words and then he flushed and ducked his head as if to hide his reaction.

Now, of course, Maggie thought, *he will wonder if Laurent only said that for Marie-France's benefit*. And honestly, Maggie didn't know either.

"Everybody sit before it gets cold," Laurent ordered.

"My," Marie-France said. "Do you always eat so formally or is this on my account?"

"Laurent likes a traditional evening meal," Maggie said. "You should see us for Sunday lunch." She nearly bit her tongue and found herself hoping that Marie-France would be gone by Sunday.

"Really?" Marie-France said flapping out her napkin across her lap. "Well, I just might."

. . .

Much to Maggie's regret, when Marie-France was on her fourth glass of wine, she began to revisit her experience at the contest. Maggie was grateful that Zouzou wasn't here at least but Mila was sure to pass along the comments and Zouzou would be just as well not to know of them.

"I mean, my first thought was that I'd been poisoned," Marie-France said. "Even Bertrand thought it was suspicious. I'd eaten nearly nothing all day!"

"Perhaps that was the problem," Maggie said lightly.

"The *problem*, Madame Dernier," Marie-France said, "is that someone drugged my coffee in order to win the contest."

"You mean Zouzou?" Mila asked, her eyes wide.

"Don't be silly," Maggie said. "Of course Madame Babin doesn't think Zouzou drugged her."

"*Non*, I do not," Marie-France said. "No one believed for a moment that the child could win. She was merely a place-holder for Frau Richter. No, it could only have been Geoff or Cheryl who did it to me."

"Is that what you really believe?" Laurent said, his voice cold.

Marie-France blinked in his direction. Laurent had a talent for saying just a few words that could nonetheless make you feel downright threatened.

"I only know that I was the only true competition in that contest," Marie-France said, "and when I was taken out of the equation, it made the possibility of one of the other two winning much higher."

Luc cleared his throat and all eyes went to him.

"May I be excused? I have homework."

Maggie was sure he also had a phone call he wanted to make to the girl Anna, girlfriend or not.

"Me too?" Jemmy said, looking at Laurent. "My science project—"

Laurent waved his assent to both boys and then turned to

Mila.

"If you are finished, *chérie*, perhaps you would like to watch television in your room?"

Mila's eyes got round in surprise and then she looked at Marie-France as it became clear that Laurent did not want her at the table listening to their guest.

"Yes, please," she said, standing up with her plate.

Marie-France waited for the children to leave before reaching for her wine glass. It was nearly empty again and Laurent leaned over and filled it up.

"I'm not accusing anyone," Marie-France said. "I mean it looks very suspicious to me but it's over and there you have it."

"Very philosophical of you," Maggie said.

"Oh, I come by that naturally," Marie-France said, slurring her words and oblivious to any possible irony in Maggie's voice. "My grandfather was a Resistance hero in the second world war."

"Oh?" Maggie said. "He must have had some amazing stories for you growing up."

"I'm sure he would have," Marie-France said, twirling the stem of her wine glass. "If the filthy Germans hadn't murdered him."

26

That night in bed, Maggie shivered and pulled the duvet up close to her ears.

"God, she's insufferable," she said as she watched Laurent get ready for bed. "I don't care how light and delicious her *profiteroles* are. And she's really polished that story about her grandfather the Resistance hero, didn't you think?"

"She has clearly told it a few times before tonight."

Marie-France had spent the rest of the evening regaling them with the exploits and detailed descriptions of her grandfather—culminating in his brutal demise at the hands of the Gestapo and somehow as the result of a trio of homing pigeons who had been used to catch him. After her own third glass of wine, the details had gotten foggy for Maggie. It had been a long, busy day.

Maggie had listened politely until it was bedtime. Laurent had long since made his escape to do the dishes and walk the dogs.

"Everybody I've ever met in this country," Maggie said, "had a relative who was a resistance hero. Did you ever notice that?"

"With so many heroes, it makes you wonder who the collaborators were, no?"

As Laurent climbed into bed, Maggie snuggled up next to him

"I didn't get a chance to tell you what I learned from my visit with Sybil today," she said.

"How did she look?"

"They're feeding her, Laurent if that's your question. I mean it's only been three days. She looks the same. Do you know if Antoine is visiting her?"

"I am sure he is."

"But you don't know for sure?"

"Why do you ask this?"

"Because she gave me a message for Mireille that made me think she didn't have another avenue of communicating with the girl."

Laurent frowned but didn't say anything.

"Anyway, get a load of this," Maggie said excitedly, sitting back up in bed "Sybil said a bird was stuffed in Helga's mouth."

"So?"

"I would've thought finding a body with a bird in its mouth was unusual."

"You saw the body too. Did you not see it?"

"I saw something but not what. Listen, Laurent, don't you see the connection here? Marie-France's grandfather was killed via carrier pigeon."

"You are making no sense, *chérie*."

"Her grandfather was killed because he was tricked by the Germans using pigeons!"

He gave her a disbelieving look.

"Think about it," she said. "Helga was confronted in the vineyard, stabbed in the heart and then had a pigeon stuffed in her mouth."

"We don't know that it was a pigeon. It looked like a black bird."

"It doesn't matter! It's a *bird*! Wait. How do you know what it looked like?"

"Detective LaBelle might have mentioned it."

"You've been talking to Detective LaBelle?" Maggie felt a sudden coldness in her core.

"Only a few emails," he said.

"Why is she emailing you?"

"Does it matter? If we get information on the case?"

Maggie grappled with her emotions, her jealousy and her annoyance.

"Okay. So let's say for argument's sake that it's a black bird. According to Marie-France, her grandfather was betrayed by the use of birds."

"You are being ridiculous."

"I've seen this kind of thing before, Laurent!" Maggie said hotly, still irked that Detective LaBelle was in contact with Laurent over the case. "Something that sounds ridiculous at first glance could hold a vital clue."

"Even accepting that Marie-France was unhappy with how her grandfather died," Laurent said, "Helga had nothing to do with the Nazis. The light, please, *chérie*."

"But she's German! You heard how Sybil called her *boche*? And Marie-France made that comment about German pastry chefs only being good enough to make gingerbread? It doesn't matter that Helga was born two generations after the war. She was still the enemy."

Laurent gave her an unconvinced look.

"You know very well that there are people in villages right around here who haven't forgiven the Germans!" Maggie said. "The fact is, Marie-France doesn't have an alibi *and* she hated Germans!"

"So what are you saying?"

Maggie sank back into her pillow.

"I think Marie-France might have killed Helga."

27

G race watched the breeze whip through what few leaves remained on the plane trees in her front courtyard and scatter them into frenetic vortexes around the pavers. It had been snowing on and off all morning but was presently in the off mode. The snow was just a dusting but it covered the two rental cars in her driveway, visible from her kitchen window.

Grace put down the envelope on the kitchen counter. It had been addressed to Zouzou but in the care of Grace Van Sant. The return address had made it inevitable that she would open it. If Zouzou was unhappy about that—and given the contents of the letter, Grace didn't imagine she would be—she could always say she thought it had been addressed to her.

Her hands felt cold and she was aware of a sour taste in her mouth.

The scent of fresh-brewed coffee mingled with the sweet fragrance of warm chocolate. Danielle stood in front of the breakfast table, wearing an apron, her hands on her hips. The table was set with mismatched French country china and colorful Provençal linens.

When they'd just started out with *Dormir* they used to make full English or American breakfasts but quickly discovered that a good cup of coffee and some sweet rolls made the guests just as happy.

Or didn't make them any less happy anyway.

"How many are we expecting?" Danielle asked.

"I don't really know."

Laurent had swung by early to collect Zouzou for school. She had begged Grace to allow her to spend a few days at Domaine Saint-Buvard and Grace had agreed. For some reason with Cheryl and Zouzou both at *Dormir*, it felt like Grace was walking through a minefield.

Bertrand was at the Hôtel Dauphin in Aix, Geoff and Debbie were in Prune cottage on the property and Cheryl was in one of the upstairs guest rooms.

"Wow! What smells amazing?" Cheryl said as she came into the dining room. "Whoa, you have a lot of nerve baking muffins for a *patisserie* chef!" She laughed. "Good for you."

"They are Zouzou's," Danielle said. "We often freeze her creations so we have them when we need them."

Cheryl sat down and Grace came to pour her coffee.

"You slept well, I hope?" Grace said.

"Like the dead, yeah. Where is Zouzou?"

"At school. But she'll stay at Domaine St-Buvard tonight."

"That is so pretentious, don't you think? Calling your house *Domaine St-Buvard*?"

Grace hesitated.

"Well, it's the name of the house."

"If you say so. These muffins are delish—even frozen and reheated. Zouzou really has a flair."

"She is very talented," Danielle said stiffly and retreated to the kitchen.

She doesn't like Cheryl, Grace thought with resignation. She tried to see her friend through Danielle's eyes. It was true she was a little loud and opinionated. Grace's shoulders slumped at the mental image.

"So what's on tap for today?" Cheryl said, slathering a large knob of butter on her muffin. "These would be better warm, by the way."

"Well, we could drive into Arles if you want," Grace said dispiritedly.

"Is everything okay?" Cheryl frowned at her and reached for her coffee cup which she'd already drained. Grace hurried to refill it.

"Yes, of course," Grace said with a smile.

"You act as if something's happened. Don't tell me somebody else got knifed while I slept."

Grace was a little surprised at Cheryl's callousness. Was it the American in her? Had it just been too long since Grace had been around her own countrymen?

"No," Grace said, sitting down and pouring herself a cup. "Actually there is something. Leave it to you to pick up on it. You always were able to read me."

"So what is it?"

"Zouzou's been accepted into the *l'Academie de Patisserie* for the summer session."

"Really? But that's great. Hey, did she amend her application online like I told her to reflect her win at the LUSH competition?"

"I don't know," Grace said.

"You don't look happy about it."

"I hate to disappoint her," Grace said. "But I don't see how she can go."

"What do you mean? Why in the world not?"

"Cheryl, I run a bed and breakfast. Summer is my high season. I can't take her to Paris for six weeks. Where would we live? How would we live?"

"I told you! She can stay with me!" Cheryl said, pushing her plate aside. "It'll be great. I've been a little lonely lately anyway. Is it the tuition? Is that the problem?"

"It...it's a scholarship," Grace said, her mind racing.

"So there you go! Free tuition. Free room. Free chaperone. It's settled."

Grace felt light-headed and her skin began to tingle unpleasantly.

Things were moving too fast.

"Well, it's something to consider," she said.

"What do you mean? It's settled! I can't wait to see Zouzou's face when we tell her, can you? Oh, I've got a million places to show her in Paris."

Grace smiled woodenly as her friend talked excitedly, unaware of Grace's growing discomfort.

An hour later as Grace was cleaning the breakfast dishes and Cheryl had opted to take a chilly morning walk in the garden, she realized she needed to bring Zouzou in on the letter.

First, she was sure that Cheryl would blurt out the "good" news as soon as she saw Zouzou and Grace needed time to process it all.

Grace wiped her hands and called Maggie.

Maggie answered on the first ring.

"Hey, you," Maggie said. "How's everything going on your end?"

"Good, good," Grace said, slipping a cup of coffee in microwave to heat it.

"What is it, Grace?"

"Zouzou was accepted into *l'Academie de Patisserie*," Grace said.

"So how is that going to work?" Maggie asked.

Grace felt a gush of love toward Maggie because of course

she recognized it wasn't wholly wonderful news. At all.

"Well, that's just it. Cheryl has offered to have Zouzou live with her for the session."

"She's just not going to give up, is she?" Maggie said. "I thought you already told her Zouzou coming to Paris with her wasn't a good idea."

"I did tell her," Grace said stiffly. "But the first opportunity was for Zouzou's last year of high school. This is only a summer slot."

"Okay," Maggie said dubiously.

"I'm not asking Cheryl to raise Zouzou," Grace said with exasperation. "Just to keep her safe for six weeks."

"I assume you haven't told Zouzou yet?"

"No. And I'm not sure why I feel so hesitant about it."

"Well, I'll tell you why," Maggie said. "Because it would be the first time Zouzou has been away from you when she wasn't with Windsor. So this is a big deal. It's nearly as bad as Luc moving to California."

"It's worse actually," Grace said with annoyance. "Luc will be eighteen years old when he leaves home. Zouzou is barely fifteen. Plus you've only had Luc for less than two years. This is my daughter we're talking about."

There was a brief spasm of silence on the phone. Grace was sorry if she'd upset Maggie but really! The two situations were nothing alike.

"Well, I guess you've got it sorted then," Maggie said stiffly. "And I've got a full day here so I'll let you go."

"Don't be like that, Maggie," Grace said.

"Look, I get that you can't go to Paris with Zouzou so it's really lucky you have someone you trust who can take her. Oh, and that reminds me. You were Cheryl's alibi for the night of the murder. Isn't that right?"

"I'm really sorry I called."

"Honestly, I am too."

Maggie stared at the phone in her hand after she disconnected with Grace. She felt a mild throb of guilt in her gut about that mean crack about Cheryl being such a good friend because Grace was her alibi.

Of course that wasn't the only reason Cheryl had offered to do Grace the favor of taking Zouzou to Paris.

Probably.

Maggie had to admit she wasn't unbiased about Cheryl. But it was for that very reason that she knew she needed to bend over backwards to give Cheryl the benefit of the doubt.

Besides, after the somewhat unpleasant dinner last night with Marie-France, Maggie definitely wanted to talk more to the French woman about her anti-German feelings. She was aware that what she'd come up with so far was far from evidence and certainly nothing Detective LaBelle would give any credibility to.

Thinking about the detective made Maggie think of how the woman had now reached out to Laurent *twice.* Maggie was used to women developing crushes on her husband. He was handsome and mysterious. But something told her that Detective LaBelle's interest in Laurent was not sexual.

Or at least not purely sexual.

It took Grace the better part of an hour to calm down from her phone call with Maggie. Not only did Maggie *not* make her feel better about the idea of Zouzou going off to Paris with Cheryl, she somehow had made it sound like Cheryl was only doing it because Grace was her alibi for murder!

And how dare Maggie imply whatever it was she was implying about Cheryl and the night of the murder!

Highly agitated, Grace brought out a heavy bottomed skillet and placed it on the stove over medium heat and added some olive oil to it. Then she pulled the bag of beef chunks from the fridge that she'd already cut and floured and added them to the skillet. Instantly they sizzled and the sound actually made her feel a little better.

There was nothing like cooking to settle your nerves, she thought. While the beef browned, she pulled out a cutting board and quickly peeled and diced a handful of carrots.

As she worked, Grace realized she felt mildly ashamed about insinuating to Maggie that her angst over Luc's leaving wasn't valid. The fact was, Maggie loved him and of course having him leave would be a wrench.

She scraped the cut vegetables into the sizzling pan and opened a can of beef broth and added that too.

Bottom line, Grace hadn't been sensitive to what Maggie was going through and while she absolutely believed there was no real comparison between Luc going off to college and Zouzou leaving for the summer, she should never have said anything!

Cheryl came into the kitchen from outside and stamped snow from her boots, making wet clumps on the floor.

"Man, all you do is cook! And as I recall, you did not like to cook in college."

Grace found a towel and tossed it onto the snow puddle. She and Danielle were very careful about slips. It was so easy to fall.

"That's true," Grace said. "But needs must. I have a different life now."

"Well, you can stop worrying about me. I'm happy to run into the village and get one of those yummy baguette sandwiches." Cheryl pulled the lid off one of the pots. "What is it?"

"It's just stew," Grace said. "Are you sure I can't make you a bowl? The bread we have in the pantry is nearly as fresh as what you'd find in Saint-Buvard. I'm happy to make you a sandwich."

"Well, if you're sure it's no trouble," Cheryl said, sitting down and pulling off her knit cap and shaking the snow crystals onto the floor. "It's freezing out there. A bowl of soup would be just the thing. Where is everyone?"

"Danielle has a busier social life than any of us," Grace said as she ladled the soup up and set it down in front of Cheryl. "A weekly card game, I think in Saint-Cannat."

"Mmm, smells good. And still no sign of Geoff or Debbie?"

"No, I knocked on their door to make sure they hadn't died," Grace said and then immediately regretted her words. "But Debbie said they were fine. I did expect to see her for lunch, though."

She cut thick slices of the country loaf and pulled a package of shaved ham from the fridge.

"I still can't believe Helga was murdered," Cheryl said, eating her stew. "Wild."

"Did you know her well?" Grace asked as she spread softened butter on the bread and layered on the ham and thin slices of Fontina cheese.

"Never met her before that night."

"It's hard to believe that Sybil would do something like this," Grace said. "She always seemed so levelheaded before."

"Well, she sure wasn't levelheaded that night. She refused to serve Helga her coffee and then did everything but accuse her of starting the war."

"I guess I didn't see that," Grace said, putting the sandwich on a dish in front of Cheryl and taking her bowl to the kitchen. "But Helga did slap her and Sybil didn't really react in kind to that."

"Probably because she was planning to sneak into the vineyard later and stab her to death," Cheryl said between bites of her sandwich.

Grace felt a tremor of nausea flutter in her gut.

"Sybil was in the vineyard," Grace said, "because she was trying to do something nice for Zouzou."

"Yeah, I think I heard something about that. Is there any more stew?"

Grace moved to the kitchen and took down another clean bowl and ladled up the stew. Her gut was twitching as her mind flashed back to the whole reason Sybil was out in the vineyard that night.

Sybil had found Grace—and also Cheryl—to say that Zouzou was hoping to get permission to watch a certain movie.

So why was Cheryl pretending she didn't know why Sybil was in the vineyard? She'd been right there when Sybil showed up.

Grace set the bowl down in front of Cheryl.

"Do you have salt or hot sauce or something? It's kind of bland."

"Sure," Grace said, moving robotically back to the kitchen to fetch both.

The memory that came to Grace as she returned to the dining room made her hands shake.

After Sybil caught up with her in the vineyard saying Zouzou needed permission for the movie, Grace had turned to go back to the house. She'd walked nearly as far as the back garden before realizing that Sybil would relay the message to Zouzou about the movie so Grace didn't need to.

Laughing off her slight drunkenness that had prompted her to turn back to the house, Grace had turned around to catch up with Cheryl.

Except she couldn't find her.

And when she finally did, Cheryl had been on her own for a good fifteen minutes.

aggie could hear the sounds of her car tires as they crunched through the snow banked up by the curb in front of the village bakery. It had been steadily snowing since she left Domaine Saint-Buvard but she'd thought it wasn't bad. Now it was coming down harder.

She squinted at the front of the bakery and saw that the sign in the window said FERMÉ but she saw Mireille inside.

Bracing herself for the blast of frigid air, she hurried out of her car and to the front door of the bakery and knocked.

Mireille opened the door. She looked breathless and pale. Maggie glanced behind her to see if Antoine was inside. She didn't see him.

"*Bonjour* Madame Dernier," Mireille said. "You are looking for bread?"

"No, thank you, Mireille," Maggie said, slipping inside. "I just wanted to have a word."

"My father is upstairs," Mireille said nervously, glancing overhead where the family's apartment was.

"It was you I was looking for," Maggie said. "I have a message for you from your mother."

Mireille's eyes filled with tears and Maggie led her to the single café table in the bakery. They both sat.

"I know you must be worried about her," Maggie said, squeezing the girl's hand.

"I am," Mireille said, a single tear streaking down her face.

"You're being so brave, Mireille. And that's what your mother needs you to be right now."

"I don't feel brave."

"That's how you know you are," Maggie assured her. "Bravery is being afraid but going forward anyway."

"I have no choice."

"You always have a choice."

"I don't," Mireille said miserably, shaking her head.

Maggie felt her heart go out to the girl and she leaned over and put an arm around her. She knew it wasn't very French to do so but she'd stopped apologizing for her American ways a long time ago.

"Your mom told me to tell you she loves you," Maggie said. "And that she didn't do this."

Mireille sniffed and nodded.

"And people who are innocent, eventually get let go," Maggie said.

"Do you really think so?" Mireille asked, looking up at her.

"Absolutely. And I don't think it will take that long either." Maggie sat with her arm around the girl and heard footsteps overhead as Antoine moved about the upstairs apartment.

"Do you have anyone to talk to?" Maggie asked. "Someone you can go to? An aunt or a good friend maybe?"

Mireille wiped her eyes with her fingers and then dug into the pocket of her *tablier*, a blue smock she wore over her corduroy jeans and sweatshirt.

"I get a lot of comfort from this," she said, opening her hand to reveal a small polished stone in her palm.

Maggie stared at it in dull shock.

"I read on the Internet," Mireille said, "that worry stones can bring luck. They don't just calm you, they can actually change bad things from happening."

"Where did you get this?" Maggie asked, taking the stone and turning it over. On the back was an elaborately carved design.

"I don't think it's valuable," Mireille said.

"I'd really like to know how you got it."

"I didn't steal it."

"Mireille, I know you didn't. As you said, it isn't even valuable. But where did you get it?"

She gave a brief shrug and looked up nervously to the apartment above her.

"My father gave it to me."

30

"Your father?"

Maggie's mind raced as she tried to imagine how or why Antoine would have a worry stone like the one found next to Helga's body.

"I think it was to say he was sorry," Mireille said. "For yelling at me in front of everyone. You were here that day."

"Do you know where your father got it?"

Mireille frowned. "Why do you keep talking about it as if it's valuable?"

"Sorry. Can I hold onto it for a bit? I promise I'll get it back to you."

"Keep it, if it's so important to you," Mireille said as she stood up. Maggie was afraid whatever good she'd done up to now she'd just ruined.

"I need to finish closing up," Mireille said. "I'm supposed to meet my friends."

"Sure," Maggie said. "I just wanted to make sure you were okay."

"Thank you, Madame Dernier," Mireille said, her face implacable. "Goodbye."

Maggie left the bakery and instantly needles of cold air peppered her face with a stinging assault.

She walked down the sidewalk to the wooden door next to the bakery. Easing the heavy door open, she waited for the motion-detection lights to flicker on but they didn't. She always carried a penlight with her but didn't bother with it now. She put a hand on each side of the walls of the narrow staircase and walked up in the dark to the single apartment door at the top.

She had one simple question for Antoine.

Where did you get the stone?

She wouldn't bother with a whole lot of chit-chat leading up to it because if he intended to lie about it, she needed to see him lying. Without giving him time to prepare she needed to see his face and watch him reach for the lie to protect himself against the truth.

And what is the truth? she wondered as she stood at the threshold in front of the apartment door.

Was it that Antoine killed Helga because she'd assaulted Sybil? And he then dropped a worry stone that he carried around?

Did Antoine strike her as the kind of man who would carry around a worry stone?

It didn't matter. None of Maggie's speculations meant anything. Antoine's answers were all that mattered.

She knocked loudly on his door and almost immediately the door swung open revealing Antoine. His hair was uncombed and his face was blotchy as if he'd just awakened. He was fully dressed but wore house slippers. His expression was stern and set in an angry grimace.

Without a word Maggie leaned into the doorway and pressed the stone against his chest. She knew that was antagonistic but she wanted to shock him just a little.

"Where did you get this?" she demanded.

The guilt formed on his face as he hunched his shoulders as if the stone burned him. He pushed it away.

"Why is that your business?" he asked.

"Because I'm starting to think you know more than you're saying about Frau Richter's murder." When he didn't answer, Maggie felt overwhelmed with fury that he could hold back when it was his own wife's life on the line here.

"What is wrong with you?" she said. "Have you no shame?"

He blushed angrily.

"Does your husband know you are here?" he asked loudly. "I think he will want to know what you are up to."

Is this guy for real?

"What I'm *up to* asking you how you got this stone. It's a simple question and I'm starting to worry that you can't give me a simple answer."

He licked his lips and his eyes darted again to the stone in Maggie's hand.

"I do not have to answer your questions," he said as he slammed the door in her face.

That afternoon Luc was deigning to play with Mila, Jemmy and Zouzou in the back garden with the two dogs. Maggie cupped her hands around a mug of coffee and watched them from the warmth of her dining room. She watched Luc automatically morph into big-brother mode. He was playful and jostling with Jemmy but also looked out for him. To the two girls, he was protective and teasing.

It was official. She and Laurent had given Luc a family and somehow, without knowing they needed it, he'd completed theirs.

"So Mireille looks well?" Laurent asked from the kitchen where he was starting the beginnings of a *béchamel* sauce.

Maggie turned and went to the kitchen counter to watch him cook—something she loved to do but rarely had time for these days.

"She's fine," she said. "But here's something interesting. Antoine gave Mireille a worry stone just like the one Sybil said she found by Helga's body."

"How do you know this?"

"Honestly, Laurent," Maggie said in exasperation, "it would be so much easier if you would just accept what I say. Trust me, it's the truth." Maggie pulled out the worry stone from her sweater pocket. "I got this from Mireille this morning who said her father gave it to her two days ago."

Laurent frowned and glanced at the stone.

"What is its value?"

"None in itself."

"What is it for?"

"It's just a stone that people rub when they're agitated."

His eyebrows shot up into his fringe. "*Incredible*."

"The point is, this stone appears to be similar to the one found by the body. The killer must have dropped it."

"And now you think Antoine is walking around with stones in his pocket?" he asked dubiously.

"I think it is highly suspicious that he has one at all when the other one was found at the scene of the murder. Don't you? Plus, he wouldn't tell me where he got it," she said.

Laurent gave a slow, disbelieving shake of his head. "You spoke with him?"

"Yes, Laurent. That is the whole point. You find clues and then talk to people. I asked him about it but he refused to tell me where he got it. And then he slammed the door in my face."

Laurent picked up the stone.

"That does not sound like Antoine," he said. "He is very agitated these days. Understandably."

"He has a hair trigger temper, Laurent and I've seen it first-hand *twice*. Plus he doesn't have an alibi for the time in question."

Laurent slid the stone in his jeans pocket.

"*D'accord*," he said. "Leave this to me."

T hinking that Antoine had a lot of explaining to do and hoping that Laurent could get to the bottom of it, Maggie went to her office

Marie-France called an Uber to go into Arles for the afternoon. She'd asked Maggie to come with her and had been annoyed when Maggie cited work as an excuse.

Speaking of work, Maggie thought as she settled down to her computer in her office, shouldn't Marie-France be rolling *pâte brisée* or doing something for the premier resto she worked at in Paris? Before checking on her newsletter subscription rate —a depressing task in any case—Maggie went to a search engine and typed in Marie-France's name. Instantly a web page popped up extolling the virtues of the restaurant, *Le Coucou Paris* where Marie-France worked. Maggie found a picture of the restaurant's chef, sous chef and *pâtissière* chef. Marie-France's picture was there—a photo that had to have been taken ten years earlier.

On impulse, Maggie picked up the phone and called the restaurant.

"*Bonjour,*" she said when they picked up. "I'm about to make a reservation for dinner but wanted to make sure you still had Marie-France Babin as your master *patisserie* chef."

There was a pause on the line.

"We do, of course, Madame," the man's voice said. "But she is *en vacances* at the moment." *On vacation.*

"Oh, that's disappointing. When do you expect her back? I was specifically looking forward to enjoying her world-famous chocolate mousse cake."

"Ah, yes. I am sorry, Madame. I believe Madame Babin has taken an extended leave of absence."

"I see. Does that mean you don't offer desserts in her absence?"

"*Mais non!* We have the delectable offerings of Georgette Blanc. She is a Ritz-Escoffier graduate and recently worked at *Mardi*. May I take your reservation?"

"I'll call you back," Maggie said and disconnected.

Marie-France was on leave from her restaurant? With an eager young replacement filling in? Maggie Googled *Georgette Blanc*. The pictures came up on the young chef's web page. Georgette Blanc was seriously adorable, mid-twenties, who was active on Instagram posting many mouthwatering photos of her latest creations.

This wasn't a fill-in. This was a replacement.

It probably wasn't motive to kill but it did underscore how important this contest must have been for Marie-France.

As it had been for Geoff. Maggie thought about putting in a phone call to Grace to see how Geoff was doing and whether he was up for a visit but her last contact with Grace had been less than affable.

She went to the French doors that looked out onto the terrace and the vineyard beyond. The land undulated, looking like someone had tossed a blanket of white over everything. At this time of year it was impossible to see the details of the grape vines.

It was this vineyard that Luc's love of the land had been ignited. The vineyard and, of course, Laurent's influence. Mila and Jemmy had experienced the same intense mentorship from Laurent but neither of them were as drawn to the land as Luc.

The thought occurred to Maggie that since they'd inherited this vineyard from Laurent's uncle, the love of the land might truly run in Luc's veins since—unbeknownst to him—Nicolas Dernier was his great uncle.

When do all the secrets stop? she wondered unhappily.

Do we drive Luc to the airport next fall to send him off into the world with his backpack and just before he gets on the plane do we let him know that he is in fact a Dernier?

The question of when to tell Luc the truth about his paternity was up to Laurent—and Maggie had no idea what Laurent's timeline was.

She sat back down at her desk with a heavy sigh.

Just because Luc was doing this internship this summer in northern California did not mean he would want to go to school there.

But it probably wouldn't help.

She typed Helga's name into the Internet search window. Instantly she saw several articles on her untimely death as well as on her *patisserie* résumé and background. As Maggie drilled down into the articles, she found the name of a sister who lived in Heidelberg.

It wasn't possible to ask Helga why she'd decided to compete in the contest in spite of the fact that Bertrand had offered to pay her *not* to come, but perhaps there was someone else who knew the answer.

Maggie had entertained different ways she could ask Bertrand that question but in every case she would have to reveal that she'd seen his emails on his phone. If there was a way to avoid that, she definitely wanted to.

She called up the website *Cherchez*, a European version of

the American skip tracer's friend, and typed in Helga's sister's name, Uli Richter.

Her address and contact information came up immediately. Without stopping to think, Maggie picked up the phone and called her.

"*Hallo?*" Uli said.

"Hello, Frau Richter? My name is Maggie Dernier. I don't suppose you speak English?" In Maggie's experience, every German she ever met spoke flawless English.

"Who is this?" Uli said in English.

"Your sister was staying with me when she was killed. I wanted to call and give my condolences."

And see if you're open to seeing me in person.

"Oh, thank you, Mrs. Dernier," Uli said. "That is very thoughtful. It was so shocking. I still don't quite believe it."

"Is there anybody else besides you? Your parents, perhaps?"

"*Nein*, they are gone many years now. It was only me and Helga."

"Again, I'm so sorry for your loss. I was wondering..." Maggie took in a big breath. "I'm going to be in Heidelberg this week and I would love to pay my respects in person."

"You are to be in Heidelberg?"

"As it happens, I am. Would you be available?"

The seconds ticked by before Uli spoke again.

"That would be very kind, Mrs. Dernier," she said. "I would like that very much."

32

That night after dinner when the children were upstairs doing homework and Marie-France was watching television in the living room, Maggie was in the kitchen with Laurent where he was finishing the cleanup and doing the prep work for the *boeuf bourguignon* he was making the next day.

"Everything okay at the monastery?" Maggie asked as she watched Laurent coat beef cubes with a mixture of seasoned flour.

He turned and raised an eyebrow at her. "What are you up to?" he asked.

"What are you talking about? You act like I never ask about the monastery."

"Everything is fine. But why not save time and just tell me what is on your mind?"

Maggie sighed and tossed down the rag she was using to wipe the counter.

"The kids have a three-day weekend coming up," she said. "I was thinking of taking Luc to Heidelberg to look at the American university there."

"He is not American."

"That's not a requirement for admission."

"Has Luc shown an interest in going to school in Germany?"

"You know he hasn't but I think he should look at all his options before he decides to move six thousand miles away to California."

Laurent gave her a skeptical look.

"And this is your only reason for wanting to go to Heidelberg?"

"Laurent, you really should do something about that suspicious nature of yours."

"It has kept me alive on more than one occasion."

"Okay, fine. I've tracked down Helga's only relative, a sister who lives in Heidelberg."

"And you believe asking *her* about the emails will stand you less chance of being arrested for hacking Bertrand's private email account than asking him?"

"Ha ha. *Très amusant*," Maggie said. "But basically yeah."

"What makes you think her sister will know?"

"I don't. But that's what sleuthing is, Laurent. Going down rat holes and blind alleys that don't look viable until *voila!* Something pops up."

"Rat holes?"

"That lost something in translation. But the point is, I'm taking Luc with me to Heidelberg and I'd like you to support me in this."

"You expect him to resist the trip to Heidelberg?'

"Don't you? He's got his whole life mapped out in northern California."

"And you want me to have a word with him?"

"He'll listen to you."

"He listens to you too."

"Yes, but tolerantly and patronizingly. He'll respect what you tell him."

"He won't respect what I tell him for long if I use his trust to manipulate him."

"I don't know why you're not more afraid of him going to California! What if he meets a girl and decides to stay?"

"How wonderful for him."

"You can't mean that."

"Are you suggesting we control how his life will go? Are we talking arranged marriages now?"

Maggie felt a burst of frustration. Laurent could be so deliberately maddening sometimes.

"All I'm saying," she said, "is that we'll be tempting fate to let him go so far from us. Don't you want him near us? At Domaine St-Buvard? What if he ends up loving California?"

"Then he will be a lucky man."

"Why are you being so reasonable?" she said, knowing even before she saw Laurent's smile how ridiculous her words sounded even to her.

33

The sound of men shouting woke Maggie the next morning. She put a hand out to touch the empty spot in bed next to her. She smelled the luscious scent of brewed coffee and looked at the clock on her bedside table. It was just after six in the morning.

She swung her legs out of bed and saw that the dogs were not in their beds. *Well, they wouldn't be. There were people in the vineyard.*

Quickly slipping into her bathrobe, she stepped into the hall and saw that the bedroom doors to all the children's rooms were open. She went to the end of the hall and looked out the window where she saw the movement of at least four uniformed policemen visible in the vineyard. Laurent and Detective LaBelle stood on the terrace below. Luc was with them.

Maggie rushed back to her bedroom where she hurriedly dressed. She flew down the broad staircase and into the kitchen where Mila and Jemmy sat at the breakfast bar. They looked up from their cereal bowls.

"The cops are here," Jemmy said.

"I see that," Maggie said as she poured herself a mug of coffee. "You two about ready to leave?"

Without waiting for an answer, Maggie let the dogs out and stepped through the French doors. She went to where Detective LaBelle and Laurent stood talking on the terrace.

"Good morning," Maggie said, noting that both Detective LaBelle and Laurent were drinking coffee. "Find anything yet?"

Laurent raised an eyebrow at her. He'd often admonished her for her failure to begin with pleasantries in conversation—essential in French discourse—but so hard for the American in her to remember to do.

Detective LaBelle wore jeans and a pullover sweater this morning. Her cheeks were ruddy from the cold. She leaned toward Laurent and dropped her voice.

"The medical examiner insists we are looking for a weapon approximately half a centimeter in diameter."

Laurent turned to Maggie. "*Chérie*, Danielle is coming to take the children to school. I am needed back at the monastery today"

"You do not want to stay and see what we find?" Detective LaBelle asked him.

"I'm sure I will hear all about it," Laurent said, before calling to Luc and going back into the house. "*Chérie*, are you coming?" he said over his shoulder to Maggie.

Maggie paused to watch one of the searchers closer to the house. He was using a metal detector. LaBelle had already walked off into the vineyard.

When Maggie went back into the house. She found that Zouzou and Danielle were there. Danielle was drinking a mug of coffee.

"You guys'll be late," Maggie said as she greeted Danielle with a kiss. "Laurent, why don't you drop the kids off? It's on your way to the monastery."

"*Bonne idée, chérie*," he said. *Good idea.*

"Aunt Maggie?" Zouzou said. "Can I stay home today? I already told *Mamère* I don't feel well."

Maggie glanced at Danielle who shrugged. "It's fine with me," she said.

Zouzou's face brightened and she looked upstairs in the direction of Marie-France's room. Clearly, the girl wanted some time with the famous *patisserie* chef.

After Laurent left with Luc, Jemmy and Mila, Maggie settled onto one of the big tub chairs in the dining room that afforded an uninterrupted view of the vineyard and the activity there. Danielle sat down beside her.

The sound of the TV came to them from the living room where Zouzou had gone.

"Why did they take so long to come back to look for the murder weapon?" Danielle asked.

"I have no idea," Maggie said. "Maybe they were afraid they couldn't make the charges against Sybil stick without it." After a moment, she said, "How are things at *Dormir*? Is Geoff still sick?"

"Oh, yes," Danielle said with a groan. "It is very unpleasant for everyone."

"I guess Cheryl is complaining a lot about her loss in the competition?"

Danielle crossed her arms on her chest and stiffened her spine.

"I am sure Grace is happy to have Zouzou out of earshot," she said. "The woman is impossibly rude."

"What does Grace see in her?"

"They are old friends, *n'est-ce pas*? Grace sees the past in her."

They watched the activity in the vineyard for a moment. Mornings at this time of year tended to leave a halo of cold fog over the vineyards. Maggie thought the mist rising up in clouds made it look like the ground was gasping for air.

"Have you heard from poor Sybil?" Danielle asked.

"I saw her the day before yesterday. She's pretty discouraged. I talked with her daughter too and tried to talk to her husband."

"Is there a problem?"

"I don't know. There might be. Sybil said that when she was doing chest compressions on Helga she saw a polished stone on the ground by the body."

"What does this mean, *a polished stone*?"

"It's like a special keepsake. Mireille called it a worry stone. It had a design carved on it."

"How strange."

"Even stranger is the fact that Antoine recently gave Mireille a stone just like it."

"That is indeed odd. But surely you are not thinking Sybil's husband had anything to do with the German woman's death?"

"That's just it, Danielle. He might have. Laurent said Antoine left the house and was gone for twenty minutes that night."

"Vraiment?" Really?

"And after the way Helga went after Sybil, he definitely had a motive to attack Helga."

"But to kill her?" Danielle pursed her lips in a doubtful expression.

"I don't know. Who knows how killers think? But I know he's got a terrible temper."

"So is Antoine the one you think killed the German?"

Maggie dropped her voice and Danielle scooted her chair closer.

"Well, honestly, Danielle, I'm not too sure about our house guest either."

"Madame Babin?"

"She detests all Germans and she has no alibi for the time in question."

Danielle frowned. "Seems a bit passionate for what I saw in Madame Babin."

"We don't really know these people, remember that. Someone who was totally charming at dinner could be a raving monster under different conditions."

"I suppose, *chérie*."

"Not to mention, I did some digging and it sounds like Marie-France is being replaced at her restaurant."

"What does this mean? Is it a motive?"

"I don't know yet."

"Uh-oh!" Danielle said and pointed to the vineyard. "Have they found something?"

Maggie turned to see that two policemen who had been working at the end of the terrace were now joined by two other policemen and LaBelle.

"I think they have," Maggie said, standing up. "Stay here, I'm going to—"

Before she could finish her sentence, the doors of the living room opened and Zouzou called to the dogs who were still outside.

"Zouzou! Let the police finish their work!" Maggie called as Zouzou ran across the terrace and up the path toward the police group in the vineyard. Maggie ran after her.

"Izzy! Buddy!" Zouzou called.

Maggie saw the dogs stop at the perimeter of the vineyard and turn to bound back toward Zouzou, who ran to them, shivering in her school uniform.

LaBelle looked up as Zouzou and Maggie reached the group.

"Leave this area at once!" LaBelle shouted. "You are contaminating a crime scene!"

"I know what that is!" Zouzou said breathlessly as Maggie put an arm around her shoulders to urge her back to the house.

Zouzou was pointing to the object that one of the policemen was holding up.

LaBelle looked at the item and then back at Zouzou as the policeman dropped the item in a clear samples bag.

"We're leaving now," Maggie said, tugging Zouzou away. "We were just chasing after the dogs."

"Stop!" LaBelle said loudly. She held her hand out for the bag and the officer handed it to her.

Maggie squinted at the item inside the bag but had never seen anything like it before. It looked like a large thumbtack with a long, tapered spike topped with a smooth dome.

"You know what this is?" LaBelle said to Zouzou who had not taken her eyes off the bag.

Zouzou nodded.

"It's a flower nail," she said.

34

A flower nail, Maggie learned, was the tool that a *patisserie* chef used in order to create icing flowers to adorn cakes and cupcakes. Held between forefinger and thumb and slowly rotated while piping a steady stream of frosting onto the surface, to produce confectionary roses, tulips, daisies, and other floral decorations.

And this particular one had also killed a woman.

In the kitchen at Domaine St-Buvard. Detective LaBelle watched Zouzou as she went through the motions of demonstrating the use of a flower nail. Maggie couldn't help but notice that the detective was at least as interested in examining Laurent's kitchen cabinets and countertops, and most especially the refrigerator with its magnets and notifications of the children's various school activities and upcoming outdoor markets scheduled.

Maggie felt uneasy at the woman's obviously ardent interest in the personal workings of her family's life.

As soon as Zouzou had demonstrated how the cake nail was normally used, Detective LaBelle instructed two of her uniformed officers to escort Maggie and Danielle to the living room, along with Marie-France, who had awakened and come downstairs, while LaBelle talked to Zouzou. Maggie overheard her warn the girl how she would not be able to tell her parents or any adults what they spoke about.

Maggie stood in the living room, her hands on her hips, furious that she couldn't be there when LaBelle questioned Zouzou.

"This is against the law!" Maggie called from the living room. "That child cannot be questioned without an adult present!"

"Madame Alexandre, please come in here," LaBelle said.

Danielle glanced at Maggie who nodded.

"I am not questioning the girl about anything related to the murder," LaBelle said in a loud voice. "I am only asking her about the culinary devices she has identified."

Maggie knew that Danielle would pay close attention to everything that was said and report back. She strained to listen to LaBelle ask her questions to Zouzou about the flower nail. Zouzou spoke in a soft voice and Maggie couldn't hear her answers.

"Did she really say it was a flower nail that killed Helga?" Marie-France asked Maggie.

"Shush!" Maggie said to her. "I can't hear them."

"Well, that implicates all of us, doesn't it?" Marie-France said. "We all have flower nails!"

One of the policemen came into the dining room with the detective and spoke to her in a low voice. Maggie strained to pick up his words. She heard "email" and "coroner" and guessed that they'd sent a picture of the flower nail to see if it could possibly have been the murder weapon.

Before Maggie could hear a definite answer to that, both Danielle and Zouzou entered the living room. Zouzou's face was flushed but she seemed otherwise composed. Danielle had a hand on her shoulder.

"You did very well, *chérie*," Danielle said to the girl.

LaBelle then appeared. "I am leaving behind a small cadre of personnel to further search the area. I need to ask you to keep your dogs out of the back as well as yourselves."

"So is it the murder weapon?" Maggie asked.

Ignoring her, LaBelle signaled to her men and left through the front door.

Maggie watched them go with mounting frustration. Marie-France wandered into the dining room to gaze out the French doors to the vineyard.

"Well," Maggie said more to herself than anyone else, "at least they can test it for fingerprints. Although they should have taken all of ours to eliminate us."

"Detective LaBelle instructed her men to get take our prints before they leave."

Maggie had to admit that made her feel a little better. At least LaBelle was doing that much—even if it was just to confirm that the prints on the flower nail were Sybil's.

She glanced over Danielle's shoulder to Zouzou who sat again in front of the TV set.

"So she just asked Zouzou about the nail and how bakers use it?" Maggie asked Danielle.

"That's right, *chérie*. She did not insinuate in any way that Zouzou might be involved."

"Well, that's good at least."

"But I did hear one of her men," Danielle said, dropping her voice. "He confirmed that they found the nail at the edge of the Domaine St-Buvard garden. It had been pushed deep into the hard ground."

"Really?" Maggie tried to imagine a likely scenario.

The killer must have run from the spot where he or she murdered Helga—the killing nail still in hand—and then pushed it into the ground a good forty meters away from there, hoping it wouldn't be found.

"And they really think this frosting nail was used to kill her?"

"Yes, *chérie*. Detective LaBelle's sergeant spoke on the phone with the coroner after he emailed a picture of the nail. The coroner confirmed that the spike fit the description of the murder weapon."

35

The sun was hiding behind the clouds already engulfing Cézanne's Mountain. Its light filtered through the skeletal branches of the plane trees in front of the main chapel of the monastery of *l'Abbaye de Sainte-Trinité* where Laurent stood.

The sprawling complex of weathered and ancient buildings had been built from the limestone of the surrounding area around the year 1100. A small stone chapel, no longer used due to its ruined roof which had been damaged decades ago by the unrelenting mistral and was still unrepaired, sat next to an old granary and a row of low-roofed buildings that led to the monastery garden where the brothers and the refugees grew potatoes, corn and cabbages.

At the moment, the garden was the setting where a blackened structure sat that had at one time been a serviceable garden shed.

"Was it deliberate?" Laurent asked Frère Jean who stood beside him. Frère Jean was a slight man with a thick head of white hair.

"It could have been an accident," Frère Jean said. "People still come to the garden to smoke."

Laurent glanced at the man.

"But you are not convinced?"

"We've had a few problems with this new bunch of refugees."

"What kind of problems?"

Frère Jean ran a hand through his hair in frustration.

"Problems beyond my abilities to handle," he said.

Laurent snorted.

He means women.

Like most monks Laurent knew, Frère Jean was much less comfortable dealing with women than men.

"Anyone in particular?" Laurent asked.

"She came from Syria two weeks ago with her family. I have been hesitant to address her behavior until I knew for sure she was to blame."

"How old?"

"Perhaps twelve?"

"You think a twelve-year-old girl burned down the monastery garden shed?" Laurent asked in incredulity.

"I don't know, Laurent. She is wily." He looked at Laurent. "I wondered if you might talk with her?"

Laurent shook his head.

"You must handle this on your own." He pointed to the garden. "Get a team together to rake up the ash. It was fortunate this happened in January and not April. The fire might have spread and damaged the crops themselves."

"She only has a mother and younger brother."

He is telling me she has no father.

"I do not have time to sort out every troublemaker at *l'Abbaye de Sainte-Trinité,*" Laurent said gruffly.

Luc had been a special case. Not only had he been willing

to change but he was a true orphan. Plus, he was Laurent's biological nephew.

Although of course nobody at the monastery knew that.

"You have a way with children," Frère Jean said, dusting his hands against his work pants. "You know you do."

"If you cannot handle her," Laurent said, turning away, "you'll need to eject her."

"I cannot do that."

"It doesn't mean you shouldn't."

Laurent drove away from the monastery, the sight of the old chapel's acicular Gothic spire in his rearview mirror.

Most of the families living at the monastery had been in transit to what they'd hoped would be a better way of life. All of them had either lost their jobs in other areas of France for various reasons or had come from as far away as Syria and Turkey escaping oppressive political regimes.

His mind flashed back to the moment when he had first met Luc two years ago at *l'Abbaye de Sainte-Trinité*.

The boy had been surly, non-communicative and ill-mannered. And even then, Laurent had known there was something special about him—something innately connected to Laurent himself.

Laurent's family background was complex and his childhood a largely unhappy one. He had few good things to say about any of his male relatives, least of all his father. So it had come as a major surprise to him years ago when he realized that being a father was a role he had been born to play.

He turned down the village road that led away from the monastery toward the village. His thoughts were unsettled.

Maybe for that reason he'd suddenly realized with surprise that he wasn't looking forward to Luc's leaving next fall either.

Not unlike his irrepressible American wife, if Laurent had his way, Luc would stay at Domaine Saint-Buvard and learn what he needed to know about the wine making business from Laurent.

Isn't that how it has been done for generations?

But more than he wanted the boy to stay, he wanted him to make his own decisions about his future and what he needed. More than anyone Laurent knew the bitterness of having those decisions made for you.

Would Gerard have turned out differently if he'd had the opportunities that Laurent and Maggie were determined to give their own children...as well as Gerard's son?

Or had he been irretrievably damaged from birth?

Laurent's phone pinged and he frowned as he glanced at it on the passenger's seat. A text message showed up from Maggie.

<Police finally gone. Pick up bread, pls>

Laurent turned his attention back to the narrow winding road that would lead him into the village of Saint-Buvard.

Usually, the lunch hour in Saint-Buvard was marked by a significantly increased activity on the terrace of Le Canard Café, the village's only café and bar. The café faced a fountain, long defunct, in the center of a lumpy square of uneven cobblestones encrusted with lichen and stained dark with years of dirt forming a concentric pattern around the fountain.

As Laurent parked his car, he recognized a few people—all men—on the terrace drinking. His eye went to one in particular.

Antoine Pelletier sat alone, a bottle of *marc* in front of him. Laurent glanced at the bakery and saw that it was closed. While he himself had suggested to Antoine that he might want to close the bakery until Sybil was released, the man had insisted that he would never do that.

Laurent strode over to him and tossed his car keys down on his table.

Antoine jumped, nearly knocking over his glass of *marc*, and looked up at Laurent startled.

"I see you decided to close the bakery after all," Laurent said. "You should have told me. I can arrange for someone else to run it until you are ready to return."

In spite of the cold weather, beads of sweat formed on Antoine's forehead.

"I...it's just for an hour," Antoine said, his fist clutching his drink. "I baked this morning."

Laurent didn't sit. He didn't want Antoine to mistake this as a social call.

"That is good," Laurent said. "Perhaps you could open it now so that I may get bread."

Antoine nodded and drank the rest of his drink. He looked in the direction where the Le Canard waiter stood watching.

"Don't worry," Laurent said. "I'll take care of him."

Antoine got up, his eye on the bottle of *marc* but only for a moment before turning toward the bakery.

Laurent followed him, his intention more to get him out of earshot of the other men at the café than anything else. If Antoine had a confession to make, he would be more amenable to doing it in private.

Antoine unlocked the bakery door and twisted the *Fermé* sign in the window to *Ouvrir*. He hurried to the counter and stood behind it.

"You want your usual *traditionale*?" he said. "I have sour dough today too."

"*Traditionale* is fine," Laurent said.

Careful not to look Laurent in the eye, Antoine quickly took two batons and wrapped them in paper. Before he could hand them over, Laurent lay the worry stone on the counter.

For a moment, Antoine just stared at it.

"Where did you get it?" Laurent asked.

Antoine refused to look at him. "In a...gift shop in Lyons."

"When?"

Antoine licked his lips. "Years ago."

"And you have only now given the stone to Mireille?"

Antoine shoved the bread across the counter toward Laurent.

"I...I had lost it until recently."

"Are you sure?"

"Of course. I remember it well."

"Where in Lyons?"

"I...in the old town."

"The name of this shop?"

"I think it is out of business."

"I see."

Sweat was dripping from Antoine's face. The drops hit the counter between them, making audible tapping sounds as they fell.

Laurent had not seriously believed that Antoine could have done something terrible and then left his wife to pay the price for it.

He took the wrapped bread and the stone and turned back toward the door.

At least not until this moment.

36

After the police left, Maggie found it difficult to settle down to work. A friend of Danielle's came by to pick her up to have lunch in Arles.

Maggie noticed that Marie-France had continued to watch the police search the grounds for a while before retiring to her room with a novel. Zouzou had gone to Mila's bedroom with her school work and shut the door.

Maggie still wasn't sure that Marie-France didn't have motive for killing Helga—*and she did seem to be inordinately interested in the police as they searched the property*—but she also wasn't sure what she could ask the woman that wouldn't prompt an out and out lie.

Thinking she needed more evidence before she could question her, Maggie went to her office where she got on the Internet. At first she just answered emails. She had a long backlist of area artisans and vendors who wanted to advertise or be featured in her newsletter and she felt it necessary to respond to all of them. While it was true that January was a slow month as far as buying local art or crafts was concerned, the spring would arrive eventually and keeping good relations would be important.

She brought up what she'd done so far in her February newsletter to fine-tune a few facts in the feature story. She wrote down in her work diary that she'd need to visit and get more pictures of Le Cigne, the village where the garlic festival would take place next month. Fortunately she'd taken pictures during last year's festival and since she hadn't run a feature on it then, she could use those pictures now if necessary.

She got up and went to the kitchen where she made herself a sandwich. She could see that Laurent had the skillet out he would use for tonight's dinner—as well as a bowl of mushrooms and a large bunch of parsley sitting in a bowl of water. She listened to determine if Marie-France or Zouzou were up and possibly hungry, but she heard nothing. She brought her sandwich and a glass of iced tea back to her office.

Wondering why she hadn't done it weeks ago, Maggie typed in the name *LUSH* into her search engine and several websites popped up. She scanned the descriptions until she found the publishing company who owned LUSH and then called the corporate office in Brussels.

"Perennial Publishing," a bright female voice with an English accent chirped into the receiver.

"Hello," Maggie said. "My name is Maggie Dernier and I was wondering if I could talk to someone about LUSH?"

"Everyone's at lunch," the chipper voice said. "Did you want me to put you through to Mr. Bertrand Glenn? He's traveling right now but I know he checks his voice mail."

"Uh, no, I was hoping to talk to someone who knew about the sponsorship side of LUSH," Maggie said.

Bertrand talked nonstop about his creative vision for LUSH and that was the last thing Maggie needed to hear.

Follow the money, she told herself as she waited for the receptionist to reply.

"Well, as I said, they're all at lunch at the moment. But I know quite a bit about it. Maybe I can help you?"

Maggie felt a splinter of excitement. A young bright girl working the phones and thinking she was better than that was exactly the sort of resource she needed right now.

"Terrific," Maggie said. "I'm on vacation here in Provence and happened to get a ticket for the *Patisserie* Competition held in Aix a few days ago for the LUSH launch."

"Oh! So you already know a little bit about LUSH," the girl gushed. "I saw the pictures that Mr. Glenn sent. It looked like a rousing success!"

If you didn't count the dead body leading up to it, Maggie couldn't but think.

"Yes, it was very interesting," Maggie said. "I was just surprised that there were so few contestants. I mean, for the 'Greatest *patisserie* chef in all of Europe,' I would have expected better representation, you know?"

"You have a good point," the girl bubbled on. "And originally there was supposed to be more contestants."

"Oh? What happened?"

Maggie had no idea what she wanted to find out from this girl. She just knew that the more she talked, the more the girl would end up saying something she didn't intend to say.

"Well, you didn't hear it from me but Mr. Glenn invited four contestants which we thought was perfectly manageable but he ended up having to uninvite one of them."

Was it possible this silly girl didn't know about Helga's death?

"Oh?" Maggie asked. "Why was that?"

The girl dropped her voice. "The higher ups decided it," she said. "From a public relations viewpoint, one of the contestants didn't rank very high in our focus groups. You know we have to do that sort of thing, right?"

"Oh, sure," Maggie said.

So a focus group didn't like the idea of Helga Richter competing for the Greatest Patisserie Chef in Europe?

"It's not American audiences who care, mind you," the receptionist said hurriedly, clearly deducing that Maggie was American, "but research showed that our French customers would not be pleased if—however unlikely—well, you know."

"You mean if a German chef were to win," Maggie filled in.

"Right. Personally, I don't see why we can't all get along, you know?"

"Sure," Maggie said.

But of course the war probably didn't directly affect you.

"So the board insisted Mr. Glenn get rid of the German contestant, you know what I'm saying?"

Maggie laughed, hoping it would encourage the girl because she didn't know exactly what she was saying but she dearly wanted to.

"They basically told him to get rid of the German or else," the girl said.

"Or else?"

"Or else, you know. They wouldn't fund his magazine."

37

That afternoon Maggie was waiting for Laurent when he came home with the children. But by then the pandemonium level had ratcheted up to the point that there was no good time to talk.

Jemmy was with his father in the kitchen working on tonight's *bourguignon,* while Luc was studying in his bedroom until dinner time. Zouzou and Mila were watching television in the living room with Marie-France.

By the time dinner was over and cleaned up and everybody had done their homework and gone to bed, Maggie was vibrating with anticipation to tell Laurent her news.

What she'd found out today meant that Bertrand had a major motive for killing Helga. The only problem was the fact that he'd been with her the whole time in the vineyard.

As soon as she and Laurent were alone in their bedroom, she spoke in a low but excited whisper, "I found out something about Bertrand today that gives him the biggest motive of all for killing Helga."

When Laurent looked at her skeptically, she felt a shimmer of annoyance but she continued on.

"It turns out Bertrand's magazine LUSH was going right in the crapper if he didn't get rid of Helga," she said.

"Is this how you do your investigations?" Laurent asked with a grimace. "Two days ago you said it was Geoff and then yesterday it was Marie-France. This morning it was Antoine. And now it's Bertrand?"

Maggie counted to five before speaking and even then she took in a deep breath first to keep her irritation at bay.

"Yes, Laurent," she said. "My process is that I look at everyone and I imagine anyone who could have done it. Don't you see? I'm telling you this is the biggest motive of all! The whole point of the contest was to launch Bertrand's magazine. If his sponsors said 'get rid of the German or we won't pay,' there is no magazine! And we already know that Bertrand tried to get rid of her by buying her off."

"What about Bertrand's alibi? Which is in fact yourself?"

Maggie frowned. "I know. I have to figure that out. Or maybe I don't have to noodle out every single detail of this by myself. I think we need to get this information to Detective LaBelle." Maggie sniffed. "Or are we calling her *Margaux* these days?"

Laurent wagged a finger at her.

Maggie turned from where she sat on the bed and squeezed out a dollop of her favorite lavender body cream and began to work the unguent into her legs and knees. She noticed that Laurent was paying close attention to her actions.

"So what are your thoughts, Laurent? You haven't weighed in yet on my theory about Bertrand."

"Your strategy appears to be to suspect everyone," Laurent said, his eyes watching her as she worked the cream into her knees. "It is very time consuming and I think leads to dead ends."

"Yes, but this is how you're *supposed* to investigate a murder case!" she said as she put the cap back on the lavender tube and tossed it onto her bedside table. "You try to eliminate people so you can focus on the more likely candidates. Like Debbie for example. I can take her off the list because she was with you at the time of the murder."

"Mostly that is true."

Maggie's mouth hung open for a moment.

"What do you mean *mostly*?"

He shrugged. "At one point she went into the salon to watch TV."

"But she was still in the house, right?"

"Probably."

"Okay, Laurent. What the hell?"

"When I came to look for her, I could not find her."

Maggie frowned. "Maybe she was in the bathroom?"

"Possibly."

"Okay then..."

"But then why were her shoes muddy?"

Maggie stared at him and then nodded. "Okay. So, no alibi for Debbie then. But no motive either."

"That we know of."

"Who else?" She began to tick them off her fingers. "Grace was with Cheryl."

"Not the whole time, of course."

Maggie looked at him. "What do you mean?"

"The whole reason Sybil was in the vineyard was to give a message to Grace to come back to the house."

Maggie stared at him. "Are you saying Grace left Cheryl alone in the vineyard?"

"At least briefly, *oui*."

She looked away. "I wonder why Grace didn't mention this to me."

"She probably thought you knew. It is not a secret. Marie-France mentioned it to me. She said she saw Grace walk away."

Laurent got into bed and pulled Maggie to him. He brushed back her hair and kissed her forehead.

"Marie-France could be lying," Maggie said. "But the point is it looks like Cheryl does *not* have an alibi for the time in question after all."

And Grace knows that.

"It appears very few people do," Laurent observed.

Maggie repositioned herself to look into his eyes. "Speaking of which, you never told me what happened with Antoine."

"First the light, *chérie*?"

Maggie twisted around and turned off her bedroom light and then resettled in Laurent's arms.

"He said he bought the stone in Lyons," Laurent said.

"And you believe him?"

Laurent sighed heavily and ran a hand down Maggie's back to her hip and then leaned in and kissed her on the mouth.

"*Non, chérie,*" he said. "And frankly it worries me greatly the reason he might be lying."

38

The next morning Maggie felt like she was just going through the motions of making breakfast and interacting with her family. Laurent again took all the children to school—except for Zouzou who had begged a second day off since Marie-France hadn't seemed interested in spending time with her yesterday.

The thoughts kept rolling over and over in Maggie's mind that Antoine was lying about where he got the worry stone. In simplest terms, if Antoine killed Helga and then dropped the stone—or deliberately placed it to indicate he was exacting his revenge—he would have every reason to lie about it. The problem with that theory was that it seemed a bit too staged and creative for someone like Antoine. Not that he was a brute exactly, but it seemed a bit too refined for him.

On the other hand Maggie hadn't given up on the idea that Bertrand had the most viable reason for wanting Helga dead but as Laurent said, *she* was Bertrand's alibi so unless he hired someone to kill Helga—*Geoff maybe?*—Bertrand couldn't have killed her.

Maggie spent the morning in her office sorting through

potential artists to showcase in her big spring newsletter. As lunchtime approached, the irresistible scent of baking cinnamon rolls lured her out.

She emerged to find Marie-France and Zouzou in the kitchen baking. Maggie's first inclination—even before being grateful that Marie-France had decided to take the time with Zouzou— was that the French woman was trying to ingratiate herself.

And if you were guilty of something, isn't that exactly what you would do?

It was too cold to eat lunch outdoors so Maggie warmed up the minestrone soup that Laurent had made a few days earlier and put together a plate of roast chicken and tomato sandwiches.

It occurred to her when she sat down to lunch with Zouzou and Marie-France that she knew very little about the French woman's personal life.

"I'm surprised *Le Coucou* can go this long without you," Maggie said to her as she handed out bowls of the soup.

Marie-France's face darkened and she glanced at Zouzou who was happily munching on her sandwich and feeding crusts to the dogs.

"I may have another opportunity opening up somewhere else soon," Marie France said cryptically.

"Oh? That's great. Any place I've heard of?"

Marie-France sniffed. "Bertrand has asked me to be the culinary editor for LUSH."

"Really?" Maggie frowned. "Not much baking happening in an editorial position I wouldn't have thought."

"I have been baking for many years now."

"So you're ready to hang up your springform pans?"

"Perhaps I am. Perhaps I am ready to make way for a younger chef with new ideas."

Now why does that sound like a big fat lie to me?

"I would've thought that good cakes and pastries were time-less," Maggie said.

"You have very pedestrian tastes, Madame Dernier. Like most of your countrymen."

"I suppose you're right. I'll always take a good *chocolatine* over a saffron and sardine soufflé any day."

"Madame Babin might be moving to Brussels," Zouzou said.

"Where LUSH is published," Maggie said.

Marie-France narrowed her eyes. "You have been doing your homework."

"So no husband to worry about? You can just pick up and move?" Maggie asked glancing at Marie-France's left-hand ring finger.

"That's right, Madame Dernier," Marie-France said coldly. "I am unencumbered by emotional constraints."

"Lucky you," Zouzou said clearly not understanding Marie-France's words.

"Yes, exactly, *chérie*," Marie-France said, looking at Zouzou with a sudden malevolence that startled Maggie. "I am well aware of how very lucky I am."

That afternoon when Laurent came in with the children, Jemmy and Mila grabbed their after-school snacks and went to their rooms. Laurent stopped to praise Zouzou for the batch of cinnamon rolls on the counter that she and Marie-France had made and then went to work on the vegetables for the *rata-touille* he was preparing for dinner.

Luc was heading up the stairs, his cellphone clapped to his ear when Maggie stopped him.

"Luc," she said. "Can I have a minute?"

He hesitated and then ended his phone call before turning to Maggie.

"Laurent already said I have to go to Heidelberg day after tomorrow," he said.

Maggie listened to Laurent move pots and pans around in the kitchen.

"I just want to make sure you've examined all your options," Maggie said.

"Is it the money? Because Laurent said it wasn't the money but I can't figure out what else it could be. After my internship this summer I'll be eligible for a scholarship if I'm accepted at Napa Valley."

"It isn't the money," Maggie said. "It's making sure that this is the right thing for you to do. But look, I'm not asking you *not* to apply to Napa Valley or California-Davis or any place else, I'm just asking you to give one day to explore a different option in Heidelberg."

"I have a paper due first thing next week and I've already put it off too long."

"It's just one day. We'll leave in the morning and be back that night."

Luc tilted his head toward the ceiling and let out a heavy sigh. His phone rang again and he hurriedly looked at it and then dismissed it as if the person he was hoping would call, hadn't.

"Is that Anna?" Maggie asked.

"No," he said. "Can I go now?"

"I don't know how close you are to this Anna, but I know both Laurent and I would love to meet her."

"Oh, for God's sake!" He turned to head back up the stairs.

"I mean, you clearly like her," Maggie called after him. "Your relationships *here* are important too."

He didn't turn around and the next thing Maggie heard was the sound of Laurent clearing his throat.

She turned and saw him watching her from the kitchen, his hands on his hips and shaking his head.

Maggie knew Laurent would have a word with her about her conversation with Luc and that night as they got ready for bed, he did.

"You must let Luc decide his school for himself," he said firmly as she sat on the bed and applied a thin sheen of body lotion to the dry spots on her elbows.

"He's too young to decide for himself," she said.

"No. This is the beginning of many decisions he must make for himself."

"Well, I disagree."

"You are giving Luc bad advice."

"No, I am not."

"Your advice to him is self-serving."

Maggie's mouth fell open. "It's not self-serving if it's the right thing to do!" she said.

"It's the right thing as far as *you* are concerned, but this is Luc's life. You must stop trying to persuade him."

"I'm *guiding* him."

"To your own ends. Stop it."

Maggie decided not to argue the point any further. She had no intention of letting Luc decide what might well be the most important decision of his life. And him only seventeen? What seventeen-year-old knew what was best for them and their future?

After spritzing her pillow with lavender scent and giving both dogs the little treats she always kept for them at bedtime, Maggie opened and closed the drawer on her bedside table.

"Have you seen the worry stone I showed you?" she asked. "I can't find it."

"*Oui.* I gave it to Detective LaBelle."

"What?! Why?" Maggie stared at him in surprise.

"Because she can test it for prints and because she can determine if it is like the one found at the crime scene."

"You should have told me first."

"Why? Are we not both on the same page? Working to free Sybil?"

Maggie hated it when he was this rational. It made anything else she could think of to say to him sound petty and well, self-serving.

"What did you find out?" she asked. "If I'm allowed to ask."

Laurent ignored her tone and pulled out his cellphone.

"She said the stone found near Helga's body had a design on it." He held up a picture that the detective had emailed to Laurent. Maggie took his phone and examined the photo. It was the first time she'd seen the stone. It wasn't unlike the one she'd taken from Mireille, but the design was definitely different.

"Detective LaBelle said the design is called an endless knot," Laurent said.

Maggie fought off the feelings churning inside her from knowing Laurent was communicating with the detective without her. She knew his connection could only help them. But she also knew that however innocent it looked on the surface, the fact was Laurent was keeping secrets.

She handed his phone back to him.

"How did *that* happen?" she asked. "You and the detective exchanging emails about this?"

"Does it matter? If she tells us information."

"Uh, yes, it matters and you know it does," she said, her eyes narrowing as she regarded him. "Or was that something I was also allowed to do when I worked with Roger?"

Roger Bedard had been a Detective Inspector in Arles when Maggie met him thirteen years ago during her first year of marriage—a difficult first year of attempting to adjust to being an expat *and* married to a Frenchman. Maggie hadn't betrayed her wedding vows that year and she had walked away with a hard-learned lesson and a stronger marriage as a result but she'd hurt a good man in the process. Roger had fallen irretrievably in love with her.

Laurent smiled. "I never for a moment feared you might sleep with Roger, *chérie.*"

"Very secure of you I'm sure," Maggie said, feeling her temper rise. "I'm not afraid that you are sleeping with Detective LaBelle either."

"*Bon.* Then we are both on the same page, yes?"

Not sure how he had sidestepped her direct question, Maggie held out her hand for his phone again. She found the email, noting that the detective gave no salutation. She squinted at the design carved into the stone.

She put the phone down and then pulled her laptop from the shelf on her bedside table and typed in *worry stones* and *endless knot graphics* in the Internet search window.

Laurent moved one of the dog beds away from his side of the bed and Maggie heard him murmur to both dogs before he got in bed beside her.

"What are you looking for?" he asked.

But by then she'd already found it. She felt the adrenaline rush through her as she turned to him, her ears buzzing with excitement.

"You're not going to believe this," she said, turning the laptop screen so he could see what had come up. "The endless knot? It symbolizes *Karma.*"

39

"Don't you see?" Maggie said excitedly when Laurent merely frowned at her. "This means Helga *wasn't* randomly killed."

"Didn't we already know that?"

"Yes, but more specifically it means it was a *revenge* killing. The killer left a signature stone at the site of the murder to say that this was payback. That means it has to be Marie-France. She's the only one with a grudge against Helga because she's German."

"The only one that we know of."

"Now more than ever, Laurent, we need to find out where that stone came from. Can't you lean on Antoine a little more?"

"I am not the French mafia, *chérie*," Laurent said with a grin.

"You could be if you tried."

"I will talk with him again."

It was infuriating that they still didn't know where Antoine had gotten the stone. For whatever reason—and possibly that reason was murder—Antoine didn't want anyone to know the truth.

"Meanwhile, I think we should focus on Marie-France,"

Maggie said. "If I had the stone I could show it to her and watch her face to see if she knows it."

"I think you are all over everywhere," Laurent said with a frown. "It makes no sense to think Marie-France killed Helga with Antoine's stone. *C'est fou.*" *That's crazy.*

Maggie snapped shut her laptop.

"Fine," she said. "I told you before some clues don't look obvious until you start rooting around them. These two things might look like nothing but I've been down this road before."

"You have uncovered a murderous village baker who drops stones around his victims?"

"Enjoy yourself, Laurent. Laugh it up. But you know I've been right in the past."

"I know you've had to be rescued from car trunks in the past before you were murdered."

"You're just a riot tonight, aren't you? You know you're a terrible sleuthing partner. You need to be open to seeing anything and everything as a possible clue."

"How is that helpful? You would soon be swamped by dozens of meaningless clues. You are creating your own haystack that hides the needle."

"I think you got that metaphor wrong but in any case this is how it's done. Or at least it's how *I* do it—I find the one clue among all the hundreds of others that points to the killer."

"It is too convoluted for a rational mind," he said with a shrug.

"Tell that to Sherlock Holmes."

"Who was a drug addict, I believe?"

"Clearly there's no talking to you tonight. But it doesn't matter. I know what I know."

"And what is that?"

"I'm not in the mood to be laughed at."

"Is Marie-France no longer in your crosshairs? Or Bertrand? What about Antoine? I admit I didn't have my eyes on Zouzou the whole night long. Perhaps she got up to something."

"The light, darling?" Maggie said, in no mood for even his good-natured teasing.

The next morning Laurent took the children to school in Aix and Maggie retreated to her office to try to get some work done. Although the air was still cool, the sun was pleasant and Marie-France was sitting outside reading a book and enjoying the mild morning.

Maggie watched her for a moment and tried to see her as Helga's killer, but the picture wouldn't gel. One thing she'd learned from the very brief time that she'd attempted to process this case with Laurent is that he was way too literal. She needed to bounce her thoughts off someone who was open to hearing sometimes outlandish theories. She called Grace.

"Wow, you're alive," Maggie said and was instantly sorry she did.

"I am in fact," Grace said coolly.

"I'm just calling to see how things are going on your end," Maggie said. "Is Geoff still sick?"

"He's still in bed at any rate," Grace said with a sigh. "Between me and Danielle, we have been walking trays into his and Debbie's cottage three times a day. I have to say it would help if his wife would give us a hand. Especially since Bertrand is only paying the base rate for their stays but I feel compelled to offer breakfast and company too."

"What does she do with her time?"

"Oh, she's off with Bertrand most days, touring Arles, lunch in Aix. Last night they caught a show in Avignon and spent the night."

"Really?"

"Before your mind goes into overdrive, I don't think there's anything between them. She's just lonely and you know Bertrand. He loves to talk."

"What does Cheryl do with her days?"

Maggie hoped she said that offhandedly enough but it was hard to tell.

"She goes for walks around the property," Grace said. "It's been lovely catching up with her."

"I'm sure. Has she gotten over the competition yet?"

"She was upset, Maggie. Anybody would be. She's as delighted as I am about Zouzou's win. By the way how's Zouzou doing?"

"Marie-France seems to have taken her under her wing. We've got *profiteroles* and cinnamon rolls to last us until summer."

"What a special treat that is for Z. And the case? Have you found out anything more to help poor Sybil?"

"Turns out Laurent has a contact in the Aix homicide division in the form of the investigating detective."

"You're kidding me. She was quite pretty as I remember."

"It's not like that, Grace," Maggie said, flushing with annoyance.

"Of course not, darling. It's Laurent so it wouldn't be. It doesn't mean the detective won't use all her wiles."

"*Anyway*," Maggie said testily, "The fact that Helga was killed with a *patisserie* tool is crucial."

"Naturally. It gives particular credence to the idea that she was killed by one of the other contestants."

"Yes," Maggie said, "and more specifically one who could get physically close to her."

"You think she was having an affair with Geoff or Bertrand?" Grace said disbelieving. "Because I have to say the woman was singularly unattractive."

"Looks aren't the only thing that attract a man."

"Oh, now I know you've been hitting the cooking sherry," Grace said with a laugh.

"Bertrand wasn't a contestant but he could have easily gotten his hands on one of those icing nail things."

"Yes, but Bertrand has an alibi, remember?"

Something was buzzing around Maggie's brain in an insistent warning. She and Bertrand had been together that evening. In fact they'd not been out of each other's sight the whole time until they ran to the clearing and discovered Helga's body.

Maggie's mind whirled as she tried to remember back to everything she remembered during the night. It was frustrating because Bertrand had the best motive! But if he had no opportunity to commit the crime, it didn't matter how good his motive was.

"So that only leaves Marie-France, Geoff and Cheryl," Maggie said.

"Not Cheryl. Remember, darling? She was with me."

"Yes, but didn't you break away from her to start back to the house at one point? I thought someone told me you did."

"What are you saying? I wasn't apart from her for more than ten minutes."

Ten minutes was plenty of time to do the deed.

"For that matter I guess *I* don't have an alibi either," Grace said stiffly.

"True, but neither do you have a motive."

"And Cheryl does?" Grace's voice began to rise shrilly. "Look, is there anything else, darling?" she said icily. "Only I've got a quiche in the oven and without Zouzou here it's not at all a guarantee I won't burn it."

Maggie could tell a brush-off when she heard it. She hated to upset Grace but she hated lying to her more. It was true Grace was upset about Maggie mentioning that Cheryl had a window of opportunity but maybe when she calmed down, she'd be able to look at it more objectively.

"One last thing," Maggie said hurriedly. "I finally talked to Sybil a couple of days ago and she said there was some kind of polished stone at the crime scene."

She debated telling Grace that there were actually *two* stones but that fact only implicated Antoine. And until she had more evidence one way or the other, she wanted to try to reserve judgment on Antoine for now and telling Grace would be essentially pointing the finger right at him.

"Okay, fine. Good to know. I'm sorry, darling, I think I definitely smell my quiche burning," Grace said before hanging up.

40

A few hours later, Maggie gave up on getting any work done that was usable. Her mind just wasn't into describing various faience-making procedures for the hundredth time.

Am I getting bored with the newsletter?

Maggie's brain was buzzing with all possible permutations of the fact that Cheryl had been on her own for ten whole minutes during the time of the murder. In consideration of Grace, Maggie realized she had really not allowed herself to seriously consider Cheryl as a suspect and even felt guilty doing so now.

The bottom line was, she didn't like the woman and couldn't trust herself to be impartial.

She needed to separate her own animosity toward Cheryl and sideline her natural impulse to blindly trust her initial judgment about people. (It had after all been wrong at least fifty percent of the time.) She needed to look at Cheryl and her involvement in this case as if she were any other person.

As Maggie came out of her office, lured out by the delectable scents from the kitchen that heralded the fact that

Laurent was back, she could see Marie-France through the French doors walking toward the vineyard with the dogs and Zouzou and Mila.

Maggie went into the kitchen where Laurent was sautéing onions and garlic in a sauté pan. He turned to look at her.

"You are all right, *chérie*?"

Maggie knew she looked distracted but she had a lot in her head pulling her from every different direction. And there was still that thing tugging at the periphery of her brain about Bertrand.

"I'm good," she said "Do you need help?" Even as she said the words, she moved out of the kitchen and into the dining room. She looked at the dining table, as yet not set for the night's meal, and tried to go through the steps in her memory of the dinner that night and then the scavenger hunt.

She tried to remember if she'd seen Bertrand's face when they'd discovered the body, but she'd been too focused on the dead body and poor Sybil shrieking beside it. She tried to think if Bertrand had acted at all oddly since the murder. But she didn't really know him so she had nothing to compare his behavior to.

As soon as Marie-France and the girls came back in with the dogs, Laurent set the girls to various chores—feeding the dogs, setting the table—and handed Marie-France a glass of Sancerre which she took upstairs with her.

"We eat in fifteen minutes," Laurent told her.

"I will be there," Marie-France said.

Maggie stood in the dining room, her arms crossed and frowned at the table which was set for seven.

"What are you thinking, *chérie*?" Laurent said as he came to stand beside her. He ran a hand down her back and she felt herself lean into it. "You might as well tell me."

"You just pooh-pooh my theories," she said.

"Never."

"I'm going crazy because I still think Bertrand has the best motive. He was willing to pay Helga ten thousand euros *not* to compete in the contest in order to save his magazine. And she showed up anyway. That must've really thrown him for a loop."

"So you no longer think it is Marie-France?"

Maggie glanced in the direction of the stairs and lowered her voice.

"I'm reserving judgement until I can get more evidence."

"Very prudent. But there is a simple flaw in your theory about Monsieur Glenn."

"Do tell."

"Frau Richter was killed in a passionate, nearly intimate way."

Maggie looked at him with surprise but realized he was right. The killer would have had to get close. A quick stab to the heart was indeed intimate. If Bertrand just wanted Helga dead, there were hundreds of other ways that were much less personal.

Not only that, but Maggie had seen the size of the spike on the nail. She didn't know if the killer had pushed it into Helga through her outerwear but if he or she had—that would involve getting closer still—enough to get a hand up and under Helga's coat.

Just about as personal as it comes.

"Was she stabbed through her jacket?" Maggie asked.

"I do not know, *chérie*," Laurent said as he sipped a glass of wine and cocked his head at her.

But you can find out, Maggie couldn't help but think.

As she moved into the dining room she realized that the indefinable amorphous *thing* about Bertrand that was buzzing around the base of her brain seemed to glimmer tantalizingly as if about to reveal itself. She knew from past experience that *not* thinking about what it could be was the best way for the thought to finally come to the foreground.

"I am not saying it could not have been Bertrand," Laurent said. "But unlikely, I think."

"That's not how this works, Laurent," Maggie said with a twinge of frustration. "If you eliminate suspects on gut feeling, you stand a real chance of missing important clues!"

"But Bertrand is firmly alibied. Was he not with you the whole time?"

"Yes, we were—"

That's when it hit her. The maddening irritation that had been relentlessly buzzing around the edges of her brain came roaring into technicolor life in one brief spasm of memory.

She groaned and sat down heavily in one of the dining room chairs as the weight of the revelation hit her.

It was true she had been with Bertrand during the scavenger hunt.

Except for the ten minutes he'd been off looking for a bush to pee in.

41

Maggie sat through dinner that night barely tasting her food or hearing the conversations around her. All she could think of was that the one person with the best motive did not have an alibi after all.

The question now was, was Bertrand gone long enough to find Helga, kill her and return?

And was he really that cold-blooded? He could easily get his hands on a pastry nail. He could steal it from any of the chefs' tool kits.

But on the other hand, Laurent was an astute judge of character and what he pointed out was also true. The murder felt personal—like a revenge. And Bertrand was basically laid back and jolly. Even his motive wasn't really *that* strong. Was he really capable of murder just to keep funding for his stupid magazine?

Surely that was a reach.

"*Chérie?*" Laurent said to her.

Maggie looked in his direction, surprised to see Luc and Jemmy were already clearing the table.

"I'm sorry," she said. "Where did Marie-France go?"

She looked around the room.

"Zouzou is showing her the bakery book she and Mila made last winter," he said.

Maggie could hear the sounds of their voices coming from the living room.

Luc stood in the doorway to the kitchen.

"Laurent," he said. "May I borrow the car tonight?"

Laurent stood and cocked his head.

Maggie marveled at how the man didn't need to speak to be understood.

"I'm going to Yves' to study for the math test tomorrow," Luc said, his eyes going to Maggie before coming back to Laurent.

"Do not be too late," Laurent said. "It is still a school night. Feed the dogs first."

"Okay."

Laurent turned to Maggie. "Grab your coat, *chérie*," he said. "We'll talk outside."

Laurent had quit smoking the month before but the custom of going outside after dinner was an even harder habit to quit.

On the way to the foyer to get her coat, she smiled at the three sitting in the living room. All of their heads were bent over the scrapbook that Mila and Zouzou had created of photos and notes of their most successful baked creations. Mila had enjoyed the project immensely but Maggie had no doubt that if it hadn't been for Zouzou, her daughter wouldn't have been interested.

She met Laurent on the back terrace. It always seemed colder in the dark. She rubbed her arms through her jacket and shivered. Both dogs had come out too and instantly bounded into the darkest part of the vineyard at the end of the garden.

Laurent handed her a small glass of Calvados. With his hand on her elbow, he guided her to the stone restraining wall around his *potager*. The slates were slick in spots.

"And so," he said as they leaned against the wall. "You will tell me what has so entranced you tonight. Although possibly it was my *ratatouille*."

Maggie smiled at him and took a sip of the apple brandy. It warmed her all the way down her throat.

"Your *ratatouille* was entrancing as always. I just don't know how I could have forgotten that Bertrand left me for a few minutes."

"Surely he did not go far?"

"Well, I wasn't listening for him, if that's what you're suggesting."

"It would have been better if you had."

"What you said about the murder being passionate bugs me. You're right about Bertrand. He's not really intense in that way. He's superficial."

"Except of course we do not know his real nature."

"True."

"Well, then what about Marie-France?"

Maggie turned in the direction of the house. Through the French doors, she could see the glow of the fireplace around which Marie-France sat with Zouzou and Mila.

"I guess the whole Nazi bird thing was a bit of a stretch," Maggie said.

"I am glad you think so. What will you do now about Bertrand?"

Maggie looked at him in surprise.

"It's not enough, Laurent. Nowhere near enough."

"What would be enough? A confession?"

"A confession would be good."

"I forbid you to confront him. At the very least you will seriously offend him."

"And at the worst?"

"You will end up in someone's car trunk."

"I'm not going to confront him," she said. "But I was

wondering if you planned on talking to Detective LaBelle any time soon."

When he didn't answer immediately, Maggie turned to squint at his features in the dark. Laurent was impossible to read even in the bright light on a clear day. There was no way she'd be able to decipher what he was thinking on a moonless night!

"If Helga was stabbed through her jacket," she said, "we need to know that. If she wasn't, then you're right, the person got up-close and personal and that will help us narrow the suspects' field."

Laurent raised his eyebrows at her.

"I'm not suggesting you ask her out on a date, Laurent. I'm just saying we should take advantage of all of our resources."

"I agree, *chérie*," he said, pulling her close to him and wrapping an arm around her shoulders. "Which is why I am having lunch with her tomorrow."

42

The next morning Maggie drove to Aix to drop the kids off at school. Jemmy and Mila were good-natured but Luc was somber, even bad-tempered. After a few attempts to draw him out, Maggie gave up and let him have his own thoughts.

The drive to Aix was twenty miles, half on country back roads winding through quaint, remote villages that still looked like they belonged to another era, the other half on the A7.

Maggie used the first part of the trip to scold herself for her jealousies about LaBelle—who was easily a good ten years younger than Maggie. She trusted Laurent and he'd had plenty of experience in the past dealing with the amorous attentions of insistent women.

The fact that Margaux LaBelle was a police detective in the area they lived in did make things a little trickier.

After letting the children out, Maggie drove to the underground parking facility at *Les Allées* next to the Aix-en-Provence tourist center. Parking anywhere in Aix—although something Laurent somehow always managed to do—was notoriously difficult. Not just too narrow lanes but simply never enough parking spaces.

After parking in the garage, Maggie decided she would allow herself a rare day to shop and wander around Aix, sipping coffee, eating beignets and *pains au chocolate.*

It was cold enough that she didn't need to worry about groceries going bad in the car. So she first went to Monoprix, the large department and grocery store immediately above the parking garage. She wandered around the store and picked up laundry detergent and sundries before going to the grocery part of the store to fill her cart with yoghurt and cheese.

By the time she'd finished and stored her purchases in the trunk of her car, it was already late morning. She took the garage escalator to the outdoor mall that fronted the famous *Fountaine de la Rotonde* at the beginning of the Cours Mirabeau.

She walked first to Bechards. Within the hour it would be so busy that the line would snake out the door and down the well-known avenue. She spent a luxurious twenty minutes enjoying the smells and sights of the famous bakery before buying a sandwich for her lunch and a small sack of *chouquettes.* Finally she bought a chocolate éclair which the woman behind the counter wrapped and tucked into a white Bechard's box that she then tied with a ribbon.

I guess if you're going to commit to the calories, Maggie thought, *you might as well make an occasion of it.*

She debated picking up a *baguette* for dinner, but Bechards was a *patisserie.* She'd been taught over the years by Danielle and Laurent to look to the humble *boulangerie* for her dinner bread. She would pick up a *baton* at the bakery in Saint-Buvard on her way home.

That would also give her a chance to check in on Mireille. And Antoine.

She glanced at her watch. It was lunch time now and

Bechards had filled up so she had to fight to squirm her way out the front door.

Looking down the broad pedestrian avenue, her eye fell on *Les Deux Garçons*, the famous *brasserie* that had once served Paul Cézanne and Albert Camus. It had burned the year before and restoration had not yet begun. She knew Laurent would not have dined there in any event. The service was notoriously terrible and the food generally considered only good enough for tourists. A part of her wished she knew where he and Detective LaBelle were having lunch.

But another part of her was glad she didn't know.

Two streets north of the Cours Mirabeau was a little park pocked with four small stone fountains of varying sizes and designs. The sun had come out so that in spite of the chill in the air, Maggie was comfortable on her bench as she ate her lunch and watched the people go by.

Aix in the summer reminded Maggie more of Disney World than a Provençal town. But in winter, it fell in step with all the sleepier, more remote towns in Provence. It was peaceful with just the occasional sounds of women's boots clip-clopping across the cobblestone streets and echoing down the boulevards and narrow alleys.

As she finished her lunch and looked around for a place to deposit her trash, she wondered if it was worth a try to go to the jail to see Sybil. But no. Laurent was already working on getting information from the detective. Probably best not to make the woman feel as if she was being inundated with civilian requests. Or used. It was in nobody's interest to create acrimony with the Aix police.

Again, Maggie found herself wondering as to which restaurant Laurent would take the detective. He definitely had his favorites in Aix and Maggie knew all of them well. What would the proprietors think when he walked in with Margaux LaBelle? Would they recognize her as a police detective?

Or think Laurent was stepping out?

Maggie shook the thought from her head and sternly reminded herself that *she* was the one who'd asked Laurent to try to get information from Detective LaBelle.

Just let him do what he does best, she told herself and getting up, straightened her shoulders and headed for the next errand in her day.

The building that housed the offices of *Maigret Catering* was like all buildings in Aix—old, majestic and imposing, with a worn limestone façade and carved figures over the massive double wooden doors.

It was situated around the corner from the popular Place Richelme produce market which had already been dismantled for the day. There was now just a pleasant terrace of largely empty tables and chairs for any brave soul who had a mind to eat their lunch outside in the cold.

Maggie looked down at the address she'd found on the Internet *Maigret Catering*. She entered through the heavy door and went up the stairs, shifting her bag of baked goods to her other arm.

She was half surprised to find a real address attached to the company. So many catering businesses today operated only virtually. She walked to the receptionist's desk.

"My name is Maggie Dernier," Maggie said. "I have an appointment with Guy Deppois."

"One moment, Madame," the young woman said, her face impassive and uninterested. She buzzed her intercom and spoke in fast French before turning back to her computer where Maggie could see she was playing Solitaire.

"Ah, yes, Madame Dernier!" a man's voice said as he entered the reception room. He was young and tall with bland good looks. He strode over to her and shook her hand. "I hope I may be of assistance."

"Me, too," Maggie said as she followed him down a narrow hall to his office.

He pulled out a wooden chair in front of his desk and she sat down.

"Now," he said, adjusting the spectacles over his plump little knob of a nose. "How can I help you?"

"Well," Maggie said, "as I said on the phone, I was very impressed with the job your firm did for the LUSH *patisserie* competition over the weekend. Especially because your food was particularly scrutinized since it was a food event."

"Ah, yes," he said smiling proudly. "Is the function you are planning about that size?"

"Er, yes. Pretty much. I'm trying to determine how many servers I'll need."

"Ah, yes. I'm sure I can help you there."

"Now I understand there was a problem with the competition itself," Maggie said carefully. "A mix-up with the ingredients?"

Guy Deppois frowned. "Our company only handled the banquet afterward."

"Oh? I must have gotten wrong information," she said, matching his frown. "You worked with Bertrand Glenn, didn't you?"

"We did."

"He said your company was entirely responsible for supplying the ingredients for the contest. Is that not true?"

He huffed out an embarrassed breath and pulled at his collar.

"Well, yes. Yes, that is true," he said finally.

"So do you know how the mix-up happened? Because one of the contestants was given emulsified garlic butter instead of softened butter."

Guy's face cleared and he leaned back in his chair.

"That was out of our hands, Madame."

"Oh? In what way?"

"We were only tasked with stocking the dry ingredients for the contest. The flour and the sugar, corn starch and yeast."

Maggie frowned.

"So to be clear," she said slowly. "You're saying you *didn't* put the butter out for the contestants?"

He shook his head emphatically.

"*Non*, Madame. Monsieur Glenn insisted he would handle that himself."

43

M aggie walked to an empty bench on the Cours Mirabeau and sat down, her eyes staring unsee-ingly at the magnificent *Fontaine de la Rotonde*, the famous avenue's most defining fountain.

The Cours ran between a double row of plane trees which provided shade in summer and gave a spooky but intensely elegant presentation the rest of the year.

Why would Bertrand say he hadn't put out the butter when he had?

Unless he's done something he isn't proud of.

On the face of it the fact that Bertrand had lied about swap-ping out the wrong ingredients—essentially sabotaging his own contest—didn't seem to have anything to do with the murder. Not that Maggie could see. Not yet anyway.

Why would Bertrand put in the wrong ingredients? Was it an accident or was he trying to ensure that Cheryl didn't win? Surely he wasn't trying to set it up that *Zouzou* would win? That made no sense at all.

The memory of a desperately sick Marie-France came to Maggie.

What if switching the ingredients wasn't the only thing Bertrand had done? Was it just a coincidence that Marie-France had been sidelined from the competition?

If Bertrand had poisoned Marie-France and then sabotaged Cheryl's workstation with the assumption that a thirteen-year-old home baker didn't stand a chance against a professional *patisserie* chef, the only person left to benefit would be Geoff.

Were Bertrand and Geoff working together?

It certainly looked as if Bertrand had set things up such that Geoff would win. And of course when Zouzou won instead...

Frustrated and not sure what this new information really told her in relation to Helga's death, Maggie glanced at her watch and saw she still had at least two hours before she needed to pick up the children from school.

The picture on her phone showed a snapshot of Grace and Maggie last September at one of the many fall festivals they'd visited. One of the kids must have taken the picture. Maggie smiled now to remember that afternoon and on impulse, she called Grace.

"Hello, darling," Grace answered.

"Hey," Maggie said. "Got a minute? I'm still trying to sort out my suspects."

She held her breath. Her last conversation with Grace had not gone particularly well. Maggie vowed to steer away from anything having to do with Cheryl and her possible connection with Helga.

"Absolutely," Grace said. "Let me just put down this dish I was drying and I'm all yours."

"Sounds quiet on your end," Maggie said.

"Well, Geoff is still sick in bed and Danielle is off shopping with one of her friends and I think Cheryl is out walking Eduard's old vineyard."

Grace's bed and breakfast was surrounded by a hundred and forty hectares of vineyard that had once belonged to

Danielle's husband Eduard Morceau, but now belonged to Laurent. While the property was now a working vineyard once more it still provided a pleasant surrounding landscape for *Dormir*.

"Well, you're not going to believe this," Maggie said, "but I think I found some reason to believe that Bertrand and possibly Geoff conspired to fix the competition."

There was a pause on Grace's end.

"For Zouzou to win?" Grace said finally.

"No, I don't think they expected that to happen."

"Why would do you think they tried to fix the contest?"

"Because Bertrand said the catering company set out Cheryl's ingredients for the contest and I just talked to the catering company and they said that Bertrand insisted on being the one to do that."

"Odd."

"Isn't it? And for what possible purpose would Bertrand have for putting the wrong ingredients in Cheryl's workstation other than to eliminate her from the competition?"

"But why invite her to compete in the first place if he was going to do that?"

"I don't know. Maybe something changed. Maybe Helga dying changed things somehow."

"Does this mean you don't suspect Bertrand of killing Helga?"

"I basically suspect everyone this point."

"Except Cheryl," Grace said. "She certainly wouldn't sabotage herself in the competition."

Except the sabotage and the murder felt like two distinct crimes in Maggie's mind. There was no way she was taking Cheryl off the table as a possible suspect.

But she wasn't going to tell Grace that.

"I had a conversation with Debbie before the contest," Maggie said, "and she confirmed what you'd found out. She and Geoff are in serious financial trouble but she suggested it was because of his gambling."

"Really?"

"So it occurred to me that him needing money and being jealous over the fact that Helga got the job he wanted—"

"Don't forget she humiliated him at dinner," Grace interjected. "Remember? With the crack about *Eatz2*? That was clearly a dig about the job they'd both gone after. And *she* got."

"That's right. I'd forgotten that."

"That would certainly be cause for a little crime of passion. What does Laurent's homicide detective say?"

"She's not his personal detective, Grace."

"At least you seem to have a friend in the police department. That should be helpful."

"You'd be surprised at how unhelpful it is so far. In fact it's pretty clear I'm going to have to do this the old-fashioned way."

"Bribery?"

"You're just a stitch today. No. Shoe leather and knocking on doors. What are you doing today?"

"I thought I'd spend some time with Debbie. Bertrand is off shooting more photos for the magazine launch and I think she's had enough of walking the antiquities in any case."

"That's nice," Maggie said, glad that whatever annoyance Grace had been feeling with her in their last phone call appeared to be gone.

Nothing feels right when your best friend isn't talking to you.

Maggie checked her watch. Laurent had his lunch engagement with Detective LaBelle at noon straight up. It was nearly three now. They were either having a very successful lunch and were still at the restaurant—not unusual in France—or Laurent had gotten what he needed and was home by now.

Would it kill him to text me and let me know? He knows I'm waiting to hear!

.   .   .

Later after a quick visit to the English bookstore on rue Joseph Cabassol where she bought three novels and enjoyed a good cup of strong English tea, Maggie hurried to collect the kids from school. When she arrived home she saw that Laurent was not there. Scanning the kitchen when she entered the *mas*, she could tell he hadn't been home all afternoon.

Is that a good sign? A bad sign? A marital counselor sign?

Luc and Jemmy went straight outside to work on a project in the shed at the end of the garden. Mila and Zouzou immediately began to pull out cake pans and mixing bowls for tonight's dessert.

When Maggie went upstairs to change clothes, she heard the radio on in Marie-France's bedroom. She assumed that if the French woman wanted company she would have heard all the noise downstairs and join them—or not.

Meanwhile, Maggie used the opportunity to slip away into her office to get some work done. She tried not to think of where Laurent might be—still at lunch?—and read through a few of her emails before focusing on her trip with Luc to Heidelberg in the morning.

Luc had still been largely noncommunicative on the drive home from school but at his age that wasn't unusual. He wasn't a pouter and so Maggie had to believe he was just absorbed in his own thoughts which had nothing to do with the trip to Germany.

Tapping her pencil against the desktop, she decided to reach out to Helga's sister Uli again and make sure she'd be available tomorrow to see her.

"*Hallo?*" Uli said, answering the phone.

"Yes, hello, Frau Richter," Maggie said cheerfully. "How are you today?"

"Yes, good."

Wow, the Germans are even worse than Americans at small talk, Maggie thought.

"I am going to be in Heidelberg tomorrow," Maggie said, "and would love to come by and see you. Would that be possible?"

"Okay. Sure," Uli said.

"Great. I'll send you my number via text. If you could send me your address, that'll be great. One more thing. I know you said your parents were gone and you had no other siblings but was there anyone else in Helga's life she might have been close to? A girlfriend? Or a boyfriend maybe?"

"*Nein.* Nobody. Not since Hans."

"Hans?"

"*Ja.* Hans Wolfe. Her fiancé."

"Helga was getting married?"

"*Nein.* It was a long time ago. Come to think of it, there was something else I was going to tell you but now I cannot remember what it was. I'm sure it'll come to me."

"Okay, well, anyway, I'm looking forward to tomorrow," Maggie said.

After they disconnected Maggie got on the Internet and typed in *Hans Wolfe* and *Heidelberg* in the search engine window.

Within seconds she was directed to a news story from sixteen years ago. Her pulse quickened as she read the headline.

Promising Bakery School Student Kills Himself.

44

M aggie stared at her computer screen.

Is this relevant? Or is it just a terrible thing that happened?

She very much wished she'd asked Uli *when* Helga and Hans had broken off their engagement and why.

As she continued to read and reread the brief news article trying to see how it might fit with Helga's death in her vineyard at the end of a very sharp pastry nail, she found herself becoming more confused by what she read. Was the dead fiancé even important? She was mildly concerned that something that had nothing to do with what happened here last week might muddy her theories.

On the other hand, one thing Maggie had learned over the years was not to discount any information—especially the traumatic experiences. It might well have nothing to do with why Helga was murdered—and it was honestly hard to imagine how it could—but Maggie would file the information away even so.

. . .

She emerged from her office to the sound of Mila and Zouzou laughing in the kitchen. She could see through the sidelight at the front door that Laurent's car was now parked out front. Amazed at how immersed she must have been with her research that she hadn't heard Laurent come home, she went to check on the girls in the kitchen before going looking for him to find out about his lunch.

"You girls okay?" she asked as she scanned the kitchen countertops. Dinner in the form of a pot of spaghetti sauce was simmering on autopilot—testimony to the fact that Laurent had indeed been there. Zouzou and Mila were pulling cookie sheets of *gougères* from the oven.

"We're good!" Mila said.

"Where are the boys?" Maggie asked.

"Luc's upstairs, Jemmy's playing video games in his bedroom. Madame Babin is napping," Mila reported.

"When did your father get home?"

"I didn't check the clock. Careful, Zouzou!" Mila said. "The pan's still hot."

Maggie turned to head to Laurent's office when she was startled by a knock at the front door.

Both dogs awoke from their endless naps in the living room to howl and announce the arrival of a stranger. Maggie shooed them away and opened the door to find Cheryl standing on the doorstep stamping her feet, her face flushed from the cold. She wore what looked to Maggie like a real fox fur coat. Under one arm she carried a scarlet Chanel clutch.

Bright red like her Tyroleon jacket, Maggie thought, *in case there was a chance one might miss it.*

"It's freezing out here!" Cheryl said with a laugh. "Hope I'm not intruding?"

Maggie recovered from her surprise quickly. "Not at all. Come in and get warm. Your timing is perfect. The girls have just made *gougères*."

Maggie led Cheryl into the living room just as Laurent appeared.

"*Bonjour*," he said to Cheryl reaching for her coat. "Would you two like a fire?"

"That would be great," Maggie said. "Have a seat, Cheryl. I'll be right back."

She hurried to the kitchen and piled a dozen *gougères* onto a plate.

"Is that Mrs. Barker?" Zouzou said.

"It is," Maggie said. "Can y'all pour two glasses of that Sancerre and bring it in?"

As she returned to the living room, she wondered why Cheryl had come over.

Laurent was just standing up from the new fire which was already warming the room.

"Oh, that's lovely," Cheryl said as Maggie set the plate of cheese puffs down on the coffee table. "It's such a cold day."

"Marie-France is napping, I believe," Maggie said.

Cheryl snorted, making Laurent turn to glance at her.

"I'm not here to see Marie-France," Cheryl said with a laugh.

Zouzou came into the room with the two glasses of wine.

"Thank you, sweetie," Maggie said to Zouzou who left the room with Laurent.

"Grace made a comment today that made me realize we really don't know each other very well," Cheryl said.

"Oh?" Maggie said.

"And since the two of you are so close, I thought that was a shame."

"I never asked Grace how it was that you two got back in touch," Maggie said.

"Oh, that was because when Bertrand got in touch with me about his idea for putting on a *patisserie* competition in the south of France to promote his new magazine, I remembered

Grace ran an inn here. I hadn't spoken to her in a decade but I'm Facebook friends with her ex-husband, Windsor. Do you know him?"

"I do. He and Grace used to live near here when Laurent and I first came to the area."

"Oh, so you know what a sweetheart he is."

"So you're Facebook friends with him?"

"Well, Grace is hopeless about social media. I don't think she even has a Facebook account. And Windsor and I knew each other very well back in college."

Oh? How well is very well?

As if reading her mind, Cheryl leaned over and said conspiratorially, "Don't tell Grace but Windsor and I hooked up one night after working late at the library."

"I don't like to keep secrets from Grace," Maggie said.

It's official. I hate this woman.

Cheryl sat upright and blinked at her.

"Well, I hope that doesn't mean you'll say anything to her because that would be mean and serve nobody."

Isn't that always what people say when they want not to be held accountable for their actions?

Maggie narrowed her eyes. She suddenly doubted that Cheryl had come here today because she wanted to get to know Maggie better. Had Grace said something? Had she revealed that Maggie wondered about Cheryl's involvement in Helga's murder?

As Maggie looked into Cheryl's eyes which suddenly appeared calculating and malevolent, she saw the truth.

That was exactly why Cheryl was here.

"Grace said you're trying to help the police with the investigation into Helga's death," Cheryl said, her face impassive as she sipped her wine.

"That's right. Sybil is a friend and she said she didn't kill Helga."

"Well, I'm *Grace's* friend. And I didn't kill her either."

"Did you know Helga before last week?"

"Why are you asking that?" Cheryl's friendliness was gone now. She replaced her wine glass on the table and straightened the lapels of her jacket.

"It's just that I was led to believe that the *patisserie* world was a relatively small one," Maggie said. "So had you two met before?"

"Did it look like I knew her?"

"Wouldn't it be easier to just answer my question?"

"You think I had something to do with her death?"

"I don't know. Did you? It seems to me you're having trouble answering a simple question. Where were you when Helga was attacked? Because I know you weren't with Grace. At least not every minute."

Cheryl's eyes flashed angrily.

"What are you implying?" she said.

"I'm just asking a question."

"A very unfriendly question."

"Only if you have something to hide."

"How dare you?" Cheryl said, raising her voice and standing up dramatically. Both dogs by the fire began to growl. Laurent stepped out of the kitchen to see why.

"Is there a problem?" he asked, his eyes going from the dogs to Cheryl.

"I need my coat, please," Cheryl said to him abruptly. "This has been a very enlightening visit. Thank you for not sugar-coating your obvious bias against me."

She marched to the front door, digging her car keys out of her coat pocket as she flung the door open and stomped out, leaving the door open behind her. Laurent stood in the doorway and watched her back out of the driveway before closing the door.

Maggie picked up the wine glasses and turned to walk to the kitchen.

"Did that go the way you'd hoped, *chérie*?" Laurent asked, cocking his head to look at her.

"Actually, it did. You saw how upset she got? That looks like guilt to me."

"Or possibly just the natural reaction of someone being accused of a crime they didn't commit?"

Maggie didn't answer. It was true that Cheryl's reaction could mean several different things. She might be innocent. She might not.

As Maggie listened to Cheryl's car roar away from the *mas*, she realized how intently she'd been refusing to consider her a suspect.

Grace would be furious if Maggie tried to find evidence against her dear college chum. It might not even matter if Cheryl was really guilty of killing Helga.

On the other hand, if Maggie went down this road and Cheryl *wasn't* guilty, Grace would probably never speak to her again.

45

Laurent drove Maggie and Luc to the Aix-en-Provence train station well before sunrise the next day, completely eliminating any chance of talking privately. As soon as Laurent parked, Luc launched from the car and hurried inside to find their platform.

By the time Maggie and Laurent had finally gone to bed last night, she had been too tired to ask him about his lunch.

"I was hoping to get a report on your lunch yesterday," she said as they walked to the terminal.

"A report?" he said, raising an eyebrow. "Am I your asset now?"

"Well, you always have been," she said patting his arm. "But that's not how I meant it."

They entered the station and bought two round-trip tickets to Heidelberg.

"Luc is not looking forward to this," Laurent said.

"It's for his own good to look at all his options!"

Laurent leaned over and kissed her.

"I would give you the same advice, *chérie*."

The train trip was a long and relatively quiet one. Luc slept the whole way, his earbuds in his ears. Maggie hadn't had the heart to wake him to force him to talk to her.

She knew that Grace thought it odd that she was reacting so strongly to the idea of Luc going away to school. After all, he'd only been living with them eighteen months.

But the fact was that after a somewhat rough beginning, Luc had slipped into the Dernier family as smoothly and comfortably as if he'd been born into it.

Which of course, technically, he had been.

Luc loved Mila and Jemmy and was as relaxed and natural with them as any big brother would be. He adored Laurent, looking up to him for advice and affirmation. And Maggie knew that Luc loved her too. Although she didn't get the sense that he was remembering his mother when he looked at her, he did allow Maggie to fuss and worry over him as though he had been hers from the beginning.

For Maggie's part, she saw more of Laurent in Luc than Gerard, his biological father. Although he had auburn hair, Luc had Laurent's deep blue eyes and full lips. Marie-France had gotten that right when she'd remarked that they looked alike. They did look alike, but more than that, Luc had that strain of decency and goodness in him that also ran through Laurent.

Maggie gazed out at the passing scenery as the train pulled into the Heidelberg train station.

So why the angst at the thought of letting him go?

She reached out and put her hand on his arm. He woke up quickly, looking around and then out the train window.

Maybe because she knew in her heart that Luc's leaving was the beginning of all of the children leaving. In a few years, it would be Jemmy's turn and then Mila's. As unimaginable as that was right now, the years would go by in a blur and she and Laurent would be as they'd started out. Just the two of them.

Her stomach roiled unpleasantly.

She'd always assumed that someday her niece Nikki would come and live with her and Laurent, but that never happened. She worried that as soon as Luc left to live overseas, he had begun the process of leaving.

And he just might not come back.

"We're here," she said to him. "Excited?"

He turned and actually grinned at her. "Yeah, okay."

"Did you know Heidelberg is the sister city to Cambridge?" she said.

He didn't answer but Maggie felt her heart lift with hope that he might in fact be open to considering a school other than the one on the coast of California. She knew he might be trying to let her down easy but at least he was making the effort to mollify her.

Thirty minutes later, she and Luc stood in front of the admissions office of American University. The buildings along the cobblestoned streets dated back to the early seventeen hundreds.

Students were riding their bikes, others hurried up the wide broad steps before them. Luc's tour of the campus was scheduled to start in a few minutes and he'd asked to take it alone. As Maggie glanced around, she noticed that no other students were being escorted by their parents.

A pretty girl with golden blonde hair to her waist and dancing blue eyes smiled at Luc.

"Are you taking the tour?" she said to him in American English.

"Uh, yes," he said, blushing.

She stuck out her hand. "I'm Danni. From Cleveland."

Luc shook hands. "I am Luc. From Saint-Buvard."

"Oh, wow! You're French!" she gushed, her face blooming with enthusiasm, making her even more beautiful. "Want to go together?"

"Sure," he said, never glancing back at Maggie but hurrying up the stairs to join the girl.

Feeding a warmth radiate throughout her body, Maggie turned to hurry down the Willy-Brandt-Platz with a definite and newfound spring in her step.

46

The temperatures in Heidelberg was even colder than in France. The snowflakes speckling the air melted on contact with the asphalt streets. Maggie stood in front of Uli's apartment off of *Hauptstrasse* and thought the row of buildings could have been found in any college town in the US.

Almost.

She was well aware that this trip could be a wild goose chase and she was totally prepared for that. But she couldn't in all good conscience say she'd done her best by Sybil if she didn't check out Helga's friends and family.

And besides she had specific questions to ask.

She needed to know what had happened to Helga and Hans and then decide for herself if that could have had anything to do with what happened to Helga on that cold night at Domaine Sain-Buvard.

She rang the apartment building bell and waited until the intercom crackled.

"*Ja*?" a woman's voice said.

"It's me, Frau Richter. Maggie Dernier."

Instead of answering, a loud buzzer and the sound of a mechanical lock alerted Maggie to the fact that the heavy outside door had unlocked. She opened it and slipped inside.

Ulie Richter was waiting for her at the top of the first landing. She looked so much like Helga that for a moment, Maggie thought they must have been twins.

Maggie walked up the stairs and they shook hands.

"Thank you for seeing me," Maggie said. "May I call you Uli?"

"*Ja,* that is fine," Uli said and led Maggie into her apartment.

It was small and uninspired, but clean. The furniture was utilitarian: a chair, a table, a couch. Nothing not absolutely necessary.

It was a dark, depressing little space and from the minute she entered it, Maggie felt a visceral urge to step back outside.

The first thing Maggie thought when she saw the apartment was that Helga must have been doing significantly better than her sister to have turned down Bertrand's offer of ten thousand euros.

"I'm afraid I never got to know your sister before she was killed," Maggie said. "And I'm sorry about that."

On closer inspection, Maggie decided that Uli was a softer version of her sister. Her eyes were grey and while she had a strong, pointy chin, her eyes helped negate any hint of harshness in her features.

"My sister was an emotional mess," Uli said sadly. "She was in a constant state of heartbreak. Oh, to anyone who did not know her, it looked like irritation, *ja*? But I was her sister. I saw her pain."

"What was she heartbroken about?"

Uli just waved away the question.

"Was it Hans?"

Uli turned to regard Maggie and then the resistance in her face melted away.

"She never got over the guilt of his death," Uli said.

The news article that Maggie had read said he'd hung himself but there hadn't been much in the way of details leading up to that.

"The night he killed himself he was high on drugs. He hung himself in his closet."

Uli went to a small writing desk behind the couch and rummaged in the drawer. She returned with a framed photo and handed it to Maggie.

"This was Hans the year Helga met him at the National Bakery School."

The photograph showed six students—all with broad smiles for the photographer, all wearing their chef whites. Hans was the only male, a tall lantern-jawed blond man sitting next to a younger version of Helga.

Helga looked nearly unrecognizably happy.

"You said she never got over the guilt of his death. Why did she feel guilty? Was she there when it happened?"

"No, he killed himself long after they'd broken off the engagement. They weren't even in touch."

"Why did they break up?"

"An old story, I think. Someone came between them."

Maggie studied the photo. So Hans and Helga were happy and going to be married. Then Hans strayed with someone and he and Helga broke up, after which he turned to drugs and killed himself.

And Helga felt guilty about it? Somehow that didn't fit.

What am I missing?

"You have a nice apartment," Maggie said.

"It is convenient to my office," Uli said, indicating the couch where they would sit.

"Oh? Where is that?"

"I work at the American University. I am a secretary."

"Oh, that's interesting. My son is touring the university right now."

"He will love it there. All the Americans do."

"Did Helga live near here?" Maggie asked.

"She was staying with me until she could move into her new apartment."

"Oh? She had a new apartment?"

"Nothing like this," Uli said. "It was on the other side of town. Very posh as the Brits would say."

Maggie wondered why Helga even bothered to compete in the LUSH contest if she didn't care about or need the money.

"Okay." Maggie glanced around the dour little apartment. "You said her new apartment was...more upscale than this?"

Uli got up and went again to the desk and brought back a torn magazine page which she handed to Maggie.

The picture showed a plush and modern setting with upscale, Danish-styled furniture.

The monthly rental amount was printed on it as thirty-eight hundred euros.

"Wow," Maggie said. "It's really nice. Pricey, too." She looked at Uli. "Her job at *La Pomme* must have paid well."

A comment like that would be considered seriously rude if directed at a French person. Maggie had no idea how Germans reacted to indiscreet money talk.

"I wouldn't know how much she made at *La Pomme*," Uli said. "She left them a few weeks ago."

"Oh, that's right. She got a new job in London, right? At *Eatz2*"

"Well, she was offered the job but I think she was going to turn them down."

Maggie felt her heart begin to speed up. "Do you know why?"

"No, but I do remember what it was I wanted to tell you."

Uli looked down at her hands and seemed to brace herself for what she had to tell Maggie.

"Helga was expecting to come into some money. She told me she was going to be well taken care of without having to work."

Maggie frowned.

"You mean like she was going to inherit?"

"No, I would have known if we'd inherited any money. This was from something else and the way she made it sound, it wasn't through a job of any kind."

Maggie knit her brow but Uli only shrugged.

"My sister was an enigma, even to me. Sometimes I thought she was so wise for her years. And other times I was astonished at her immaturity."

"Sure. I get it," Maggie said. But she was only half listening. She was too busy thinking about the big windfall of money Helga was expecting.

From what? From selling something?

Or maybe from blackmailing someone who then decided to get rid of the annoyance of being blackmailed?

Permanently.

47

Grace stood in Zouzou's bedroom, her arms full of neatly folded laundry. From the bedroom window there was a view of the vineyard behind the house that stretched nearly to the horizon. As Grace gazed out the window, she thought of how this house used to be Danielle's as a young bride. Childless, Danielle and her first husband Eduard Monceau had lived here for thirty years.

Now the house rang with children's laughter, from Maggie and Laurent's two, as well as Zouzou and Philippe. Grace often found herself wondering how Danielle processed living here again. She'd moved out of the old *mas* when she married Jean-Luc. When Laurent bought the estate and renovated it as a *gîte* that Grace would run after Jean-Luc's death, Danielle had moved back in to help.

Grace ran a hand across the dresser. Unlike most girls her age, Zouzou had photos and posters of people like Gale Gand and Elizabeth Falkner tucked into the frame of her bureau mirror. Both were American pastry chefs, both winners of the Top Chef competitions many years running. Grace was grateful that Zouzou had strong women as her role models.

Would she ever have developed such a passion for baking if not for Laurent's influence? Grace smiled at the thought.

What would any of us be doing anything if not for Laurent's influence?

She heard the door open downstairs and she walked into the hallway.

"Danielle? Is that you?"

"*Oui, chérie,*" Danielle called upstairs. "Do you need help?"

"No, but if you could check the legumes on the stove that would be good."

Grace had put them on low but cooking was not her strongpoint. She'd burnt them before.

"Okay," Danielle said. "Should I put a pot of coffee on?"

"Sounds good. I'll be down after I finish putting the laundry away."

Grace gave Zouzou's room one last look and felt a shiver of sadness ripple through her. She didn't mind Zouzou preferring to stay at Domaine Saint-Buvard this week. It was always more exciting particularly now with one of Zouzou's culinary heroes staying there.

Grace walked down the hall to Cheryl's room. Grace had finally convinced her to get out and take a tour of Arles. While it was true Cheryl had lived in Paris for a year, she never ventured into the country. In fact, Paris was only a three-hour trip by train from Saint-Buvard. It was odd that she and Cheryl hadn't gotten together before now. They'd been so close in college. In fact all three of them had—Windsor too.

Life interferes, she thought as she went to Cheryl's dresser.

Cheryl was very tidy which Grace couldn't say for most of her B&B guests. Her suitcase was tucked away next to the armoire and the only thing on the dresser was a brochure for the Musée Granet in Aix and a pair of gold earrings.

Cheryl had finished her undergraduate courses at Ole Miss with Grace and Windsor—largely to please her parents because anyone who knew her knew she was going to be a professional baker someday.

After graduation, Grace and Windsor had married and embarked on their whirlwind disaster of a life together. For Cheryl, after college she'd worked in hotels and restaurants on the west coast before attending *l'École de Cuisine Alain Ducasse* in Paris and going on to win dozens of bakery competitions that would garner her jobs and awards and finally a reputation that today easily put her at the top of her profession.

Grace on the other hand had no work résumé and was divorced with two children—one of whom hated her.

She jerked open the dresser drawer to place the neatly folded stack of socks and undies inside. She'd told Cheryl it was absolutely no trouble to do her laundry too since she was doing hers and Zouzou's anyway.

Inside the top drawer was a tidy stack of two t-shirts side by side.

In Grace's experience, most people put their socks and underwear in the top drawer.

Leave it to Cheryl, she thought with affection, *to be different*.

She set the stack of laundry briefly down on the dresser top and pulled open the second drawer.

And froze.

Because there nestled on top of a silken camisole were three grey worry stones.

48

After leaving Uli's apartment, Maggie hurried to meet Luc at the café inside the Heidelberg *bahnhof* for a rushed lunch of *sauerbraten* and *wienerschnitzel* before boarding the train back to Aix-en-Provence.

Maggie had only managed to get a few uninspired remarks out of Luc about his experience on the campus tour. But because her own head was spinning with all she'd learned from Helga's sister, she didn't press him.

About halfway through the trip a light snow began to fall on the passing countryside. Maggie spent the first few hours of the trip going over and over the facts she'd learned from Uli Richter, not at all sure what to make of them.

Luc leaned against the window, his eyes closed, his earphones securely strapped to his head. There was no one else in their train compartment. Even though Maggie still felt stuffed from the heavy German lunch, she decided to step out for a hot cocoa—and to make a phone call to Laurent.

She walked four train cars away to the dining car, which was not at all crowded, and ordered two hot chocolates and took a seat by the window before calling Laurent.

"*Allo, chérie*," Laurent answered.

"I think Helga was blackmailing someone," Maggie said, glancing around to see if anyone had overheard her.

"*Vraiment?*"

"Her sister said she was expecting to come into a lot of money. That would explain why Bertrand offering her money didn't convince her not to come."

Laurent snorted. "On the basis of *that* you are saying she was blackmailing someone?"

Maggie felt a splinter of annoyance pierce her at his words. "Can you think of a better explanation?" she asked.

"Perhaps she sold her couch or was moonlighting at a second job."

"Blackmail is a common reason why people are murdered, Laurent."

"Where is this fact written? I have never heard it."

Why is he being so resistant to my theories?

"Are you at home?" she asked. It sounded like he was in his car. She tried to imagine where he might be going.

"I think it is a big leap from an unexplained source of income to blackmail," he said.

"Look, a lot of what I do is gut reaction and instinct. You would be surprised how not knowing something one day turns into...oh never mind! Just trust me, her behavior is very suspicious. *Follow the money*. Have you never heard of *that*? That's all I'm doing."

"*Bon, chérie.* You sound tired. We will talk when you are home."

"You never told me about your lunch with Margaux."

"Frau Richter was stabbed from inside her jacket."

Maggie let out the breath she didn't even realize she was holding.

"So it was someone she knew well. A lover? Were she and Geoff or Bertrand sleeping together?"

"It is a theory. Among many. You were saying about following the money? Because in France we have a saying too—"

"Yes, yes, I know: *cherchez la femme*. But that doesn't necessarily mean a *woman* did it. And honestly, I think that's a little old-fashioned. If you watch any decent TV mystery today it's almost always about the money."

"*Tant pis*. It is a sad evolution of affairs when money trumps love."

"No pun intended," Maggie said with a smile. "Anyway I'm going to try to put together a blackmail motive and see how it fits with an intimate relationship with someone and see where that gets me."

"That all sounds very vague to me."

"Well, that doesn't surprise me."

"How did Luc like Heidelberg?"

"Well, he left the college application on the café table at lunch, but I'm sure he can apply online. That doesn't mean anything."

"Of course not," Laurent said in that way he had of saying one thing but meaning another that so totally infuriated Maggie.

"Well, it doesn't. He met a girl for one thing."

"Always there will be girls," Laurent said with a shrug that Maggie couldn't see but could definitely hear.

"Well, I guess we'll just have to see," she said, finding her annoyance with her husband measuring high on the temperature scale of wifely ire.

"*Oui. Bien sûr*," he said blithely.

Once back in the train compartment, Maggie set both hot cocoas down on the pull-down tray table and nudged Luc with her foot. He roused himself, looking around as though surprised to find himself on a train. His eyes went first to her and then the paper cup of cocoa.

"*Merci*," he said, reaching for it.

"That seemed like a nice girl I saw you talking to," Maggie said. "The one from Cleveland?"

"*Oui.*"

Maggie heard Laurent's voice in her head and to a certain extent she knew he was at least a little right. She didn't want to put her own needs first when it came to Luc's future. Even if in her mind, those two things comfortably coincided.

Or if she were honest, she didn't want to be *perceived* as doing that.

Why is it so hard for everyone to believe that I really do know what's best for him?

"Was she visiting or going to school there?" she asked.

"Je sais pas." I don't know.

"Really?" Maggie felt a splinter of annoyance pierce her and she fought to keep her voice steady. "You spent all afternoon with her and didn't find that out? So what did you talk about?"

Maggie could hear the tone of the words coming out of her mouth and she felt powerless to stop it. She knew she sounded nagging. Luc confirmed that when he put down his cocoa and looked at her.

He gave her a disarming if rueful grin.

"I know you do not want me to go to California."

"I *do* want you to go! I just want you to come back."

Instantly Maggie heard Laurent's voice again in her head. Whether or not Luc came back was not the question right now. Not really. Because if it turned out he didn't come back, then that would clearly be the right thing for Luc.

Did she really want him to return just to make her happy?

"I will miss all of you," he said. "You know I will. And I am a little...nervous, too."

Maggie reached out and took his hand.

She felt a flood of tenderness toward him.

It suddenly dawned on her that she wasn't the only one who knew down to the kilometer exactly how far away California was from Saint-Buvard. She wasn't the only one who felt like she was poised on a high dive over a cliff.

Of course he was afraid. He wanted this amazing new experience that looked so incredible in theory but he'd never been out of France until this morning. She took a deep breath and smiled at him.

While it was true that, unlike Luc, she wasn't about to embark on a grand, scary adventure, in her own way she would be tested by his experience.

"I'm sure you'll come to the right decision for you, Luc."

"I haven't always made good decisions," he said, looking pensively down at his cellphone.

"We all make mistakes when we're young. But we wouldn't let you go if we didn't think you could handle it."

"*Are* you letting me go?" he asked, looking up at her, his eyes full of doubt. For a moment Maggie knew exactly what Luc must have looked like as a small child. Her heart went out to him and the thought of the childhood he must have had—largely motherless and full of hunger and fear—made her eyes fill with tears that she fought to conceal.

Maggie smiled. "Well, not right his minute, no. But when the time comes, you'll be ready. And I guess so will I."

"Thanks," he paused, looking like he was about to say her name but he blushed instead.

"I wish you'd call me *Mom*," Maggie said, "unless you think that would take away from your real mother."

Maggie was aware that they never spoke of Luc's mother, the beautiful young woman killed in a car crash with Luc's stepfather when Luc was only eight years old.

"She will always be *Maman* to me," he said and then looked at her, his eyes shining.

"Well, then it's settled," Maggie said patting his knee and letting him go back to his music.

She picked up her own cocoa and stared out the window feeling sadder than she had before her conversation with Luc. But also happier. And she was proud of herself. It might not feel like the right thing for *her*, but it felt like the right thing for Luc.

After a few minutes, and with nearly another two hours before they arrived in Aix, Maggie opened up a browser on her phone and did a search for Helga's pastry school. She scanned some of the archives looking for the photo that Uli had shown her today but there was nothing there.

She found it tricky trying to do this sort of research on her phone. She jotted down a few notes for later when she was at her desktop computer. For the rest of the trip, she tried to put Helga and Uli out of her mind.

She closed her eyes and let the comforting motion of the train rock her until the insistent vibrating of her phone made her realize she'd dozed off. She picked up her phone and saw Laurent's photo on the screen.

They were still an hour from the station in Aix.

"Hey," she said into the phone. "You're not there yet, are you? We're still an hour away."

"I just had a phone call from Detective LaBelle," Laurent said. "And I thought you would want to know as soon as possible."

Maggie felt a lightness form in her chest. "What's happened? Has somebody confessed?"

"In a manner of speaking. Can you speak? Is Luc with you?"

Maggie glanced at Luc but his eyes were closed. She could hear his music through his earphones.

"He's listening to his music. What's happened?"

"It seems the police have a note in their possession that was found in Helga's suitcase."

"They're just now finding it?"

"I believe they have had it for a while now."

"What kind of note?"

"A threatening note promising to kill Frau Richter if she competed in the contest."

Maggie could barely sit still in her excitement. "That's great! Do they have any idea who it's from?"

"Some idea, since it was signed by Marie-France Babin."

49

"No way a boche will take France's top honor for patisserie. Bow out of the competition now or bow out permanently."

Maggie sat at the kitchen counter at Domaine Saint-Buvard looking at an email of the note that Detective LaBelle had sent to Laurent. It was late, nearly one in the morning, and everyone but Laurent was in bed asleep.

Laurent had picked up both her and Luc thirty minutes earlier and, after making them both ham and cheese sandwiches—which Luc promptly took up to his bedroom—he poured Maggie a glass of wine and handed her the printout of the note.

Maggie stared at the note and shook her head in disbelief.

The woman who'd written this note was sleeping not twenty feet above her head in her upstairs guest room.

Was it also the woman who had cold-bloodedly murdered Helga Richter?

"So why is Sybil still in custody?" Maggie asked. "This is an overt threat! And it's in writing! Why are we just finding out about it now? The murder was eight days ago!"

"I do not know, *chérie*."

Maggie narrowed her eyes at him.

Did the sudden reveal of this note have anything to do with Laurent's lunch with Detective LaBelle?

"I never got any details about your lunch with the detective. What else did you two talk about?"

"Just the case."

"Nothing else?"

"Like what?" he asked.

"I'm not going to give you multiple choice answers, Laurent, just so I can get your famous monosyllabic yes or no answers."

"You sound like you need another glass of wine." He turned to bring the bottle back to the counter to refill her glass.

One thing Maggie knew if she knew anything about her husband was that there was no way Laurent would talk about something he didn't want to. There was no ploy she could use to make him tell her something he wasn't ready to discuss. This habit of his was supremely annoying and in thirteen years of marriage she'd not yet gotten used to it.

"What I need are answers about why this note was ignored for eight days while Sybil was rotting away in prison."

"It is not a prison. It is a detention center."

"It's still not a very nice place!"

"Perhaps the police felt they needed more evidence," he said, pushing the glass of wine toward her. "*C'est suffit.*"

"How much more evidence do they need? It's a murder threat in writing!"

"It is possible it is only a threat from an impassioned *artiste*."

"Oh, please spare me the impassioned artist defense."

"That defense exists for a reason. The police believe that

the note was not an admission of intention but one of pique or perhaps jealousy."

"Is Marie-France upstairs?"

"Yes, but you are not to talk to her."

"Why not?"

"Because you are going to be unforgivably rude. I can see it in your face."

"She might be a murderer, Laurent! You're allowed to be rude to murderers."

"Not in my house," he said firmly. "*Non.*"

"Well, why isn't she in Aix being grilled by the cops?"

"Because this is not new evidence, *chérie*," Laurent said patiently. "As you say, they have known of this note for eight days."

"Exactly! And ignored it!"

"You will not talk to her," Laurent said firmly, his hands on his hips as he glowered at her.

"Talk to who?" a voice said from the stairwell as Marie-France appeared in the living room.

Maggie instantly stood up.

Marie-France came into the kitchen wearing a dark plum silk dressing gown over matching silk pajamas. She nodded at Maggie's full wine glass.

"Perhaps you would be so kind as to pour me a glass of that, Monsieur Dernier," she said to Laurent.

Knowing that Laurent was momentarily torn between being the consummate host that he was to his core, with the urge to clap a hand over his wife's mouth because he knew what was about to come out of it, Maggie moved out of his reach.

"The police have discovered a threatening note in Helga's personal belongings," Maggie said.

Marie-France held out her hand for her wine glass. Maggie noticed there wasn't a tremor in it.

"The note was from me?" Marie-France asked.

"Unless you know of anyone else who might want to threaten Helga with her life," Maggie said.

"*Maggie*," Laurent said in a low warning voice.

Rarely did he call her by her first name. Maggie didn't know if he was warning her to keep her voice down because of the children or because he didn't like her being rude to a guest in his home no matter how many other houseguests Marie-France had killed.

"Yes, I wrote that note to her," Marie-France said. "I hated the filthy *couchon*."

"*No way a boche will take France's top honor for patisserie. Bow out of the competition now or bow out permanently,*" Maggie read. She looked up at Marie-France. "That's a death threat."

Marie-France arched an eyebrow.

"I think you are the only one who thinks so. Where are the police if this note is so damning?"

"They're clearly building a case against you, Marie-France," Maggie said, watching to see the effect her words had on the woman.

Marie-France snorted.

"You don't know what you're talking about. They have their murderer."

"Yeah. The wrong one," Maggie said heatedly. "And a fellow countrywoman? You're going to let her go down for a crime you committed?'

"*Chérie*," Laurent said, his voice tight with anger. "Not another word."

"It is all right, Monsieur Dernier," Marie-France said, finishing her wine and setting the glass on the kitchen counter.

"I am tired and will return to my bed, but thank you for your hospitality."

Laurent stopped a few feet from Maggie, his hands on his hips. Maggie knew she'd embarrassed him. But she also believed that the fact that he hadn't intervened meant that at some level he knew she was handling it just right.

Her initial intention had been to prod Marie-France—a mercurial and volatile *artiste*—into blurting out a confession. Because of Laurent, she'd held back but in the end, Marie-France had surprised Maggie with her self-possession.

Perhaps after all, threatening note or not, Marie-France didn't have the passion to have committed this murder?

"I will be packed at first light," Marie-France said as she turned toward the stairs. "But you have made an enemy of me, Madame, with your accusations."

"That's doesn't bother me," Maggie said.

"It might bother Zouzou though," Marie-France said coldly. "Her career in baking might be adversely affected as my name and reputation still carries much weight."

"That's true," Maggie said. "Although perhaps not so much from a prison cell."

50

T he next morning after Marie-France called an Uber and left, Maggie drove Luc to school. She was surprised to realize that Jemmy and Mila were in fact not in the house at all. Zouzou had gone back to *Dormir* for the night and Jemmy and Mila had been allowed to have a sleepover on a school night.

Assuming that the kids had used the opportunity of her absence to wear Laurent down, Maggie thought no more about it. As for Laurent, while he clearly understood her strategy with Marie-France the night before, he still seemed annoyed with the way she'd handled it. Nor, he made it clear, was he at all convinced that the Frenchwoman was guilty of murder.

After dropping Luc off at school, Maggie debated trying to get in to see Detective LaBelle to ask why the threatening note hadn't made a difference in Sybil's case. But since it was clear that the detective was open to talking only to Laurent, she decided to save the effort.

Danielle had a late afternoon hair appointment in Aix and had volunteered to pick up the children after school, which meant Maggie didn't need to spend the day in town. Even so, she felt at loose ends. From Marie-France's threatening note to everything else that she'd stumbled across in this case—from Bertrand's motive and Helga's secret influx of money—she felt further away than ever from the truth.

She sat down at a café on the Cours Mirabeau and ordered a *noisette* and a *pain au chocolat* and sent a text to Laurent reminding him he was supposed to follow up with Antoine on where he got the stone.

Clues and more clues and none of them leading any place, she thought in frustration.

Maggie drank her coffee and her thoughts turned to Grace. She hadn't heard from her since their conversation the day before.

Surely Cheryl had gone straight to Grace to complain after her visit to Domaine Saint-Buvard that Maggie thought she was Helga's killer? But whatever Cheryl had or hadn't said to Grace, clearly Grace wasn't interested in discussing it with Maggie.

Trying to push thoughts of Grace out of her mind, Maggie turned her attention again to the photo that Uli had shown her yesterday, the one Maggie hadn't been able to locate online. She'd tried again this morning before taking Luc to school. She kicked herself for not examining the faces of the other students better. People changed physically—especially young people.

She texted Uli and asked her to send a copy of the picture to her phone.

"Hello, there! Fancy meeting you here!"

Maggie looked up to see Bertrand, dressed in jeans and a black shirt, approaching her table. They greeted each other the French way with cheek kisses, and Maggie invited him to join her. The waiter appeared and took his order.

"So what brings the luscious Madame Dernier to Aix?" he said with a flirtatious grin.

"Dropping my son off at school," Maggie said, reminding

herself that except for an obvious lack of passion, this man had no alibi and the best motive for killing Helga.

"Jolly good," Bertrand said as the waiter brought his coffee.

"I'm glad I ran into you," Maggie said. "I was wondering about the cash prize for Zouzou. You know? The twenty thousand euros?"

"Ah, yes," Bertrand said uncomfortably. "About that. I probably should have mentioned this before now."

"Mentioned what?"

"There was a clause in the contract, just a basic boilerplate sort of thing, that disqualified Zouzou from winning the money."

Maggie wasn't surprised that Bertrand was going to squirm out of his promise of the cash prize.

"On the basis of what?" she asked.

"Well, it states all contestants needed to be over twenty-one. I'm pretty sure I mentioned it to Zoe's mother when she signed the contract."

Maybe he did, Maggie thought tiredly. It didn't matter Grace would still have allowed Zouzou to compete even with no winnings.

She stirred her coffee and let an uncomfortable silence grow between them. She felt him shift and just when she was sure he was about to go find another table, she asked the question she'd been trying to find the answer to ever since the murder.

"How well did the chefs know each other before last week?"

Bertrand frowned as if giving it serious thought, and Maggie couldn't help but think he was putting on an act.

"Well, let me see. Friends, no. Obviously they all knew *of* each other, I'm sure, being in the same incestuous industry. I think Helga knew Geoff personally. I don't know why I say that except for the fact that they were both up for the same job."

"But you don't have any reason to believe they knew each other before last week?"

"Not really. I know he didn't like her. Thought she was arrogant. And while it's possible that Helga was a bit of an acquired taste, perhaps that was because he'd known her before. You should ask him."

"I will. I guess he's still pretty sick?"

"Oh, aye, as the proverbial dog. But I've been doing my bit to keep the ball and chain out and away."

"Grace mentioned she thought Debbie was getting bored."

"Oh, darling, it's a tad more than that. I know I shouldn't say anything but I've known Geoff on and off for years. Frankly he's lost the plot. And that's saying it kindly."

"What does that mean? Lost the plot? He's nuts?"

Bertrand laughed. "Oh, not really. But then again maybe not far off. Unstable, I'd say."

"Because of their money troubles?"

"Or just because he's Geoff. Debbie has been a saint to stay with him this long."

"Is she thinking of leaving him?"

"She won't have much say in the matter soon," he said ominously.

"Geoff is leaving her?"

"In a manner of speaking." He leaned across the table and looked both ways before speaking. "I'm not supposed to say anything until the cops have all their ducks in a row but I have a contact who has a contact in the lab that the Aix police use out of Nice."

"Forensics? On this case?"

"Yes."

Bertrand eased back into his chair with the air of a man who'd just delivered momentously important information. He crossed his arms and nodded at Maggie.

A pinging sound from her phone made Maggie glance at her phone to see a text had arrived from Uli.

<I dropped the framed picture after your visit and the glass damaged the photo so I threw it out sorry. Was important?>

Maggie felt a wave of discouragement.

One step forward, four steps back.

She looked at Bertrand.

"You were saying you have information from the forensics lab?"

"You could say that."

"Well?"

"You know the pastry stabby thing that killed Helga?"

Maggie nodded.

"It had Geoff's fingerprints on it."

51

G race stood at the kitchen window and cupped a mug of coffee that she'd allowed to get cold. The temperature had dropped further and the day promised to be another miserably cold one.

Her view out the window was limited to the two guest cottages which faced each other on the other side of the driving pad. Since Marie-France had moved to Domaine Saint-Buvard, only Cheryl's guest room and Prune cottage were occupied.

Debbie had mentioned last night that she was afraid she was catching whatever it was that had laid Geoff so low for the last couple of days. When Grace brought her a breakfast tray this morning, she'd said she intended to spend most of the day in bed.

And the way she'd looked—pale and red-eyed like she'd been crying or fighting allergies—Grace had thought that a very good idea.

Windsor had called last night to allow Grace to talk to Philippe, although at five the child was easily distracted and the conversation had been largely one-sided. Truth be told, she was glad Windsor had agreed to his visit. Philippe was a darling child and because he was living in France with Grace there was little chance of Windsor really getting to know him.

Still, she would be glad when the little dear was back home. The house felt unsettled and incomplete without him. She was nonetheless grateful that Philippe was not here at the moment. There was doubt and betrayal in the air at *Dormir* right now that she would not want Philippe feeling.

Starting with his own grandmother.

And coming from the fact that she didn't trust a dear old friend.

As soon as Grace had discovered the karma stones in Cheryl's drawer, she'd felt an overwhelming nausea come over her that in many ways hadn't abated since. She felt like a bad friend not telling Cheryl what Maggie had told her—that a worry stone had been discovered by Helga's body. Why would she keep that information from her? Why, unless she really believed that Cheryl was involved in some way?

And then there was the fact that she'd kept the discovery of the stones in Cheryl's drawer from Maggie.

I'm two for two, she thought sadly. I'm keeping secrets from both of them.

What kind of a friend does that make *me*?

There had been so many moments since she discovered the stones that she'd resolved to confront Cheryl—or at least ask her about them.

She wasn't very good at this—not like Maggie. Her plan at first had been to casually mention to Cheryl that a worry stone had been found by Helga's body and then wait for Cheryl to offer up the information that she herself had one.

And then try to read her face to see if she was trying to cover her guilt.

But Grace knew she was not good at dissembling. Her face revealed every emotion and intention she was feeling. And now she'd kept the secret of the found stones too long. The second she casually mentioned to Cheryl that a stone had been found by Helga's body, Cheryl would know that Grace knew that she herself owned similar stones.

No, it was best now to say nothing.

Besides, just because Cheryl owned worry stones, and just because one had been found by Helga's body, didn't mean anything.

Oh, Maggie would definitely say it did! Which was why Grace had resolved not to tell her. Besides, Maggie didn't like Cheryl. Maggie had no reason to want to protect or defend Cheryl. She would go all out to unearth the truth to clear the name of the baker's wife—someone whom neither of them had ever given two thoughts about before—but if it was a friend of Grace's? Not a chance.

Grace threw her cold coffee into the sink and scolded herself for her line of thought.

I'm getting as bad as Maggie, she thought, rinsing her mug out. Just as she was about to attend to that leaky faucet in the upstairs bath she'd been avoiding, she noticed a motion outside.

It was Geoff leaving the cottage and pausing on the doorstep long enough to button his jacket before turning and walking away toward the village road.

Grace frowned. While she was glad to see that he was clearly feeling better—he was practically jogging—she would have advised against a walk in the cold so soon after shaking off whatever his recent illness had been.

Although she had no doubt after being cooped up for three days he was probably desperate for a little fresh air, she seriously considered running after him to tell he wasn't dressed warmly enough when she saw another figure coming from around the house.

Bundled up in her garish red boiled wool jacket, her white cotton neck scarf flowing behind her, and following the exact same path Geoff had taken—was none other than Cheryl.

Cheryl.

Who had told Grace not an hour ago that she intended to stay inside and read all day.

Cheryl was hurrying after Geoff and looking over her shoulder as if she was doing something she knew she shouldn't be doing.

fter tossing down a few euros and giving Bertrand a hurried goodbye, Maggie bolted from the café table and raced to her car.

Geoff's prints on the murder weapon had to mean he was the killer! Didn't it?

She ran down the long Cours Mirabeau and jabbed in Grace's phone number on her phone. When Grace didn't answer, Maggie called Danielle's phone. The call went straight to voicemail.

No wonder Detective LaBelle didn't want to look at Marie-France for Helga's murder! She knew that Geoff had motive, opportunity and now evidence that he'd handled the murder weapon!

Surely this meant that Sybil would be released any moment! Maggie found her car in *Les Allées* and as she sped out of the underground parking garage, put in a call to Laurent

"*Allo?*"

"Laurent, you're not going to believe this!" Maggie said breathlessly as she roared up the on ramp to the A8. "But first, you need to get to *Dormir*. Grace might be in danger. I just found out—"

"Grace has just come, *chérie*," Laurent said.

"Oh, thank God!"

"What has happened?"

"I just had coffee with Bertrand and he told me he knows someone who knows someone in the forensics lab in Nice who said they've pulled Geoff's prints off the murder weapon!"

Laurent was silent.

"Laurent? Did you hear me?"

"Yes, *chérie*."

"It means that Geoff is the killer. Wait. Where's Debbie?"

Maggie heard Laurent turn to talk to Grace. He came back to the phone.

"She is still at *Dormir*."

"Laurent, Geoff is a murderer! I don't think Debbie's safe there. You need to call the police straightaway. Do *not* go there yourself!"

"I would say the same thing to you, *chérie*," Laurent said.

"What about Cheryl?"

Again Laurent turned to confer with Grace.

"Grace says Cheryl went out. In fact, Grace says that Geoff is gone too."

"So Debbie's there alone?"

Maggie heard Laurent tell Grace to call the police.

"*Chérie*? Call me back when you are close, yes?"

"Okay." Maggie came within a hair of asking him to tell Grace she was sorry she ever thought her friend Cheryl was the killer but of course that was something she needed to do face to face.

"And *chérie*?" Laurent said before disconnecting, "I'm pretty sure you owe Marie-France an apology."

∾

The forty-minute drive back to Domaine St-Buvard seemed interminable to Maggie. Her mind whirled with thoughts of what this new information meant and how it affected everything she knew up to now. She'd been so sure that Marie-France had been the killer but in fact Geoff had always been a close runner-up.

And with his prints on the murder weapon? There was no doubt that Detective LaBelle would be swooping in for the arrest any time now. Maggie was sure LaBelle would enjoy arresting a British national and releasing the Frenchwoman currently held for the crime.

As she neared the village of Saint-Buvard, which signaled that the family *mas* was only a few minutes away, Maggie called Laurent again.

"I'm nearly home. Has anyone talked to Danielle yet?"

"She is at the school to pick up the children. All is fine, *chérie.*"

"Have you heard anything? Was it Geoff's pastry nail? He might try to say his prints would logically be on it."

"I don't know, *chérie.*"

"Do you know where he is? Is he in custody?"

"The police are not as reliable as I might desire for letting me know their timelines."

Maggie snorted. "Have you and Margaux had a tiff? Because I'm pretty sure she'd hand over the murder file to you if you asked."

"I will see you when you get here," Laurent said, the wry amusement evident in his voice.

Grace was still at Domaine St-Buvard by the time Maggie arrived. She had wanted to go back to *Dormir* but Laurent wouldn't allow it.

Cheryl called to say the police had arrived at *Dormir* and she herself would be heading to Domaine St-Buvard.

Maggie went to the kitchen where Grace greeted her coldly.

"Look, I'm sorry, Grace. All I can tell you is that Cheryl looked like a possible suspect to me."

"Be honest. You took an immediate dislike to her and used that as the basis for your suspicions."

"I really don't think so. I mean, I admit I don't like her, but I can't apologize for how she appeared to me."

Before Grace could respond, Maggie turned to Laurent. "Where's Debbie?"

"She is being questioned by the police at *Dormir* about Geoff's whereabouts," he said before pouring two mugs of coffee.

Grace turned and walked into the living room.

"She is upset," Laurent said to Maggie.

Maggie knew Laurent was asking her to be sensitive to Grace's mood but she was way past that. She brought the two mugs of coffee into the living room where Grace was sitting on the couch flipping through a home and garden magazine.

"You can be mad at me if you want, Grace," she said. "But implying that I'm so shallow that jealousy over your relationship with another friend made me suspect her of murder is beneath you. And if you don't think so, then the hell with you."

"Ah," Laurent said as he came into the room with a plate of *chouquettes* on the tail end of Maggie's words. "Making up, I see?"

"Just Maggie being Maggie," Grace said with a sniff.

"Fine. I tried," Maggie said and took her coffee and one of the *chouquettes* into her office.

For the next hour until she heard Danielle and the children arrive, Maggie went back to *Cherchez* on the Internet and from there to an international news archival system to try to find any information she could on Helga Richter. Scrolling through the long list of news articles, she was able to find a few old newspaper articles on Helga from her teen years. Helga had been a moderately good volleyball player and her teams had won several regional awards.

Just as Maggie was about to give up and switch off her computer, she found something that caught her eye. It was an article of a summer tragedy that happened on a scouting trip when a twelve-year-old boy fell to his death from the trail.

One of the student minders was a teenager listed as H. Richter.

Maggie stared at the old newspaper article. The tragedy happened in the Black Forest, about eighty miles from Heidelberg, during an overnight scouting trip sponsored by a branch of the European Scouting Group. There were details on the boy who died—a twelve-year-old named Dieter Schmidt—but nothing on the particular group of children on the hike—or on the teenagers or adults who were supposed to be watching out for the children's safety.

Before Maggie could dip any further into it, she heard a shriek that came from the living room. She jumped up and jerked open her study door to see that Cheryl and Grace were in each other's arms. Laurent and Danielle stood by watching.

"What's happened?" Maggie asked. "Is it Geoff? Have they found him?"

"They have," Laurent said solemnly.

"So he's in custody?" Maggie asked, still looking at Grace and Cheryl, her confusion mounting.

"No, *chérie*," Laurent said solemnly, "He's not in custody. He is dead."

53

Grace didn't know why she was acting like such a bitch to Maggie.

Maybe it was because Maggie had been so right and she'd been so wrong. Maybe it was because Maggie had seen the true nature in Cheryl and Grace had breezed right past it.

Maybe it's because I'm just a shallow vain person who can't accurately judge evil even when it's sitting at my breakfast table.

The minute Cheryl arrived at Domaine St-Buvard, Grace took her outside on the terrace. She had no doubt there was a good explanation for why Cheryl had gone after Geoff this morning. She didn't doubt that for a minute. But she still needed to know what that good explanation was.

"I saw you follow Geoff this morning," Grace said, searching Cheryl's face for the perfectly reasonable explanation.

"What? No, you didn't," Cheryl said, her eyes cold and unreadable.

"Cheryl, yes, I did."

"I don't know what you think you saw but I didn't go after anyone. I never left my room."

Grace just stared at her, the shock riffling through her in nauseating waves.

"If I were you I'd be careful what you say to people, darling." Cheryl looked meaningfully at Grace. "I was in my room reading all morning."

Cheryl then turned on her heel and went back into the house leaving Grace shocked and aghast.

When Grace reentered the house, the police had arrived. The whole downstairs level looked like barely contained mayhem. Three policemen stood in the dining room. The scent of brewing coffee filled the air.

Grace inched her way into the room and leaned against the dining room wall. She felt the onset of heart palpitations.

Maybe even chest pain.

"Are you all right, Grace?" Cheryl asked, turning to Grace and giving Grace's arm a solicitous squeeze.

It was all Grace could do not to pull away from her.

You lied! What did you do that you needed to lie?

Cheryl turned to go into the kitchen and Grace felt a tingling sensation as if she was having trouble getting enough oxygen.

What's happening to me?

Danielle was in the kitchen with Laurent. Grace craned her neck until she spotted Zouzou and tried to catch her eye but she and Mila were being hustled upstairs by Luc and Jemmy.

"We have to go to our rooms," Zouzou called down to her. "*Oncle* Laurent's orders."

Grace smiled wanly and nodded.

Laurent's orders.

She turned back to the kitchen to see Maggie talking to Laurent and Danielle. Suddenly it felt like all the conversation and noise in the house wasn't making sense to her. It was all a discordant mishmash. She felt hot and cold at the same. She found a chair in the dining room and eased into it, afraid she might faint if she didn't sit down.

From where Grace sat she could see Cheryl in the foyer talking to the woman detective. A sudden terror gripped Grace.

Would Cheryl tell them the truth? That she'd followed Geoff?

If she did, then Grace would need to tell the truth about what she saw. But what if Cheryl lied? If Grace told the police what she saw—Cheryl hurrying after Geoff—Cheryl would be charged with obstruction at the very least.

Not to mention whatever Cheryl's reason was for lying.

Grace watched Cheryl and the detective walk to the back of the house, toward Maggie's office.

The police were taking statements.

A film of perspiration broke out across Grace's face. She licked her dry lips. Maggie was still in the kitchen talking with Laurent and Danielle. Grace hated that she'd been so sharp with her.

Now when she really needed to talk to her, to tell her what happened and ask what she should do, she was all alone.

Laurent came over to her and handed her a glass of water.

"You are not well, Grace?" he asked with concern.

Grace took the water. "I'm fine," she said. "I didn't sleep well last night."

"And it is a shock. The Englishman's death."

"Of course," Grace said. "Such a shock."

Laurent went back to the kitchen and Grace heard the dishes clinking.

She took in a deep breath and tried to control her breathing.

When Cheryl finally came out of Maggie's office, the police detective was right behind her. Grace studied her friend who looked completely relaxed and unworried.

Was that the face of someone who'd just lied to the police?

Cheryl came into the dining room and turned her attention to Laurent who was bringing in a tray of coffee and a platter of *chouquettes* and *Madeleines*.

Cheryl was smiling and seemed totally at ease as she picked up a coffee mug and selected the cookie she wanted from the tray.

How was anyone totally at ease after being questioned by the police? What did it mean that Cheryl appeared so unaffected by everything that was happening?

A man has died! Someone Cheryl knew!

Someone with whom she'd had a secret rendezvous just hours ago!

Grace's mind raced as she tried to fit in all the pieces of memory and thoughts that were popping into her brain.

Is she sitting here drinking Laurent's coffee and smiling as cool as anything when three hours earlier she'd killed a man? Does this mean she killed Helga too?

Grace glanced at Maggie who was watching her and Grace felt an irrational pulse of fury erupt inside her.

This was all Maggie's fault! If she hadn't suggested Cheryl didn't have an alibi, none of this would be playing out like this.

That sounded insane even to Grace's ears.

Grace wondered what poor Debbie was doing right now. Was she identifying Geoff's body? Was she trying to explain to the police why she had no idea what her supposedly sick husband was doing in the woods on a frigid January day? Was she being asked if her husband was having an affair with someone?

Grace tried to envision Debbie looking up from her book in the library of *Dormir* to the sight of two police cruisers with flashing lights coming up the front drive.

Coming with the news about her husband.

Some people just can't catch a break.

"Madame Van Sant?" the detective said, suddenly appearing in front of Grace, her demeanor cold and unfriendly.

Grace cleared her throat, her heart pounding in her chest like a sparrow trapped under a basket.

"Yes?"

"Will you come with me to the back room to give your statement?"

This was it. This was the moment she was going to lie to the police.

Forcing herself not to glance at Cheryl, Grace got up and followed the police detective into Maggie's office.

She sat on the leather couch, glancing briefly at the framed photos—most of them with herself in them—and the awards or childhood projects that Jemmy or Mila had won or made over the years.

Detective LaBelle sat at Maggie's desk and set a hand recorder down facing Grace. For the benefit of the recorder the detective identified herself and Grace and gave the date and time.

She turned to look at Grace.

"Tell me what you saw, Madame."

Grace blanched, sure her face was giving her away.

"Ex-excuse me?" she stuttered. "When?"

"Today, of course. Unless you have information of another time you think would be pertinent?"

Grace took in a breath.

"After Madame Alexandre, Danielle, left, I washed up the breakfast dishes," Grace said.

"Where did Madame Alexandre go and at what time?"

"She left after breakfast to go to Aix for a hair appointment. Eleven o'clock, I think."

"Who was at breakfast?"

"Cheryl, Danielle and myself."

"Not Geoffrey or Debbie Fitzgerald?"

"No. They'd asked me to send in a tray."

"Who brought this tray and at what time?"

Grace felt her mouth go instantly dry. She licked her lips.

"I did," she said. "At around ten-thirty."

"Continue."

"I did the dishes. Danielle left. And Cheryl went upstairs to her room."

"Cheryl is staying in the main house?"

"Yes."

"But Monsieur and Madame Fitzgerald were staying in a separate cottage?"

Prune cottage, Grace nearly said. It was how she'd kept them straight in the beginning. Naming the three little one or two bedroom cottages on the grounds after fruit.

"That's right."

"And then?"

"I stacked the dishwasher and wiped down the counters and got out the leftover stew for lunch."

"What did you *see*, Madame?" the detective asked again.

Sweat formed on Grace's top lip.

Half-truths, she thought. The key to not being caught lying was to tell half-truths.

"I saw Geoff leave his cottage."

"I thought he was sick."

"Yes, he had been for several days. I assumed he felt better."

"And his wife?"

"She wasn't feeling well."

"Did you see her?"

"When I delivered the breakfast tray."

"But she was not with Monsieur Fitzgerald when he left?"

"No."

"And you have no idea where he was going?"

"None."

Grace prayed the detective wouldn't ask any other questions. Questions like: *did you see anyone else leave after he did?*

"Was he alone?"

Grace swallowed hard. "As far as I could see, yes."

And there it was. The direct question. And the lie.

The detective watched her for a moment.

"You are warm, Madame?"

"A bit."

Grace didn't dare bring any more attention to her perspiration by trying to wipe off the sheen from her face but neither could she bear the feeling of it much longer.

A sharp knock on the door broke the spell.

The detective turned off the recorder.

"Enter," she called.

A uniformed policeman stood in the door.

"Thank you, Madame," Detective LaBelle said.

Grace realized she was being dismissed and nearly wept with relief.

She came out of the room and without thinking walked over to where Maggie was seated on the couch. She eased herself down next to her.

"You okay?" Maggie asked in a low voice.

Grace nodded. Her stomach buckled and she didn't trust her voice to speak.

Danielle and Cheryl sat opposite the couch while Laurent spoke in low tones with the detective. It appeared that she and her squad were about to leave.

"We overheard them say they scoured Geoff's phone," Maggie said to Grace. "But there was nothing on it to indicate he was meeting someone."

"What makes them think he was meeting someone?" Grace said, her voice a little too shrill.

Danielle pushed her glass of sherry to Grace.

"Drink something, *chérie*," she said. "You look pale."

Grace gulped down the sherry and looked guiltily at the police detective, hoping she hadn't seen her.

"The cops think it's suicide," Cheryl said.

"Really?" Grace looked at Maggie for confirmation.

"His throat was slashed," Maggie said. "And a knife was found in his hand."

"But why would he do that out in the woods?"

"Maybe because Debbie was back at the cottage?" Cheryl suggested.

"Does anyone know how Debbie is?" Grace asked.

"She's staying in Aix tonight," Cheryl said. "She called while you were in with the detective. She wanted to thank all of us for our kindness."

"Does Debbie think Geoff committed suicide too?" Grace asked trying not to look at Cheryl. "Because of his debts?"

"Try not to worry about her, Grace," Maggie said, taking Grace's hand. "Debbie's got family back in the UK and lots of support."

"That's good," Grace said. "You need your friends at a time like this."

Grace watched Cheryl who was swinging her foot and looking around Maggie's living room appraisingly.

All Grace really knew for sure was that Cheryl and Geoff had left at roughly the same time and had gone in generally the same direction.

Perfectly innocent.

Right up until Geoff ended up with his throat cut and Cheryl lying about where she was.

54

Maggie tried to remember the last time she'd seen Grace this rattled. She'd been on the questioning end of a police investigation before so Maggie had trouble imagining that was the problem. She did notice that as the evening dragged on, Grace spent less and less time talking with Cheryl.

As in none.

Had something happened between them?

Maggie saw that Luc was in charge of serving dinner. She popped her head into the kitchen to see that Laurent was gone. She looked at Luc but he only shrugged.

"He just told me to take over," he said. "Hey, Jemmy. Get the dogs out of the living room!"

Maggie reran her memory to see if she could remember if Laurent had hinted at where he might have gone. They had plenty of bread and wine. The dogs were here, the children were here. Not unlike many things Laurent did, it was a mystery. But even so, if she had to guess, she'd guess that he was off to talk to Antoine about the worry stone.

Did that even matter now?

Clearly, Laurent seemed to think so. If nothing else, he probably wanted to get sorted the fact that Antoine had lied to him. That wasn't the sort of thing Laurent could easily let go of.

As the children settled down to eat in front of the TV in the living room and Cheryl stepped outside to smoke, Maggie, Danielle and Grace sat together in the dining room.

Nobody had been very hungry, except for the children who'd each had at least two helpings of spaghetti and meatballs.

Grace had managed to eat a little salad with wine.

"Please don't worry about Debbie," Maggie said to Grace. "I'm sure she'll be fine."

"I'm not," Grace said. "I mean, I'm sorry for what she's going through."

"Then what's on your mind?"

"Nothing, Maggie. Can we drop it, please?"

"So something *is* on your mind?"

"Nothing I want to share," Grace said firmly, focusing on her wine glass.

Maggie felt a flash of annoyance and hurt race through her as Danielle leaned over and tapped her wrist with her forefinger.

"Like a dog with a bone, *non*?" Danielle said.

At first Maggie didn't get the reference and then she realized it was what Laurent tended to tease her about. Her tenacity reminded him of a dog with a bone. And yes, whether that was tracking down clues or trying to get to the bottom of why her best friend was sitting here looking like she'd just gotten very bad news, it was hard to let things go.

"I guess you're right," Maggie said to Danielle. "Bad habit."

She tried to shake it off but she didn't understand why Grace wouldn't just tell her what was bothering her.

It wasn't like the two of them hadn't been through plenty in the past ten years. And if setting the stage with a betrayal that ended with Mila being kidnapped hadn't ended their friendship—although granted it had come close—then Maggie was pretty sure nothing would.

After Danielle poured herself a coffee and went to the living room to join the children, Maggie noticed that Cheryl was still outside smoking.

"Your friend acts nervous," Maggie said without thinking. Then she looked at Grace to see if she'd taken offense but Grace didn't even appear to have heard her.

"Grace?"

Grace didn't answer.

"You don't have to tell me what's going on," Maggie said, "but on the remote chance that I might be able to help, I wish you would."

"Cheryl is a...a nervous sort of person," Grace said slowly.

"I noticed that. She smokes a lot."

"She's just one of those people who fidgets," Grace said, glancing out the window at the shadow of Cheryl's form. "She jiggles her foot, fiddles with her napkin, smokes." Grace cleared her throat. "When she can't smoke, she has a little talisman she rubs. I guess to calm her."

"What kind of talisman?" Maggie asked, her senses starting to heighten.

"A stone." Grace turned to look at her. "I hated keeping it a secret from you. I don't even know why I did."

Maggie gave her an incredulous stare. "Cheryl uses a worry stone to calm herself?"

"After you told me about the stone found by Helga's body, I found a set of three stones—all with different designs on them —in Cheryl's underwear drawer."

"Why are you telling me this now?"

"I guess because, well, if Geoff really did kill Helga..."

"...then you don't have to worry that Cheryl might have," Maggie finished for her.

"Yes."

"Were you afraid she might have?"

Grace rubbed the back of her neck.

"I don't know. You said a stone was found next to Helga's body and I...I am ashamed of what I thought. Cheryl is my friend. I should have trusted her." She looked at Maggie. "I don't blame you for being suspicious of her. You don't know her. But I shouldn't have doubted her."

Maggie thought about telling Grace that even as they spoke Laurent was likely off trying to sort out what another of the stones could mean—and how Antoine had come to have one. She decided it would just complicate the issue.

They were silent for a moment.

"I suppose the police think Geoff killed himself out of remorse?" Grace asked as she and Maggie watched Cheryl toss her cigarette into the garden and turn to head back to the house.

"Or it might have been his money problems," Maggie said. "He didn't strike me as a very reflective kind of guy."

"Poor Debbie."

Maggie was glad she didn't have enough time before Cheryl came inside to remind Grace that Geoff's prints on the murder weapon could have a perfectly reasonable explanation, as in, the cake tool belonged to him.

She was glad she didn't have time to mention it to Grace because of course if Geoff *wasn't* the murderer, then Grace had just put her good friend Cheryl smack into the frame as a viable suspect.

"Oh, my God it's cold out there!" Cheryl said as she came into the dining room and hugged her coat tightly around her. "Any of that coffee left?"

"In the kitchen," Maggie said, not getting up. "Just use any mug."

Grace raised an eyebrow at Maggie but Maggie didn't care.

Even if she wasn't the murderer, Cheryl could damn well serve herself.

Danielle came into the dining room.

"I see Mila's cold is better," Danielle said. "I told Laurent it was probably nothing."

Maggie frowned and craned her neck to look toward the living room.

"Mila has a cold?"

"I am sure it was just an excuse to come home," Danielle said. "I told Laurent that. Is there any more spaghetti left?"

"Come home from where?" Maggie asked.

"From her little friend Gigi's," Danielle said. "The night before last? I think Laurent thought you and Luc would be spending the night in Heidelberg so when she called wanting to come home I needed to go get her. I brought her back to *Dormir* with me. Did Laurent not tell you?"

Maggie stared at her.

"Where was Jemmy?" she asked.

"At a friend's house, I believe. What is wrong, *chérie*?"

"Why didn't Laurent go and pick up Mila himself?"

Danielle frowned and glanced at Grace. She looked discomfited.

"Perhaps you should ask Laurent," Danielle said.

"I'm asking *you*, Danielle. Why were both kids out of the house and where was Laurent that he couldn't go get Mila himself?"

"I believe he had an emergency of some kind," Danielle said, now not looking at Maggie.

Maggie felt Cheryl's presence as she came into the dining room with her coffee and stood behind her.

Laurent was gone while she was out of town?

Maggie's mind flashed back to that night when Laurent had picked her up at the train station. It had been after midnight and she had been so mesmerized by the news about the death threat from Marie-France that she hadn't really paid much attention to anything.

Like why Laurent was dressed in a white shirt and dress slacks.

And why the gas gauge showed the petrol tank was nearly empty when Laurent had had all day to fill it.

Her mind suddenly remembered seeing the tip of a yellow speeding ticket that had clearly been jammed into the overly full glove compartment.

As if someone had been racing through the night to get to the train station on time.

Laurent had been gone that day and evening.

Maggie felt a wave of nausea.

"I think I remember now it was an emergency with one of the mini-houses," Danielle said, referring to the small one-bedroom homes that Laurent had built on his property for the influx of monastery refugees. She was clearly distraught at having caused the distress she was seeing in Maggie.

"I believe he said he wanted to use the unexpected free time to repaint one of the homes that was vacant."

"Are you sure, Danielle?" Maggie asked dully. "Because I happen to know for a fact that all five of the mini-houses are full. There was no house needing emergency painting two nights ago or any other night."

"Maggie, stop it," Grace said. "*Wherever* Laurent was, I'm sure he had a good reason."

"For not telling his wife?" Cheryl said with a smirk from behind Maggie. "Yeah, pull the other one."

Maggie stood up and felt Danielle's hand shoot out to grab her wrist. She used the moment to calm herself.

"I'm okay, Danielle," Maggie said, patting Danielle's hand. She looked at Grace. "I'm sure you're right." Then she turned to Cheryl. "It's time for you to leave."

Cheryl looked at Grace as if expecting her to say something, and when she didn't, Cheryl put her coffee mug down hard on the counter, sloshing coffee down the sides.

"I'll meet you in the driveway," Cheryl said to Grace before turning and walking to the front door.

"There's plenty of room for you here, Grace," Maggie said.

"No," Grace said. "I'll go back with her. She's upset. She'll want to talk."

Maggie fought down her irritation that Grace had been obviously upset all night long and Cheryl had been oblivious to it.

Clearly their friendship was a seriously one-way street.

"*I* will stay, *chérie*," Danielle said. "If that's all right."

"Of course," Maggie said, standing up with Grace.

Grace went to the living room to kiss Zouzou goodnight and then joined Maggie in the foyer. Cheryl was waiting outside in her rental car, the taillights glowing angrily in the dark.

As she opened the door to let Grace out, Maggie hesitated.

"I can't help but think there's something you're not telling me," Maggie said.

Grace searched her eyes for a moment and then impulsively leaned over and hugged Maggie.

"It's nothing, darling," she murmured. "Just the culmination of a long, very bad day."

Then she turned and walked to her car parked next to Cheryl's.

As Maggie watched both cars disappear into the night, she realized she couldn't remember the last time Grace had out and out lied to her.

55

The moment Antoine opened the door to his apartment, Laurent grabbed him by his shirt front and yanked him out into the hallway. He had no problem confronting the man inside his apartment but he did not want to upset Mireille.

To Antoine's credit, he must have felt the same for he didn't struggle or make a noise but allowed Laurent to drag him onto the landing and slam him up against the wall.

"I...I knew you would be back," Antoine gasped when Laurent released him.

"In that case I am irritated I was forced to make the effort," Laurent said.

"You don't understand."

"That is what I am here to do. To understand."

"I owe you everything. I know that."

"You do not act like you know that."

Antoine rubbed an agitated hand across his face and glanced back at the door to his apartment. Laurent knew the man wasn't stupid enough to be contemplating making a run for it. First he'd never make it. And secondly, he had to know only broken bones lay at the end of *that* decision.

He gave Antoine a moment to catch his breath. There was no mystery as to how this interaction would end. Antoine knew as well as Laurent.

"May I smoke?" Antoine asked.

Laurent grunted an assent but he felt a flinch of vexation over and above what he was already feeling. He wouldn't mind a cigarette himself and it annoyed him that he was being forced to deal with that on top of everything else.

Antoine's hands shook as he pulled the blue packet of *Gitanes* from his shirt pocket and began patting his clothes for matches.

Laurent took the moment to study him. He didn't believe for a moment that Antoine had killed anyone. Whatever explanation he had for the worry stone, Laurent was sure it did not lead to Antoine's involvement in the German woman's death.

No, Laurent's intentions today had to do with his future working relationship with this man. And that future did not look good for Antoine.

Antoine took a long drag on his cigarette.

"I didn't steal it," he said. "I found it."

"Where?"

Antoine licked his lips. His eyes darted around the enclosed space as if looking for a way out.

"At Domaine Saint-Buvard," he said, finally. "The night of the scavenger hunt. I knew it was wrong," Antoine said, his eyes looking downward. "But it was a rock! I didn't think it was worth anything."

"Should I be relieved you didn't find something more valuable in my house to walk off with?"

"It was wrong," he repeated. "I put it in my pocket before I even knew I'd done it."

"You stole from my house," Laurent said slowly. "From a guest in my house."

Antoine breathed out a long sigh. "Yes."

Antoine had to know he was finished. Laurent wouldn't bring in the police but Antoine would lose everything now, the bakery, his apartment, his job. And when the news of *why* he'd lost the bakery got out—because something like this could never stay quiet in a small village—his reputation, too. He would have to move.

"Where was it when you found it?" Laurent asked.

"On one of the dining room chairs."

Laurent narrowed his eyes. "Which chair?"

"*Comment?*" Antoine looked at him in confusion.

"Who had been sitting in that chair?" Laurent clarified patiently.

Antoine's face cleared as if grateful he could at least provide the answer Laurent wanted.

"The American woman called Cheryl," he said.

56

By the time Maggie got all the children settled for the night, she was so exhausted from the day's events she found she didn't have the energy to wait for Laurent. She was however very invested in hearing *why* he hadn't shared with her whatever his secret mission had been on the day she'd gone to Germany with Luc.

Had he always planned to do whatever it was, or had her being gone for the day given him the idea?

As she fell into bed and pulled the duvet up to her chin, she realized she wasn't really worried that Laurent had betrayed her. But she'd learned from past experience that some things that he felt worth doing would not be sanctioned by Maggie—and honestly vice versa—and would therefore need to be done surreptitiously.

In any case, she would get to the truth.

Just not tonight.

The next morning Laurent was gone before Maggie was up. He'd taken Danielle and all the kids to Aix. Frustrated at not getting her one-on-one with him and the answers she'd been dying to hear, she checked her watch to confirm that he should have dropped the kids off by now and called him.

"*Allo, chérie.* I am just pulling into *Dormir.* I will call you back."

"Fine," she said with ill-humor and disconnected.

Maggie knew that Danielle would have told him by now that she'd spilled the beans about his extracurricular activity the day Maggie was in Heidelberg. Which, with a normal man, would have given him plenty of time to get his story straight.

But she knew Laurent. Not only did she trust him not to lie to her face—although clearly that lie-by-omission-thing was still an issue—but she knew he had a perfectly good reason for where he was. It was just the not knowing what it was that was driving her mad.

Maggie cleaned the kitchen although even after making everyone breakfast and getting them ready for school—and having been out late himself the night before—somehow Laurent had managed to leave the kitchen in its usual spotless state.

Maggie pulled out a heavy ceramic mixing bowl and measured out flour, salt and sugar. With Zouzou always baking pastries there was rarely any need for Maggie to roll out pie dough.

But sometimes she just needed the therapy of it. After all, even without Zouzou there were only about a dozen amazing bakeries between her house and Aix so the pastries themselves were not the sole reason to make the effort.

As she cut pieces of shortening into the flour and brought them together with water to form the dough, she found herself glancing at the clock in the kitchen and wondering if perhaps Grace was showing Laurent something that needed his attention at the B&B. Even though Grace had a handyman, because Laurent owned *Dormir*, he was the one ultimately responsible for its upkeep and maintenance.

As she shaped the pie dough into two discs, Maggie found herself wondering what to make of the fact that Cheryl had a drawerful of worry stones like the one found at the murder scene.

Now that Maggie thought back at it, Cheryl *was* always fidgeting and Maggie could distinctly remember her doing something in her lap at the table at dinner.

Maggie had thought it was a nervous affectation. Plenty of people had them.

Cheryl kept worry stones.

And somehow one of them had gotten to the vineyard and next to the body of Helga Richter. Did that mean Cheryl had killed Helga and dropped her stone?

The phone rang and Maggie saw it was Laurent. She quickly dried her hands and picked up.

"Hey," she said. "Everyone okay over there? Is Debbie back?"

"*Non*, she is still in Aix."

"What about Cheryl? Did you see her?"

"Why do you ask?"

"Because Grace told me she found a drawer full of worry stones in Cheryl's underwear drawer."

There was silence on the line.

"Laurent?"

"Antoine told me last night he found his stone on Cheryl's chair the night of the scavenger hunt."

"Well, that fits. So the stones are definitely Cheryl's."

"Does this matter?" Laurent said with a tone of frustration. "The killer has been identified. Margaux called a few moments ago to say that Sybil was being released."

"Oh my gosh, Laurent! That's great! Way to bury the lead!"

"*Comment?'*

"Never mind. That's amazing. Are you going by the bakery?"

"*Non.* I am giving that family some space to heal. And I am instructing you to do the same."

"Settle down, darling. I'm not going to bother anyone."

"Then why are you still talking about Cheryl and her stones? It means nothing. Just as Antoine and his stone meant nothing! And Marie-France and her angry note meant nothing!"

"Why are you getting so pissed off?"

"Because this case is closed and you are acting like it isn't! The police have determined that Geoff Fitzgerald killed Helga Richter. I insist you leave Cheryl Barker alone."

"The hell I will," Maggie said, suddenly furious.

"Grace is right. You won't stop because you are jealous."

Maggie felt the fury well up inside her.

"You know what? If that's who Grace wants as her friend, then fine. I'm totally fine with that. And if that's what she thinks, no problem. But I'm not going to be browbeaten into ignoring what I see when it's right in front of me. I won't pretend that all these incriminating clues that point to Cheryl don't mean anything."

"The detective has closed her case!"

"Oh? Is that what *Margaux* told you?"

"You are not trying to free Sybil now. You are trying to implicate a friend of Grace's out of spite and jealousy."

"I can't believe you're saying this to me. Do you know me at all?"

"I know you this well. I know how you are when you do not want to give up or when you don't like the answer you have been given."

"Well, that just goes to show how little you *do* know me, Laurent Dernier, and yes we will definitely be getting to the topic of your little excursion the other night when I was out of town, trust me. But before then, answer me this: if Geoff was Helga's killer why didn't he wipe his fingerprints off the murder weapon?"

Laurent huffed a breath out in frustration.

"It probably slipped his mind in all the excitement," he said.

"Or maybe the real killer wore gloves," Maggie said, "and Geoff's prints were on the nail because it belonged to him?"

"Why are you trying to *un*solve this case? *C'est incroyable!*"

"Because it's *not* solved! What was Geoff's motive? He stabbed Helga because she got the job he wanted? That makes no sense at all!"

"So everyone is wrong and only you are right. Is that what you are saying?"

"If everyone is saying that Geoff killed Helga and then offed himself, then yeah, I guess that's what I'm saying."

"I am going to give you a moment to calm down," Laurent said. "I will see you when I am home."

"When will that be?'

"Whenever it is."

And he disconnected.

Maggie stood for a moment in the kitchen and realized she was shaking. It had been a long time since she and Laurent had gone toe to toe and she was frankly surprised he was doing it now.

She maneuvered to one of the kitchen stools and sat down.

Why did he care so much? Why did he want her to stay away from Cheryl? Why was he so invested in believing that Geoff was the killer?

None of it made sense!

She got up to fill a glass of water from the tap and drank most of it down before she realized her phone was vibrating. Hoping it was Laurent, she snatched it up to see it was a call from Uli.

"Hi," Maggie said.

"Maggie, *hallo*," Uli said. "I hope I am not interrupting you?"

"No, not at all."

"I just wanted to call because I felt bad about throwing away the photograph and got to thinking and suddenly remembered that there was some other drama before Hans and Helga got together."

"What do you mean?"

"Remember I told you that a girl stole Hans from Helga?"

"Yes."

"Well, before that, now that I remember, I guess Helga stole Hans from a girl too."

"Okay," Maggie said, feeling a bit impatient and wondering where this was all going.

"I am sure it is not important but as I remember it when Hans broke up with this girl to be with Helga, things got quite ugly. Stalking, bags of dog *scheisse* on the front step, a rock though his bedroom window. That sort of thing."

"How old was everyone about this time?"

"It would have been in the beginning of their pastry classes. But Hans' girlfriend was a year ahead."

So she wouldn't have been in the picture that Uli showed me.

Maggie felt her heart begin to speed up.

"Do you know her name?"

"I do not. I am sorry. But I remember she was American."

57

I
t was clear now.

Cheryl had known Helga from years ago but had lied about not knowing her. And she'd had her boyfriend stolen by Helga—a boyfriend who then went on to die tragically.

That was major motive.

Maggie looked around the kitchen before pulling off her apron. She needed to talk to Cheryl. There was no way the detective was going to unhook from the easy answer that Geoff Fitzgerald had killed Helga and then killed himself due to guilt. Maggie was going to have to find irrefutable proof and lay it right in front of her big Gallic nose.

She hurriedly let the dogs out and then filled their bowls with kibble. She didn't know when Laurent was coming back and she had no idea how long her errand might take her. If Cheryl decided to comply, they could drive together to Aix so she could confess to Detective LaBelle.

If not, it might be a long night.

She let the dogs back in and they instantly ran to their bowls. Maggie checked that the stove burners were off and that her phone had plenty of battery power. Then she grabbed her purse and hurried out the front door to her car.

As she drove down the icy village road to *Dormir*, five miles away, she went over and over again what she'd learned that made her now believe that Helga's killer had to be Cheryl.

First, Cheryl had been in Germany as a student. Second, she had gone to *patisserie* school there. Third, she was American. And fourth, she owned the worry stone found by Helga's body.

Plus, this murder was personal.

You didn't stab someone underneath their shirt unless there was some serious passion involved.

Cheryl had killed Helga.

But how did Geoff's suicide come into it? Why would he kill himself if he wasn't involved? And if he was involved, how was he?

Maggie blamed herself for missing the obvious clues. She'd been trying so hard *not* to look at Cheryl for the murder that she hadn't seen what was right in front of her.

Maggie pulled into the gravel driveway at *Dormir* and saw that Grace's car was gone. That was good. The last thing Maggie wanted to do was confront Cheryl with Grace there.

This has nothing to do with me and Grace.

She parked next to Cheryl's rental car and hurried to the front door. Cheryl was waiting for her.

"Grace isn't here," Cheryl said, barring Maggie's entrance into the house.

"Move out of the way," Maggie said. "I own this house."

Something in Cheryl's cheek flinched but she stepped back.

"You're just making things worse for yourself," Cheryl said. "Even your own husband thinks you're not thinking rationally."

"What would you know about husbands?" Maggie said coming into the room and pulling off her wool scarf.

She'd hit pay dirt with that comment. Cheryl blushed and crossed her arms angrily.

"Grace told me you have a set of worry stones," Maggie said.

She could tell that Cheryl hadn't expected that. She hadn't expected Grace to know about them and she certainly hadn't expected Grace to tell Maggie.

"So?"

"So a worry stone was found next to Helga's body the night she was murdered."

Cheryl's face whitened. "You're lying."

"Nope. It's the truth. You were dropping breadcrumbs and all along you never knew it."

"It wasn't mine."

"How do you know it wasn't? You haven't even seen it."

"There are millions of worry stones of all shapes and designs."

"This one had a karma design on it but it shouldn't be a problem for you to bring your collection down to the Aix police and have them look it over and see how the one they have matches up."

"I'm not doing anything like that. They'll have to get a warrant."

"I'm sure that can be arranged but in the meantime it does tend to make you look guilty."

"Grace will be furious that you're doing this."

"Since *she* was the one who told me about you having the stones, I don't think so. Didn't you go to school in Germany? Heidelberg to be specific?"

"So what? Millions of American kids did."

"But not all of them left with hatred and revenge in their hearts."

"Bit dramatic, don't you think?"

"Let's see what a jury of your peers thinks when they hear all the details of you and Helga. Starting with how Helga stole Hans from you."

Cheryl's mouth dropped open and Maggie knew she'd gotten it right.

"Why are you doing this? The cops have Geoff for Helga's murder. Everybody's happy," Cheryl said.

"I'm not sure Helga's all that happy. Or Debbie for that matter—who's just been named the wife of a murderer."

"I didn't kill Helga."

"Neither did Geoff."

"Even if that's true, it won't ruin *his* life if people think he did it! It *will* ruin mine!"

"Maybe you should have thought of that before you stuck a five-inch nail into Helga's heart."

Cheryl licked her lips and patted her sweater pockets as if looking for something and then rubbed her hands together.

"I can't believe you're doing this! I'm a fellow American," she said.

"Please don't remind me."

"I can't let you ruin my life."

"You did that yourself when you killed Helga."

"Stop saying that! Grace will never forgive you for this."

"I'm pretty sure it's *you* she'll have trouble forgiving. You kill someone and then continue on with plans to take Zouzou to Paris with you? You'll be lucky if Grace doesn't break into your holding cell and kill you herself."

"Are you saying that Zouzou wouldn't be safe with me?"

"A murderer? Yes, that's what I'm saying."

Maggie would later berate herself for not seeing that Cheryl had been steadily moving closer to her and increasingly ramping up her fidgeting. Maggie had been so fixated on what she was saying to Cheryl that she didn't realize until Cheryl was an arms-length away that her eyes looked crazed and unfocused.

"Back off," Maggie said, the palms of her hands suddenly clammy.

"Why? So you can tell Grace I'm a danger to her child? Or a murderer? How about *no!*"

Cheryl lunged at Maggie, raising up in her right hand and revealing the heavy ceramic vase that Maggie hadn't seen her pick up from the hall table.

Maggie only had a moment to try to swivel away from her but even then she knew she was too late.

The crash of pain exploded in her head, engulfing her senses in a tsunami of all-encompassing darkness.

58

The sound began as a low thrumming at the base of her skull and rose to a loud thunder. The pain chiseled into her forehead like twin drills competing for depth and intensity.

Maggie groaned and when she did she was aware of the cold tile beneath her cheek and the pain in her head that made her stomach swirl in nausea.

She opened her eyes and saw a pair of shoes and closed them again.

At least it's not a car trunk, she thought miserably.

"Danielle! Help me!"

Grace's voice was louder and more discordant than anything Maggie had ever heard before in her life. She groaned again and tried to wet her lips.

"Maggie, darling!" Grace said, her voice now close to Maggie's ear. "Darling, can you hear me?"

Make it go away, Maggie squeezed her eyes closed.

"She's alive," Grace said.

Maggie felt strong hands grip her shoulders and pull her

slowly to a sitting position. Her stomach heaved with the motion and she knew she was going to be sick.

"Help," she said in a small voice before throwing up on the floor.

"It's all right, darling," Grace said, her voice less loud and strident now. "We've got you."

Twenty minutes later, Maggie was on the plush sofa in the small annex room off the kitchen in *Dormir* that was heated by a Franklin stove.

Her stomach felt better but her head still clanged unbearably.

"Eat the paracetamol, *chérie*," Danielle said, nudging a small cup of water toward Maggie.

"Don't tell Laurent," Maggie whispered, her eyes clenched shut as she felt for the pills.

"Too late," Grace said, sitting down beside her. "He's on his way."

Damn.

"Can you tell us what happened, *chérie*?" Danielle asked as Maggie took the cup of water from her and drank deeply.

"Cheryl attacked me," Maggie said. She wanted to open her eyes to see how the news affected Grace but she couldn't do it just yet.

"Dear God," Grace whispered. "We saw the vase on the floor. Did she hit you with that?"

"That and a small truck," Maggie said and opened her eyes.

"I'm going to make coffee," Danielle said, patting Maggie's knee. "Laurent was in Aix so he will not be here very soon."

"What was he doing in Aix?"

"I do not know, *chérie*."

Maggie put her hand to her forehead and felt a lump but no blood. It was very tender.

"Maggie," Grace said. "I'm so sorry, darling."

"It's not your fault."

"Yes. It is."

Maggie opened her eyes wider and turned to look at Grace. "Tell me what you know," she said.

Grace licked her lips.

"I saw Cheryl leave to go after Geoff minutes after he left here yesterday."

Maggie's thinking felt fuzzy and she strained for the natural conclusion from that statement. She frowned.

"You're talking about the afternoon he was killed?"

"Yes! I lied to the police when they asked me if I'd seen anyone but Geoff. I saw Cheryl leave right after he did."

"You...you think Cheryl followed Geoff and killed him?" Maggie asked, still fumbling to get her thoughts straight.

"I don't know. Maybe? I mean, he's dead, isn't he?"

"Did you ask Cheryl about it?"

Grace reached over and took Maggie's hand.

"She lied to me," she said. "She said she didn't leave *Dormir*. And now she's attacked you. This is all my fault. I brought her here and she's obviously unstable. I can't believe I was even thinking of letting her take Zouzou!"

Maggie drank more water and felt better. Her head was only mildly vibrating now and her thoughts were somewhat clearer.

"Maggie?" Grace asked. "Do you really think Cheryl could have killed Geoff?"

"I do," Maggie said. "And Helga too."

Maggie accepted the cup of coffee from Danielle as she sat in Grace's salon at *Dormir*. Her phone rang and she saw immediately it was Laurent.

"*Chérie!* Are you all right? I am caught in traffic! I am still thirty minutes away."

"I was just about to call you," Maggie said, grateful that she felt so much better after Danielle's good strong coffee.

She was also grateful that the lie she was about to tell Laurent would be much less discernible over the phone.

"I wasn't attacked," she said. "Grace got that wrong. I hit my head on the low beam in the kitchen and I guess I went down. There's not even any blood."

There was silence on the line.

"Laurent?"

"You were not attacked?"

"Nope. Just me being clumsy. So do not come rushing to *Dormir*. Do you have the kids with you?"

"*Oui.*"

"Great. Just go on home. I'm going to visit a little longer and then I'll see you back there."

"*D'accord*," he said. "Margaux called. The police are now treating Geoff's death as a murder. His prints on the knife did not line up."

I knew it!

"So who do they think killed him?"

Cheryl killed him. Cheryl followed him and killed him!

"It does not matter, *chérie*. Sybil is free."

"Well, she won't be for long if it turns out Geoff didn't kill Helga."

"Let the police handle it from here."

"Sure. Okay."

Lie Number Two.

"And you are sure you are fine?"

"Perfectly."

After she hung up, she looked up and saw both Grace and Danielle staring at her.

"Why did you not tell him the truth?" Danielle said. "And

why are you not calling the police about Cheryl's assault?"

Maggie stood up and dropped the cloth she'd held to her forehead.

"Because it would be Cheryl's word against mine and I have bigger fish to fry."

"Do you really think Cheryl killed Geoff?" Grace asked.

Maggie couldn't help noticing that Grace's face was white and her lips seemed to tremble.

"Look, why don't both of you go to Domaine St-Buvard tonight? I don't know where Cheryl's gone but if she comes back here, she's already shown herself to be unpredictable. I'd feel better if you're not here."

"I think that is a good idea," Danielle said.

Grace looked at Maggie. "Where are *you* going?"

"I have an errand to run in Aix."

"Oh, no you don't," Grace said. "You're going after Cheryl, aren't you? There's no way I'm letting you do that on your own."

"Grace, I don't have enough evidence for Detective LaBelle and Cheryl did not seem in the mood to make a full confession the last time I saw her. Plus, Laurent just told me that Geoff's death is no longer being ruled a suicide but a murder."

Danielle gasped and put her hand to her mouth, her eyes wide with horror.

"Oh, my God," Grace said. "I can't believe it. Cheryl killed Geoff!"

"And I'm pretty sure Helga too," Maggie said. "So you can't come with me because I'm a hundred percent certain that would make her go off the deep end."

"What if something happens to you?"

"I have my cellphone and I'm in Aix surrounded by about a million people. Plus, I intend to call Detective LaBelle and force her to hear what I have to say."

"How are you going to find Cheryl?"

"I've got a plan that I'm afraid to tell you about," Maggie

said.

"Because it's so dangerous?" Danielle asked.

"No, because it sounds so stupid. If Cheryl isn't where I think she is, I'll turn around and come home, letting her go free to murder again. No problem."

"You can't do that," Grace said.

"Well, I won't have enough proof to go to the police so I'll just have to."

"I could get her to confess," Grace said.

"Or she could just kill you. Fifty-fifty."

"You're not even a little bit funny."

"I wasn't trying to be."

The three women stared at each other for a moment.

"You know Laurent is going to blow a gasket when he finds out you lied to him," Grace said.

"I know. I'm hoping having two adorable children together will work in my favor."

"Don't count on it. Laurent prizes veracity above all else."

"Isn't that ironic given that he lied about everything under the sun for the first thirty-two years of his life? But it doesn't matter. It has to be this way. Can I trust you two to go to Domaine St-Buvard and not spill the beans just yet?"

"Put a time limit on it," Grace said. "If you don't call by six o'clock, we tell Laurent what's going on and send out the cavalry."

Maggie looked at her watch.

"That only gives me two hours and it's forty minutes just to drive to Aix."

"Take it or leave it, *chérie*," Danielle said, crossing her arms.

"Especially since Laurent will be asking me later why I did not sit on you to prevent you from going at all," Grace said.

"Okay. Fine. Six o'clock."

"Promise you won't get yourself killed, darling," Grace said, her eyes shining. "I'm pretty sure I would never forgive myself."

59

Maggie put her wipers on to combat the onslaught of snow as it hit her windshield as she drove. At this time of year, the daylight was gone by four-thirty and she already had her headlights on.

She didn't want to admit to Grace that her plan for finding Cheryl first involved finding Bertrand. He, Debbie and Marie-France were all staying at the Hôtel Dauphin. It stood to reason Cheryl would go to those three first to tell her side of things before Maggie accused her of murder—or maybe just to be among friends when the hammer came down.

But on the plus side, Maggie was pretty sure Cheryl wouldn't be swinging a five-pound Egyptian vase at her head with witnesses in the room. Although of course that was no guarantee.

On the drive to Aix, Maggie received a text from Uli saying she might have gotten the years mixed up. With the picture gone, she couldn't say for sure which *patisserie* classmate did what.

Maggie immediately called her.

"What do you mean?" Maggie said. "I thought there was just the one pastry class?"

"There *was* but there was also the other thing that happened. Ten years before that. A boy died. I told you that Helga was heartbroken over Hans but she saw a terrible thing when she was younger and that might have contributed too."

Maggie recalled the newspaper article and her mind reeled back to try to recollect the salient points.

"Remind me?" she said.

"Helga was working a summer as a lead scout and an ESG guide. This particular group was made up of international students. A boy named Dieter Schmidt fell off a cliff and died. There was some talk that perhaps it wasn't an accident, but nothing was ever reported."

"They thought he might have been pushed?"

Did Helga kill a kid? Was her heartbreak the result of wracking guilt?

"Nobody is knowing for sure. But my sister always acted very strange about it. She'd been close to where it happened but she was never questioned by the police."

"Are you saying Helga might have seen Dieter go over the cliff?"

Maggie felt her excitement ramp up. If Helga actually saw Dieter fall, she'd know whether it was an accident or not.

"There's more," Uli said. "The boy who died was dating one of the other scouts—a girl from England. When Dieter fell in love later that weekend with a girl from Basel—the English girl was very angry."

"How angry?"

"She stabbed Dieter in the leg with a fork in his tent."

"That's pretty angry."

"*Ja*, but the head ESG guide agreed not to send her home if she promised to behave herself. I fear he thought it would reflect badly on the program."

Maggie mulled over the new information for a moment. It was awful and probably devastating for Helga and everyone else on the hiking summer trip but she couldn't see how it fit with Helga's death.

Whether a jealous teenager from Bristol killed her German boyfriend or he fell to his death in the Black Forest didn't seem to have anything to do with Helga dying twenty years later in France.

Maggie thanked Uli and asked her to call or text if she remembered anything else.

Maggie parked in front of the Hôtel Dauphin. She opened up an Internet search engine on her phone and ran a search for *Geoff Fitzgerald* but found nothing current on him and no mention of his death yesterday. Then she Googled for the Black Forest tragedy twenty years ago but found even fewer details than Uli had given her.

On impulse, she put a call in to Detective LaBelle. After waiting on hold for a few minutes, she disconnected.

A phone call was coming in from Laurent. Maggie hesitated and then declined it.

It would be just like Grace and Danielle to blurt out the truth as soon as they crossed the threshold of Domaine Saint-Buvard. Laurent tended to have that effect on people.

She debated calling Roger. Although she knew that Laurent would not be pleased if she reached out to Roger, he might be able to fill in some missing details on Geoff's background. As she was trying to decide, Detective LaBelle called her back.

"Thank you for returning my call, Detective," Maggie said. "I was hoping you could tell me if Geoff Fitzgerald did in fact have gambling debts. His wife said he did and that the debts were impoverishing them."

"Is Laurent there with you?"

"Ah, no. It's just me."

The detective hung up on her.

Well, that's rude.

She saw that Laurent was trying to call her again and she felt a splinter of urgency. She needed to get some answers before she went inside and made a total fool of herself.

She put the call in to Roger.

"Why are you calling?" he said by way of greeting.

Maggie didn't take it personally. How could she? The last time she'd seen Roger, he was in the process of being demoted after a twenty-year career in the police service. He'd gone from a Detective Inspector to doing something in the department of motor vehicles in Nice.

Because of what he'd done to help her.

"I need you to look at something on your police database," she said.

"*Non.* Wait. Are you in jail under suspicion for murder?"

"No."

"Then *non.*"

"Roger, I just need you to pull some financials on an Englishman named Geoffrey Fitzgerald. He was murdered yesterday. That's all I need. Just confirmation that he was a gambler."

There was a pause on the line. "That's it?"

"I swear. How's Chloe?"

Roger's daughter was Zouzou's age. When Roger had had to move to Nice, his wasn't the only life unhappily affected.

"She is fine. I will call you back."

He hung up and as Maggie waited, drumming her nails on the car dashboard, she saw that she had only fifteen minutes before the time that she'd promised to check in with Grace. Fifteen minutes.

Something was bothering her about all the clues she'd gathered so far. She ran over them quickly.

Cheryl had to be the American who'd known Helga in Germany all those years ago. She'd essentially admitted that an hour ago with Maggie had confronted her. Plus, the dates matched up. And she was the one who had the karma stone—and who'd dropped it in the vineyard next to Helga's body. Grace had seen her racing after Geoff the afternoon he was killed.

And finally, she'd attacked Maggie when confronted with the evidence of her guilt.

Everything pointed to Cheryl.

So why was Maggie starting to feel unsure?

Somehow, the clues had started to feel weak and coincidental.

Suddenly Maggie saw the clues the way Laurent saw them. The way a normal, rational person would see them.

They appeared to her as reasons why Cheryl was not worthy of Grace's friendship.

But not as evidence that she had killed anyone.

Maggie glanced at her phone and silently urged Roger to call her back.

Had she really used her personal bias against Cheryl after all? Had she set things up to see what she'd wanted to see?

Suddenly her phone rang in her hand, making her jump. Instantly she recognized Bedard's number.

"Geoffrey Fitzgerald did not have gambling debts," Roger said.

"But his wife said he did."

"Well, he didn't."

Why would Debbie lie?

"But they were in debt?"

"Yes."

"Okay. Thanks, Roger."

"Call me some time when you don't need something," he said and hung up.

Maggie deserved that, she knew. She chewed on a nail and tried to understand what this information might mean. Why would Debbie lie? Maybe she was ashamed of the real reason they were in such debt.

Maybe *she* was the reason.

Maggie swallowed hard and glanced up at the hotel where she knew Debbie was staying.

What reason for debt is worse than an out-of-control gambling addiction?

The thought came to Maggie like a snake sliding into her sleeping bag: *what about paying a blackmailer?*

Her mind raced back to Heidelberg when Uli told her that Helga had started getting an influx of money early this year.

Maggie called Uli back.

"Is there any way you can find out the name of the girl from Bristol? The one who Dieter jilted? I've found newspaper articles but none of the kids' names are listed."

"*Ja,* of course. That is to protect the children."

Maggie felt a ripple of frustration.

"But I remember this girl because Helga talked of her," Uli added.

"She did? Why?"

"Because the other kids used to make fun of her name."

Maggie felt a chill as she waited for the words she already knew were coming.

"The crazy girl in love with Dieter," Uli said, "was an English girl named Debbie Humper."

60

Maggie's mind began to whirl.

There was mud on Debbie's shoes the night of the murder. Why would any sane person go for a midnight stroll in forty-degree weather?

Debbie must have slipped away from the house that night. She must have found and killed her blackmailer, then buried Geoff's pastry nail on her way back to the house.

She had opportunity and means.

But her motive was the timeless one of all victims of blackmail.

Maggie looked up to see Bertrand and Marie-France leave for dinner. She glanced at her cellphone. Her deadline was up. She debated sending Grace a text saying she was fine and on her way home, but the lies were starting to stack up. Even though she knew that *not* calling meant Grace would tell Laurent where she was, she switched off her phone.

It didn't matter anymore.

It was Debbie all along.

A thought slithered into her brain and made her stomach drop painfully.

Cheryl.

Maggie glanced at the façade of the Hôtel Dauphin. She needed to get in there and make sure that Cheryl was safe before she did anything. She got out of the car and made her way to the Hôtel Dauphin.

Maggie entered the hotel and went first to the front desk. The old man at the desk watched her approach. He was ninety if he was a day, but his eyes were shrewd and calculating as he watched her come.

"I'm looking for an American guest named Cheryl Barker," Maggie said. "Can you tell me if she's registered here?"

"*Non*," the old man said and went back to the magazine he'd been reading.

Maggie put her hand on her purse but remembered she didn't have cash. If he was waiting for a bribe, it wasn't going to happen.

"I'm her sister," she said. "It's really important that I see her."

"You are her sister and you do not have her phone number?" he said without looking up.

"We had a fight."

"I do not care."

Maggie glanced behind the man and saw there was a glass enclosed office.

"I think your hot plate is on fire," she said.

"Eh?" He jerked his head up to look behind him in the office. He'd taken nearly two steps before realizing he didn't have a hot plate. He swiveled around to face Maggie.

"If you are finished, Madame," he said, his lip curling. "Only paying guests are allowed in the Hôtel Dauphin."

"Sure, no problem," Maggie said, turning to walk back to the lobby.

She hadn't gotten a very good look at the registry—which was upside down and faced away from her.

But she'd seen that Debbie Fitzgerald's room number was 14.

She stopped in the lobby to pretend to look in her purse for something and saw that the desk clerk had lost interest in her. Then she silently slipped down the corridor on the other side of the lobby and hurried to the elevator.

Maggie raked open the wrought-iron grill door of the elevator and stepped inside, punching the button for the fourth floor.

French elevators located in nineteenth century buildings had mostly been retrofitted to the available space—usually squeezing the shaft into the middle of ancient spiral staircases. This usually resulted in extremely small elevators that could accommodate only one person at a time.

Once at the fourth floor, she stepped out into the hallway. There were only two rooms on this floor. Maggie stood for a moment before Debbie's door and could hear an American TV show playing inside. She knocked on the door.

"Maggie, hello," Debbie said, looking genuinely surprised when she came to the door. "Is everything okay? Come in."

Maggie stepped inside and glanced around the room.

"I was looking for Cheryl," she said.

"Cheryl? I haven't seen her. I thought she was staying at *Dormir*."

"She was," Maggie said, beginning to feel a little warm. "So you haven't seen her?"

As soon as the words were out of Maggie's mouth she saw it. It was partially visible under the bed. A red Chanel clutch.

Cheryl's purse.

Debbie followed Maggie's eyes and with a sigh she went to her dresser and picked up a very large knife and turned to Maggie.

"Kindly step away from the door," Debbie said. "I think I've adequately demonstrated I have no qualms about using sharp objects."

61

A room that just moments before had been too hot was suddenly freezing.

All Maggie could see was the red handbag and the big knife in Debbie's hands.

"What's going on?" Maggie asked, her breathing coming in short, panicked puffs.

"Hmmm. Well, let's just see," Debbie said as she walked over to Maggie and held out her hand to her. "Your phone please."

Maggie hesitated and then handed over her phone. She watched as Debbie turned the phone on and gestured for Maggie to stand away from the door. Then she positioned herself between Maggie and the door. She held the knife easily at waist level.

"Password."

Maggie debated for almost a full second before giving it. Mila's birthday.

"I don't know what you think my phone is going to tell you," Maggie said, her first thought going to the last text she'd received from Uli twenty minutes ago.

"I see you've got a few voice mails from your buddy Grace," Debbie said, scrolling through the texts. "And oh! One from that sexy hunk of French Brie you climb into bed with every night. I do envy you that. But let's get to the good stuff, shall we?"

Maggie licked her lips. Debbie had moved her away from the door and she could see there were bars on the windows.

"Look, I was hoping we could talk, Debbie."

Where is Cheryl? Why is her purse here?

"Sure, absolutely," Debbie said, still looking at Maggie's phone. "Oh, here's a good one from...who's this? Uli Richter? Let me guess. Helga's mom? Sister? So she writes: *<Not sure you heard me say that the English girl's name was Debbie Humper>*"

Debbie looked up at Maggie. "Well done, you." She looked back at Maggie's phone. "Looks like she sent another one about ten minutes ago. *<Helga was sure this Humper girl pushed Dieter to his death. Hope this helps!>*"

Debbie smiled at Maggie.

"Germans. Aren't they just so efficient? She really wanted to make sure you got the complete picture. So do you, Maggie? Do you have the complete picture?"

"You might as well give up, Debbie. What are you going to do now? Travel to Heidelberg and kill Helga's sister too? The truth is out."

Debbie shrugged. "Is it? But that's a good idea about going to Heidelberg."

Maggie was sick that she'd suggested it.

"What have you done with Cheryl?"

Debbie followed Maggie's gaze again to Cheryl's purse. She went over to it and picked it up.

"Sloppy of me," she said. She dug Cheryl's phone out and set it on the table next to Maggie's phone. The moment she turned the knife around, Maggie nearly rushed her. But she could see the knife was heavy and very sharp. She might reach her in time but there would be a battle with a wicked, deadly knife between them. Instead, she waited.

Debbie brought the knife handle down hard on the first cellphone and Maggie flinched at the noise and the destruction as plastic shards flew across the room. Then Debbie smashed the other cellphone and turned to look at Maggie.

"People know where I am," Maggie said.

"As I recall your husband has you on a pretty long leash. When you have a crap marriage like I did, you notice things like that. I'm sure he knows you're out somewhere. Maybe even in Aix. But I'd be willing to bet he doesn't think you're here with me. Why would he? Cheryl just got through telling me that you thought *she* killed Helga. *And* Geoff." Debbie laughed and shook her head.

Maggie's mouth went dry at Debbie's cold-blooded recitation of the facts.

"So you did see Cheryl tonight," Maggie said.

"I did. Keep your hands where I can see them and I'll tell you what happened to Helga. Honestly, if you thought *Cheryl* killed Helga, you really didn't have a clue, did you?" Debbie waved to the pieces of electronic debris on the floor. "For all your so-called research."

Maggie edged over to the bed and sat down, her eyes scanning the dresser top for anything she might use as a weapon.

Debbie leaned against the dresser and observed Maggie before speaking. She held the knife loosely in one hand but Maggie wasn't fooled. She knew how quickly the knife could be raised up against her.

"The night before we went to your place for dinner," Debbie said, "Geoff, Bertie, Marie-France, Cheryl and I all met for dinner at *Nino's* and I happened to comment on the worry stone Cheryl kept rubbing. The woman is a total basket case if you haven't noticed. I was only trying to be polite but she actually gave it to me and said she had more. I put it in my jacket pocket intending to throw it out later but I forgot about it and —wouldn't you know it?—I discovered later that my pocket had a hole in it."

"She gave you the Karma stone," Maggie said, envisioning the stone falling out of Debbie's pocket in the vineyard that night.

"Spare me the irony. Anyway, Cheryl came here tonight raving about the stone she'd given me and how it had been found next to Helga's body. Really tiresome."

Of course! When Maggie had told Cheryl about the karma stone today, Cheryl must have realized then that it was Debbie who killed Helga.

"Where is Cheryl now?" Maggie asked.

"You're really stuck on that, aren't you? I didn't kill her if that's what you're thinking. She went back to her room."

"Without her purse?"

"Apparently. She was rather distraught when she left."

Maggie saw that Debbie appeared to becoming a little agitated herself and Maggie didn't know how much longer the conversation could go on before a knife fight was in her future. There was no way she could get to the door, get the chain off and get out before the knife was in her back.

Was there another way?

"You killed Helga because she was blackmailing you about Dieter's death, right?" Maggie asked.

"Aren't you clever?" Debbie made a face and a nerve twitched over her right eye.

"My question is why now? Dieter's death was twenty years ago."

"Geoff and I ran into Helga at a cupcake conference in London last spring. Even with my married name, Helga recognized me and I guess she saw an opportunity."

"So the night of the scavenger hunt you slipped out of the house, found Helga, used your husband's cake dart to kill her and ran back."

"Pretty slick, huh? Especially since as it turned out practically everyone in the vineyard that night tripped over Helga's body," Debbie laughed. "Bertie must have shown up right after I did the deed because Geoff told me he found him staring at the body and when he yelled out his name, Bertie ran off! So Geoff assumed *Bertie* killed her."

"So Geoff wasn't in on the murder with you?"

Debbie snorted. "Please. My husband had the imagination of a penne noodle."

"What was the point of the bird?"

"Absolutely none except possibly to confuse the cops. I had a small bird keychain I'd bought at the Nice airport. I just pulled off the chain. Because I wasn't a suspect, they didn't take my DNA. If they had, they'd have found the bird coated with it."

"And then Sybil was arrested for the murder."

"Is this the part where I'm supposed to feel guilty?" Debbie laughed. "No, the only bad part of the whole thing was when my dunce of a husband went to Bertie and told him to make sure he won the contest or he'd tell the cops he saw Bertie leaning over Helga's body."

"But Bertrand didn't kill Helga."

"No, but I imagine he figured just being arrested on suspicion of it would kill his magazine before it was even born. Plus, as I later found out from a drunken confession he made to me, Bertie had written a few dodgy emails to Helga that wouldn't go down well. Honestly, he might not have gotten off. More than one person has gone to prison purely on circumstantial evidence. In any case he decided to take the easy route. I don't know how he did it although I'm sure it wouldn't have been that hard but he somehow poisoned Marie-France and then sabotaged Cheryl's ingredients."

"But Geoff didn't win."

"It didn't occur to Bertie to mess with the kid! After all, Geoff was a professional pastry chef for God's sake! Bertie must have assumed Geoff could beat a kid home baker. I got such a good laugh out of that."

"And when Geoff didn't win, he went back to Bertrand and raised the stakes?"

"Have I mentioned how much I hate blackmailers? Geoff told me what he was going to do and I'd had just about enough. The more he meddled, the more he was going to get the attention of the police."

"And he still didn't know that *you* were the one who killed Helga?"

"Not a clue. I'm telling you I married a total idiot. But one thing was sure, if I let things go on the way they were *someone* was going to blab the wrong thing. My idiot husband couldn't just let it alone and let the stupid baker's wife take the rap. No, he had to get his payday out of it. It's thanks to him it ended the way it did."

"By that you mean you killing him?"

"Haven't you heard? It was suicide."

"Except the cops know now he was murdered."

Debbie frowned. It was the first time since Maggie had walked in where she didn't look completely sure of herself.

"You're lying."

"Turns out you can't place a weapon in a dead person's hand. The grip doesn't line up right."

"Well, that's annoying. But it doesn't matter. They're not looking in my direction."

"Not yet. But now that it's murder, the spouse is usually on a pretty short list. So how did you do it?"

"I let the moron think he was meeting me for a canoodle in the woods. Can you imagine? It's forty degrees outside! He met me in the woods, I killed him, planted the knife and ran back to the *gîte*, nobody the wiser."

"Except Grace saw you leave."

"No, petal, she saw *Cheryl* leave." Debbie said with a smile.

"Because you were wearing Cheryl's jacket."

"Is any of this making you feel better?" Debbie asked.

"I don't understand why you didn't just take your chances with the law. You were a kid at the time of Dieter Schmidt's death. I'm sure the evidence is either gone or would have been your word against Helga's."

"It's all so clear in hindsight, isn't it?"

"What are you going to do now?" Maggie didn't know what made her ask. It was the last thing she wanted to know. Her heartbeat was racing, nearly exploding in her chest.

"I think you know what I'm going to do. I realize we aren't exactly close but I'm still rather sorry about having to do it."

Even in the cold room, Maggie felt a steady line of perspiration crawl down her back.

"Do you really think the cops won't think it suspicious that *three* people died around you in the space of a week?" Maggie asked. "*Four* if you've hurt Cheryl too."

"Just between you and me I've decided French cops are not very smart."

"Listen, Debbie, everything up to now can have a plausible explanation for why it happened," Maggie said. "Even Helga's murder."

"You must be joking." But there was something in Debbie's eye that wanted to believe what Maggie was saying. "How?"

Maggie licked her lips.

"Since Geoff was the second person on the murder scene after Bertie and since his prints were on the murder weapon, he's the prime suspect. And since he's dead, he can't defend himself."

"What about Bertie? He can testify that he was there before Geoff."

"Yes, but why would he? Just the fact that he was there before Geoff puts *him* in the cops' crosshairs. Plus, as you said, he has motive and evidence on his phone that he tried to pay Helga not to come."

"And Geoff's murder?" Debbie asked with a frown.

"You can always say you killed him in self-defense."

Debbie's grip shifted on the knife. Her eyes tracked the room as if she were trying to digest what Maggie was telling her.

"There's just one problem with all of this," Debbie said.

"And that is?"

"*You* know the truth," Debbie said, her eyes boring into Maggie's. "What's to stop you from telling the cops the truth?"

"I only started investigating this murder because Sybil was being held for it. Now that she's free and I understand why you did what you did, I won't say anything."

"Why should I trust you?"

"I have no reason to speak against you. All I ever wanted was for Sybil not to pay for a crime she didn't commit."

Debbie glanced around the room and bit her lip as if trying to make up her mind about something.

"Come with me to the cops," Maggie said gently, trying not to look at the knife in Debbie's hand. "Tell them you fought with Geoff and to protect yourself you were forced to kill him. You can tell them *he* confessed to killing Helga and was afraid you knew too much."

Debbie looked at Maggie with hope and longing etched across her face.

"Do...do you think they'll believe me?"

"I do. I think they'll want to believe Helga's killer has paid for his crime. And in Geoff's case, that would be true."

"And you'll stand by me when I talk to the police?"

"I promise. We can go there right now."

The tension seemed to release from Debbie's shoulders as the knife in her hand sagged. She walked over to Maggie.

"I'm trusting you," she said, her bottom lip trembling. Then she handed the knife to her, handle first.

"It's going to be okay, Debbie," Maggie said, relief spilling out of her as she felt the heft of the big knife in her hand. She slipped it into her coat pocket.

They walked to the door and Debbie picked up her jacket and her purse and turned to look back at the room.

"I honestly don't think I've ever felt so exhausted in my entire life," Debbie said. "When this is over I'm going to sleep for a month."

"You've been carrying a terrible burden."

"You don't think they'll arrest me tonight, do you?"

"No. I'm sure they won't."

The relief across Debbie's face was evident as she turned and walked ahead of Maggie to the door. Once outside in the hall, Debbie let out a long sigh. They walked to the elevator and Maggie reached out to pull open the elevator door.

All of a sudden, Debbie took a step back.

"These tiny elevators freak me out," she said. "We'll need to take the stairs." She motioned to a door next to the elevator that Maggie hadn't seen before.

"Do you mind?" Debbie asked, her brows knit together as she regarded Maggie.

"No, that's fine," Maggie said. She moved past Debbie and pulled open the door. It was an old wooden door and obviously not used much. As soon as she got the door open there was a blast of mustiness and rot that spiraled upward toward her. She fumbled blindly for the light switch. Not finding it, she took a step closer and tried to peer into the darkness.

Suddenly she felt Debbie's hands slam into her back.

She pitched forward, her hands scrambling to find purchase in the narrow space. Instead of steps, her feet found nothing. She flailed frantically on the lip of the chute and then lost her balance and plunged down the long dark shaft.

62

Maggie hit the side of the narrow wooden shaft, her arms desperately wind-milling to grab for anything in the space.

Her hands found a rope cable but were too slick with sweat to hold on. She slid down the rope, her hands burning all the way down but she was too terrified to let go.

Pain thundered through her as she landed on top of a soft mound at the bottom of the shaft. The impact knocked the cable from her grip.

She grabbed for the rope again, ignoring the fire in her burning hands, and pulled herself to her feet, craning her neck to look upward.

Her first impulse was to scream but if Debbie believed she survived the fall, she might do something worse to ensure Maggie was finished her off.

A reluctant groan escaped Maggie as her knees gave way and she sat down hard on the soft mound beneath her. Immediately, she felt its warmth.

With a shriek, she jumped up and pressed her back against the shaft wall.

Whimpering but determined not to let her panic totally control her, Maggie leaned toward the soft mound, her heels pressed onto the two-inch rim that circled the shaft.

"Help me." A small strained voice near Maggie's feet.

"Cheryl?" Maggie said in a horrified whisper as she frantically dug into her coat pocket for her flashlight. She flicked it on and saw that she stood in a rusted narrow shaft surrounding a wooden platform.

Cheryl lay on her side, no coat on. One leg was bent unnaturally underneath her, and her arms were cradling her chest. Cheryl's body was on a slant.

Dear God! Maggie had landed on her when she fell!

Maggie knelt next to Cheryl.

"Help me," Cheryl said again her voice even weaker than before.

"I will, sweetie," Maggie said. "Where...where does it hurt the most?"

Maggie gently touched Cheryl's arm and the woman moaned hoarsely. Maggie licked her lips. What was the point of examining her further? Whether she had two broken legs or one Maggie could do nothing for her.

"Hang on, Cheryl," Maggie said. "We're going to get out of here." She played the light from her flashlight upward and saw what she thought was the hotel floor she'd fallen from. It was around thirty feet overhead.

She shined the light on the walls, looking for a trapdoor or conduit—anything that might allow an escape. But there was nothing. She looked again at the platform they were on and sucked in a tight breath when she realized how flimsy it was.

One wrong step or even just a good sneeze could send both of them falling to the basement.

From where Maggie knelt she could see one side of the platform was held in place by a rusting, ancient bracket. She could see no such bracket on the other side.

Because the platform was tilting.

Suddenly her flashlight beam flickered and dimmed. Before she had a chance to pray it would hold, the light went out leaving both of them in the dark.

"Maggie?" Cheryl said. "Are you there?"

"Yes, I'm here."

Maggie's teeth began to chatter in spite of her. She felt the adrenaline shoot through her system as she shrugged out of her coat, instantly feeling the cold drill into her bones. She draped the coat over Cheryl's body. The woman groaned.

"I was jealous," Cheryl said softly.

Maggie was shaking with the cold, as she listened to Cheryl's breathing become more and more regulated and she realized the woman had passed out.

Probably for the best, Maggie thought as she looked upward again although in the dark, it was impossible to see anything. Thank God she'd already checked the walls when she had a light because moving about on the platform in the dark could prove fatal for both of them. She didn't know how far they'd fall if it gave way but she was pretty sure Cheryl wouldn't survive it.

Hoping that Debbie didn't have the patience to wait this long, Maggie took in a huge breath and screamed as loudly as she could. She waited and strained to listen. There was absolutely no sound coming from above her. She filled her lungs and screamed again.

How is it nobody can hear me? she thought as she sagged against the freezing wall, her limbs shaking with the cold, her breath coming in short hitches.

As she tried to picture where she and Cheryl must be in the ancient elevator shaft, she got a sudden sickening thought that hit her with the swiftness of a razor blade slash.

Where was the elevator car? It didn't make sense that the platform they were on would be on top of the car. It only made sense if the platform was fairly close to the bottom of the shaft.

Maggie felt her bowels go to water as she realized the elevator car had to be above them.

63

Maggie didn't know how long she sat in the elevator shaft, shaking with cold and nerves. She could hear the wind whistling through the cracks in the walls and somewhere there was water dripping. The scent of wet stone and rotting vegetation filled her nostrils.

"*Allo*?"

Maggie jerked her head up at the sound of the voice.

"Hello?" Maggie called. "Is there somebody there? Help, please!"

"They are here!"

The voice seemed to hover over Maggie like a disembodied angel looking down on her.

A blinding light erupted in the space. Maggie squinted into the light, refusing to look away, and then the light beam softened and shifted to Cheryl and Maggie saw a woman suspended on a rope poised over her.

For one mad moment Maggie thought Debbie must have thrown her down the shaft too.

But no, the woman was talking on a walkie-talkie. Maggie

heard discordant crackling and voices on the other end of a radio but she couldn't make out the words.

"You are hurt, Madame?" the woman asked.

"No," Maggie said, licking her chapped lips. "But Cheryl is. I don't know how badly."

"No!" the woman on the rope bellowed and Maggie jerked back, placing her hand on the shaft wall and then recoiling as her wrist erupted in pain. "Tell them to use the damn schematic! We don't want the whole thing coming down on us! Where is Monsieur Dernier?"

Laurent? Maggie squinted at the dangling form of the woman on the rope.

Astonished, she realized that the woman was none other than Detective LaBelle.

"It's Debbie Fitzgerald!" Maggie blurted. "She threw us down here! She is the one who killed—"

"Yes, Madame," Detective LaBelle said. "She is in custody. Now if you will kindly shut up so I may converse with my team?"

Maggie slumped against the wall in relief.

Within seconds, Detective LaBelle was standing over Cheryl, balancing her feet on the rim that ran around the shaft, careful not to step onto the platform. She craned her head to look up.

"Just drop it!" she shouted into the walkie-talkie before jamming the device into her coat pocket.

Maggie saw a silver cloud float down into the shaft before being snagged by the detective.

"Can you stand, Madame?"

At first Maggie thought the detective was talking to Cheryl but she quickly realized nobody in their right mind would ask such a stupid question.

"Yes," she said, not at all sure if it was true.

"I am going to step onto the platform to examine Madame Barker but to be safe I will need you to stand on the ledge as I am doing. Do you see?" She shined her flashlight beam on her feet.

Maggie unstretched her cramped legs and tried to stand but the cold and the inactivity had frozen them. When she tried to move, she realized she'd hurt her ankle too. Pain shot up to her knees and radiated back down to her foot.

"I...I don't think I can," Maggie said.

"Never mind," LaBelle said. "There is a handle one meter from your head. Do you see it?"

Maggie turned and noticed a rusted protuberance. Was it a door or hatch of some kind? How had she missed it before?

"I see it."

"Grab it in case the platform gives way."

Maggie gripped the handle with her good hand and watched as the detective stepped gingerly onto the platform. It groaned and tipped sharply. Maggie held her breath as LaBelle stripped away her coat and lay the emergency foil blanket over Cheryl. She knelt by her for a moment, checking her pulse.

"Where is the elevator car?" Maggie asked, between chattering teeth.

LaBelle tossed her the coat.

"On one of the upper floors presumably," LaBelle said.

Maggie shakily pulled on her coat. Her fingers were frozen and stiff and it took her several long seconds to get the coat on. There was no way she could button it. A second later Maggie heard the sounds of some kind of drilling equipment on the other side of the narrow shaft.

"What's happening? Is my husband here?"

LaBelle pulled out the walkie-walkie again.

"We need the brace first," LaBelle said. "Can you tell how far down we are?"

The voice came crackling from her radio, "You are nearly ten meters down. We have sent someone to get a heavier support bolster."

"Well, hurry," LaBelle said testily and then switched off the radio. "Yes, he's here," she said to Maggie. "This is not the main elevator shaft. It was used decades ago. When they built the new one they sealed this one up."

"Except they didn't," Maggie said burrowing deeper into her coat, her ankle and her wrist now throbbing in dull unison.

"It seems Madame Fitzgerald discovered from the desk clerk that access to the old shaft existed."

So they had never been in danger of one of the elevator cars pummeling them to dust.

Just of never being found.

Maggie pushed her hands into her pocket for warmth and felt the knife in her pocket.

"How did you know it was Debbie?" Maggie asked.

LaBelle gave a short harsh laugh.

"We didn't. We were looking for Cheryl Barker because your husband said you were convinced *she* killed Frau Richter so we were hoping to find you with her. We ran into Bertrand Glenn and Marie-France Babin who told us Cheryl was with Deborah Fitzgerald. We came to the Hôtel Dauphin to see Mrs. Fitzgerald to ask her if she had seen you or Cheryl and she made a full and unexpected confession."

Maggie was stunned. "I guess she thought you were coming to arrest her."

"*C'est ça.* So she confessed everything. When she realized that we hadn't suspected her for any of the murders, she stopped talking until she could speak to her lawyer."

The sounds of the electronic equipment had gotten louder and more insistent, making further conversation impossible. Maggie felt the vibration of the drilling from the other side of the shaft through her shoulder where she leaned against the shaft wall, when a large section of the wall suddenly disappeared.

"About time," LaBelle muttered, shifting her stance back to the shaft ledge.

Laurent was the first one up the ladder. He shone the beam of his flashlight around the space until it rested on Maggie.

"Take her first," LaBelle said. "This platform is going to come down any minute."

"Don't move," Laurent said to Maggie before reaching out across the shaft and grabbing her by the shoulder. "I have you. Crawl to me. Slowly."

Maggie focused on inching her way toward Laurent. She kept one knee on the platform—and it tilted crazily when she put weight on it—and the other knee partially on the metal ledge. When she reached him, he took her firmly under the arms and pulled her against his chest where he stood on the ladder. He moved down the ladder with her in his arms and stepped away so the EMT personnel could scramble up with a portable stretcher.

Laurent sat Maggie down on a wooden bench and ran his hands gently down her arms and legs.

"Sprained ankle," Maggie said. "And maybe my wrist."

Laurent gingerly picked up her hand.

"From the fall?"

Maggie nodded. She realized that tears were streaking down her cheeks.

"I'm sorry, Laurent," she said, her chest aching with emotion.

"I know. It's all right. You're safe."

"How did you find us?" She had heard LaBelle's story but she needed to hear it from Laurent. "How did you know to come looking for me?"

Laurent picked her up in his arms and made his way through the small scrum of police and hospital personnel toward the exit.

"It is lucky for you that Grace does not lie as well as you do," he said.

64

The next morning at Domaine Saint-Buvard, Maggie was drinking a cup of coffee. The buttered toast drizzled with lavender honey which Laurent had prepared for her sat on the dish uneaten.

Laurent had taken her directly from the hotel to the emergency department in Aix where her wrist and ankle were wrapped. She'd waved off the pain medication and had fallen asleep on the ride home, overcome with exhaustion.

Laurent had taken the children to school this morning and returned before Maggie woke up. She heard him now in his office.

January was not a busy time of year for him as far as the vineyard was concerned. The harvest was long done and it was too early for pruning or the general field maintenance that would busy him as they got closer to spring.

But he was still a hands-on landlord to the tenants in his six mini houses on the perimeter of his land.

Maggie heard her cellphone vibrating and hobbled over to the easy chair in the dining room where she found it in the cushions.

It was Grace.

"Hey," Maggie said.

"In my defense," Grace said without greeting, "Laurent knew as soon as we walked in the house that you were up to something. Sorry, darling."

"It's all right." Maggie eased herself into the chair. Her foot was throbbing and she was having serious second thoughts about not taking the pain meds offered last night.

"And since he was determined to haul off to Aix with guns blazing," Grace said, "I went ahead and filled him in on how I'd seen Cheryl go after Geoff that day. Honestly I don't know who he was madder at, you or me."

"Trust me, it's me."

"I'm just so glad everything turned out the way it did," Grace said.

"How's Cheryl?"

Maggie knew from the texts she'd exchanged with Grace last night that Cheryl had been taken to Aix hospital with a broken arm.

"She'll heal," Grace said. "I'm going over there later today. Can Laurent pick up Zouzou from school? Danielle is having one of her ladies-who-lunch meetings."

"Wow. Life goes on, doesn't it? I'm sure that's fine."

"That must have been quite a shock when you saw Detective LaBelle rappelling down to your rescue."

"I was never so glad to see anyone in my life."

"I'll bet. So tell me what happened," Grace said. "How did it all go down?"

Maggie didn't feel great about getting into the details about last night. She hurt everywhere and had discovered a lump on her forehead from the fall, not to mention the smack on the head that Cheryl had dealt her earlier in the day was starting to bother her too.

"He called Detective LaBelle," Maggie said. "She met him

and they went to the Hôtel Dauphin where they thought Cheryl was and ran into Bertrand and Marie-France who hadn't seen me but had seen Debbie and Cheryl together."

"At this point they still didn't know that Debbie was Helga's murderer?"

"No. They were looking for me by way of Cheryl. But by then I'd pieced together that the killer wasn't Cheryl," Maggie said.

"Why didn't you call and tell us?"

"I figured I'd already cried wolf too many times. Who would believe me if I now said the murderer was Debbie? The last time I saw you I was convinced that *Cheryl* was the killer."

"So you went to confront Debbie?"

"I had to! Cheryl and Debbie both knew Helga from years ago. After I'd accused Cheryl of killing Helga, there was no way she wasn't going straight to Debbie. When I told her the karma stone had been found by Helga's body Cheryl knew immediately Helga's killer had to be Debbie since she'd given Debbie the stone."

"So how did the cops nab Debbie?"

"They were just hoping to ask her some questions but she thought the jig was up and blurted out that killing Geoff wasn't her fault or something to that effect."

"I'll bet that got Detective LaBelle's attention."

"Yes, except, unfortunately, when Debbie realized she'd jumped the gun, she was so mad at herself that she refused to say any more. If it hadn't been for Laurent, I'm not sure we'd have been found yet."

Maggie shivered at the thought.

"How did you get found?" Grace asked. "The ER doctor said if Cheryl had been left down there another hour she would've died."

"Laurent saw my busted-up cellphone in Debbie's room and since Debbie wasn't talking, he went to the desk clerk to ask for a map of the building. He figured Debbie hadn't had time to leave the hotel with us. Turns out the old guy had talked with Debbie when she complained about the elevator feeling dangerous to her. He mentioned the second defunct elevator chute."

"So the cops knew roughly where the two of you were."

"*Roughly* being the operative word. The ancient elevator shaft hadn't been used since the turn of the century. I'm not kidding. That's where I hit my ankle and my wrist on the way down. But the worst of it was that once past that bend, no sound carried upward. I screamed my head off and heard nothing. Speaking of Cheryl, have you talked to her yet?"

"Briefly on the phone this morning. Why?"

"Did she give any explanation why she hit me?"

"She feels terrible about that. She was just upset about what you told her. She realized it had to mean that Debbie had killed Helga and all she could think of was getting to the hotel to confront Debbie."

"Stupid."

"You know how ironic that sounds coming from you, right?"

"Yeah, yeah," Maggie said. She turned to see Laurent standing in the door of the dining room with his arms across his chest. The children were all at school. The house was empty. He was waiting for her and she couldn't put it off any longer.

"I need to go, Grace," she said. "Laurent wants a word."

"Oh, darling, stiff upper! You know he loves you. And you know you deserve whatever he's going to deal out."

"I know. I'll talk to you later."

Maggie hung up and turned to face Laurent and the inevitable music.

～

Maggie limped over to the table and sat down, determined to hear his completely justified anger without excuses.

"You lied to me," he said, his face implacable except for a barely perceptible pulsing vein over his eye.

"I'm sorry," Maggie said. "Truly."

"That's it? That is all you have to say?"

Maggie licked her lips. "I'm very *very* sorry. I wish I hadn't had to do that."

He cracked his knuckles and glared at her.

"Oh, so you still believe you had to do it?"

"No, Laurent. I have no excuse."

"And if you had it all to do over again?"

When Maggie hesitated, Laurent kicked the dining chair in front of him. Always before he was measured and even circumspect with her, but Maggie knew he had a temper and had seen evidence of it many times before.

With other people.

"We have had this conversation before, yes?" he said. "More than once. Only then it was *you* demanding complete honestly from *me*."

"I still believe in complete honesty. I do."

"When the time is right."

"Laurent, you have every right to be angry."

"I do not need you to justify my right to be angry! Can I no longer trust you? If you find a reason that outweighs the need to tell me the truth—"

"You're right! I did think that...which was incredibly arrogant. You're absolutely right."

"You think you are saying words I want to hear."

"Well, I can't go back in time! I can't erase what I did! I knew if I told you that Cheryl had attacked me and that I was going after her you would try to stop me."

"*Absoluement.*"

"I'm sorry, Laurent, but I felt strongly that Cheryl's attacking me—especially since there was no long-term damage done—"

"That we know of."

The ER doctor had said there were possible signs of a concussion. Laurent had been in the room when he'd said it.

"Okay, but I was so close I couldn't stop just yet! You and I had just had a big ugly conversation about Cheryl where you told me I was jealous of her and my judgement was impaired."

Laurent came to stand close to her. Maggie felt a flinch of discomfort from the near presence of the man who normally only generated comfort and security in her. She wasn't afraid of him but she wasn't pleased he would try to use his size to intimidate her.

"Step back, please," she said calmly. "I know you're frustrated and I know you're angry."

"Yes, Maggie. I am. I am angry at your insistence that you needed to lie to me."

"No, I didn't *need* to lie to you," Maggie said with a sigh, the dull ache in her ankle and wrist now intensifying the more frustrated she got. She was tempted to take his hand but was pretty sure he wasn't ready for that. "I admit I *chose* to do that. What can I do to...?"

"To earn my trust back?" He snorted and crossed his arms again.

"Oh, come on, Laurent. I know it's bad but if I can remind you *you've* done worse."

"And I swore to you that I never would again. I assumed I would not need to extract the same vow from you. Clearly, my assumption was ill-founded."

"Doesn't the fact that I took such a chance with your trust in me—something I hold precious—doesn't that indicate how critical I thought the situation was?"

"Again, you are rationalizing what you did. You are saying that lying is acceptable under certain circumstances."

"No, I'm not saying that!"

Except of course it was true.

"I'm saying *I'm sorry*. I made a mistake."

His face closed in a way she had seen many times before. Just never at her.

"I am done," he said before turning and leaving the room.

65

Six days and nights after Debbie was arrested on two counts of murder and three days after Luc received his acceptance letter from Napa Valley College, Laurent was in the kitchen putting together a celebratory meal of *Coquilles Saint-Jacques.*

It had begun to snow heavily. The front drive and gravel parking pad flanked by the fir trees that lined the drive looked like a winter wonderland of snowbanks and dangling icicles.

Laurent checked the baking sheet of ramekins filled with the creamy scallops and mushroom mixture and glanced into the living room where Maggie, Danielle, and Grace sat with their drinks discussing Luc's big news.

It had been difficult for Maggie, Laurent knew, but she was trying hard to keep Luc from seeing how conflicted she was. Even now, she smiled proudly whenever she caught sight of Luc.

As well she should. Two years ago Luc was a teenage refugee who'd missed more school than he'd attended. Only hard work, together with his natural aptitude, had been suffi-cient to get him into Napa Valley. He'd need to enroll in a special English as a Second Language program, and if he couldn't keep up with the basic curriculum, he would be back home soon enough.

Laurent seriously doubted that Luc would have trouble keeping up.

So of course Maggie was proud of him. They were all proud of him.

That this amazing young man was Gerard's son was one of the more amazing mysteries of Laurent's life.

Nurture over nature?

Except nobody had nurtured the boy until he came to live at Domaine Saint-Buvard. Perhaps the real answer was that Luc was genetically more Laurent's than Gerard's.

"Laurent? Won't they burn?" Luc said as he came into the kitchen.

Swearing, Laurent shook himself out of his reverie and turned to the broiler to rescue the ramekins just in time.

"Don't you think it is time you called me *Papa*?" Laurent said gruffly, his back turned to Luc. "Or are you too old for that?"

There was a silence and Laurent turned to see Luc staring at his shoes, beet red.

"I'm not too old," Luc said. "It's just...the first time is the hardest."

Laurent hid a smile and grunted, turning away.

"Besides Jemmy and Mila call you *Dad*," Luc said.

"Is that what you would prefer?"

"Maybe."

Laurent set the tray of bubbling ramekins on the stovetop.

"Go and feed the dogs," Laurent said. "Then check to see that everyone in the living room has their drinks refreshed. Then you can help me bring in the *Coquilles Saint-Jacques*. Where is Jemmy?"

"Upstairs playing video games."

"Get him down here. *He* can feed the dogs."

"Okay." Luc turned and made it as far as the entranceway to the dining room.

Laurent heard him take in a long breath.

"Thanks, Dad," he said and then sprinted toward the stairs to fetch Jemmy.

Crusts of broken bread, along with bowls of tapenade, pickles and small relishes, were scattered across the table,

Maggie loved *Coquilles Saint-Jacques*—especially the way Laurent made it. The lemon and garlic seemed to temper the heavy sherry and cream. Besides *Coquilles Saint-Jacques* was a classic celebration meal in their house. It took time to cook—which Laurent did with loving attention and obvious pleasure. And because they didn't have it very often, it indicated without words that tonight's meal was special.

Maggie was sitting between Zouzou and Mila across from Luc. She tried to remember the last time she'd seen him smile so much. Twice she tried to catch Laurent's eye to share a moment with him, but he was too busy putting the meal together and ordering the children about.

It had only been a week since the near-catastrophe at the Hôtel Dauphin. Cheryl had gone back to Paris. She'd decided she was tired of living in a country where she didn't speak the language and so had applied for the London station chef position at *Eatz2*.

Marie-France and Bertrand were arrive in Brussels working together on the first issue of LUSH. And Debbie was being held in a maximum-security detention center in Nice.

Maggie's wrist had healed faster than her ankle, which had a cast on it. Laurent told the children they must fetch and carry for her—which wasn't the same as offering to do it himself, Maggie was keenly aware.

In fact the tension between Maggie and Laurent had been palpable all week and the children had all felt it. Because of her injuries, she couldn't help Laurent in the kitchen—normally a natural opportunity to connect with him. And when the household chores or errands related to the children were done, Laurent was away at the monastery or mini houses, or in the vineyard.

Anywhere but alone with Maggie.

Not for the first time during the week, Maggie noted with dismay that for the first time in her marriage, she found herself on the receiving end of his often rigid and unforgiving nature.

They still slept in the same bed but back to back and unspeaking. Maggie's overtures to him were met with grunts or words of one syllable. She knew she was in the wrong. The only thing she could do was wait him out. But as the days passed, the divide between them felt more and more permanent.

"You look tired, darling," Grace said, frowning at Maggie. "Is it your ankle? You've spent too much time on it, haven't you?"

Danielle turned to look at Maggie with concern too.

"No," Maggie said. "I'm fine. Just a little tired. But so happy."

She hadn't told either Grace or Danielle about her disconnect with Laurent.

How could this be just a blip in her otherwise ideal marriage if Danielle and Grace were reduced to asking her with concerned looks on their faces *how were things going with her and Laurent?*

And the hell of it was, there was no high road to take. She'd brought all of this on herself. And not because she was saving anyone from jail. Sybil had already been released by the time Maggie had lied to Laurent.

No, she had done it solely because she was powerless to

control her own nature. She had truly believed she was the only one who knew the truth about Cheryl, and she couldn't hand off the job to someone else who didn't see that.

Hubris, she thought sadly. *That's all it was in the end. Stupid, meaningless ego.*

She watched Laurent as he passed a basket of warmed baguette pieces down the table, then he turned to pick up the wine bottle. This was the moment he would normally glance at her, his eyes asking or confirming what he didn't need to bother saying with words.

Not tonight. He tapped Jemmy's wrist and the boy immediately snatched his napkin from the table and put it in his lap. Then Laurent refreshed everyone's wine glass.

Maggie kept her eyes on her own wine glass as he filled it forcing herself not to look at his face, not to see him deliberately refuse to look at her.

Of course he had every right to be mad. Absolutely. She'd screwed up. No question.

But on the other hand, up until last week when Laurent had turned away from her, she'd thought he not only accepted her tenacity but even appreciated it.

Now everything was changed. She no longer knew what he thought or felt about her or indeed even loved about her.

If he still did.

66

With Mila's help, Zouzou was just serving the *gâteau au chocolat à la ganache,* her competition masterpiece, while Luc showed Jemmy the leather work diary that Danielle and Grace had given him as an early graduation present.

Laurent poured hot water into the French press for coffee when he heard the doorbell ring. He looked out the kitchen window and saw that Antoine's bread truck was parked at the end of the drive as if the man hadn't the courage to come all the way up to the house.

"Maggie," he called as he positioned the plunger in the coffee press.

Maggie appeared in the kitchen doorway. She leaned on a single crutch, her foot held up.

"Who is it?" she asked.

He found himself startled to see how vulnerable she looked. She was wearing her hair down to her shoulders and her eyes were large and unsure as she regarded him. She looked beautiful but fragile.

"It is Sybil and Antoine," Laurent said. "Go to the living room. I will bring them in."

She turned and hobbled away and Laurent made his way to the front door.

The baker and his wife were on the threshold with their daughter Mireille. Sybil looked like she'd lost weight. Her face was pale. Mireille stood beside her with her eyes cast down. Antoine looked tense and fidgety. He refused to look Laurent in the eye.

Until this moment, Laurent had not made up his mind as to what to do about Antoine. Suddenly, before the baker had even said a word, Laurent knew he would need to work with him. It wouldn't be easy and he certainly wouldn't expect thanks for his effort. But he couldn't let him walk away—not with Sybil and Mireille as helpless and dependent on him as they were.

"*Bonsoir*," Laurent said as he shook hands with each of them. "Come in."

"We cannot stay," Antoine said. "But we would have a word with your wife."

"She is in the salon. She would come to the door but she has an injured foot."

Sybil straightened her shoulders. She reached for Mireille's hand and moved past Antoine into the living room. Finally Antoine's and Laurent's eyes met.

"We have come to thank your wife—and you—for what you have done for my family," Antoine said stiffly.

"Of course," Laurent said.

When he and Antoine entered the living room, Sybil was sitting beside Maggie on the couch and they were holding hands.

"What a nice surprise," Maggie said to Antoine. "I wish you would join us for chocolate cake and coffee."

"*Non*, Madame Dernier," Antoine said. "*Merci*. We just wanted to thank you. As a family."

"Well, I'm just glad everything turned out all right," Maggie said, smiling.

Sybil stood up, her eyes shining. She leaned over and hugged Maggie and whispered something to her before straightening up.

As Laurent walked them to the door, Sybil grabbed his hand for just a moment. Laurent stepped outside and watched them walk down the driveway together.

Just then, his phone vibrated in his hip pocket. He dug it out and glanced at the screen before answering.

"*Oui?*"

"Ah, Laurent," Detective LaBelle said briskly into the phone. "All is well, I trust?"

"Yes. We are having a celebration dinner for my older son who was just accepted into viticulture studies in California."

"I am sure you are very proud. Do you have time tomorrow to attend to a delicate matter?"

Laurent felt a sudden desire for a cigarette.

"Where?"

"At *l'Abbaye de Sainte-Trinité*. One of the refugee children was caught stealing music CDs at Monoprix tonight. Frère Jean insists she has never stolen before. But she is very young. Only twelve."

"Where is she now?"

"We have released her to Frère Jean's care. Will you work with him? He is expecting you tomorrow morning."

"Was my involvement a provision of the girl's release?"

"Partly. So will you?"

"I have not worked with girls before."

"They are just like lost boys," LaBelle said briskly. "Only with longer hair."

After agreeing to meet with Frère Jean and the girl in the morning, Laurent disconnected and turned around to see Danielle standing on the front steps. She looked beautiful in her ivory wool wrap coat as she stared up at the sky. It was still lightly snowing.

He stood beside her.

"I know you don't smoke, Danielle," he said. "And it is too cold to be stargazing."

"Something is the matter with Maggie," Danielle said, her eyes on the night sky.

"She has a sprained ankle," Laurent said blankly.

Danielle turned her eyes on him and regarded him balefully.

"I think you know what I mean," she said. A moment of silence passed between them.

Danielle rubbed her hands down her arms.

"Did you ever tell Maggie where you were the night she was in Heidelberg?" she asked.

Laurent let out a long sigh. Danielle was famous for having her say and it was just as well to let her say it rather than try to distract or dissuade her.

"Maggie is on the back foot with you, Laurent. She won't feel she can ask you about it. But you need to tell her."

"It was not a rendezvous if that's what you're thinking," Laurent said.

"I'm not thinking anything at all. But I am not your wife. It is still something you're keeping from her."

Laurent sighed again.

"You are making something of nothing," he said. "I knew Margaux LaBelle many years ago."

"Oh? She doesn't look that old."

"She was a child at the time. I was friends with her brother."

"Ah. I see. Does this brother have a sad story?"

"He's in prison outside Lyon. That is where I went the day Maggie was in Heidelberg. For years he has refused to see his sister. Margaux asked if I would talk to him."

"Did it work?"

"Sadly, no. He has been in prison a long time. He killed a man and is bitterly ashamed. But I told her I would try."

"So the detective doesn't hold your own criminal background against you?"

"I think she still sees me as the man she used to know when she was a little girl. Perhaps she even thinks I am the man her brother could have been if he had taken a different path."

"Perhaps her brother will come around?"

"Perhaps."

"You must tell Maggie about the detective's brother and your connection to Detective LaBelle. There have already been enough secrets between you and Maggie, don't you think?"

When Laurent again didn't respond, Danielle huffed out a breath in frustration.

"I am not saying Maggie wasn't wrong to lie to you," she said, the agitation evident in her voice. "But she's admitted that. I think you are having trouble forgiving her because of the fear you felt that night when you thought you'd lost her."

He scrubbed an agitated hand over his face and through his hair.

"When I saw her broken cellphone, Danielle, I knew that something terrible had happened to her."

"I know, *chérie*. I know." Danielle slipped her arms through Laurent's. "But your wife is not a doll you can program to stay safe or act the way you want. She is an original, is our Maggie. And honestly, would you really have her any other way?"

"I find lately I am rethinking many things I thought I wanted."

"Fair enough. But as you rethink these things I would ask you to remember one thing, Laurent."

"Yes?"

"I would ask you to remember how you felt when you

thought you had lost her. And also to realize how lucky you are to have felt it."

Laurent snorted and glanced at her with a frown.

"Yes, very lucky, *chérie*," Danielle said. "Because that feeling of fear and helplessness is the price of love."

67

Maggie watched the snow come down outside her bedroom window for a few moments before turning and climbing into bed. Laurent was still letting the dogs out for the night and locking up the house.

She pulled out her lavender lotion and then hesitated. Tears had unexpectedly gathered in her eyes. She put the cream tubes away and felt a longing to have her little dog Petit-Four with her in bed tonight.

Of all the nights that she and Laurent were disconnected—and there had been very few of those over the years—tonight of all nights she missed their being able to confer over their thoughts and feelings of Luc's success. Only Laurent truly understood how it felt to love a child with her and to delight in his achievements and still feel sad about that child leaving.

And right now Laurent was not available to share that with her.

The night had been perfect, with the glittering candlelight on the table, the delicious *Coquilles Saint-Jacques* that all four of the children equated with celebration and special occasions, and the love they all showered upon Luc.

Maggie had never seen Luc smile so continuously. The fear was gone—at least for now. Tonight had only been about basking in the congratulations and pride of his adopted family. Luc had turned his life around. So many times tonight Maggie had wanted to ask him, *Two years ago, could you ever have imagined this night was waiting for you?*

And some night in the not too distant future she and Laurent would have this night all over again for Jemmy and then for Mila.

Maggie quickly wiped away her tears as the bedroom door opened and Laurent came in.

Laurent glanced at her in bed and then snapped his fingers. Both dogs ran to their beds and settled down.

"Luc was so excited tonight," Maggie said. "It's still seven months away but he acts like he's ready to go now."

Laurent grunted and pulled off his pullover. He'd left his jacket downstairs but Maggie could see snowflakes still clung to his dark hair. He went into the bathroom and she heard the shower go on.

She pulled her basket of lotions onto her lap, selected a tube and carefully squeezed out a dollop on each knee and massaged them into her legs.

Even lonely, divorced women probably need to keep their knees from chapping, she thought miserably. She admonished herself for the thought and then turned to the novel she was reading.

After a few minutes Laurent came out of the bathroom toweling his hair. He pulled on pajama bottoms and sat on the bed with his back to her as he wound the clock on his bedside table.

Maggie watched him and wondered sadly if this really was the way things were going to be from now on.

"Next time it'll be Jemmy and then Mila packing their bags to go," she said.

And then you can leave me without upsetting the children too badly.

"Yes, but that is the way of things," he said.

Maggie perked up, taking the fact that he was at least talking to her as a good sign.

"And that doesn't make you sad?" she asked.

He turned to glance at her.

"That this chapter is ending for Luc and a new one is beginning? *Non.*"

"You French are so philosophical."

"And you Americans are so dramatic. Luc is not dying. You still have him."

Maggie found herself fighting back tears again. She turned off her bedside lamp to hide her emotion. Laurent stood up and walked around to her side of the bed and sat down.

"But more importantly," he said, "you still have me, *chérie.*" He leaned over her and lifted her chin with his fingers and looked into her eyes.

"Do I?" she whispered as the book she'd been holding fell to the carpeted floor.

Without thinking, she wrapped her arms around his neck and lay her head on his chest, a warmth radiating throughout her body.

"I am sorry for my behavior this week," he said. "Danielle was right."

Maggie lifted her head. "Danielle?"

"She made me see it was not really the lie that I was angry about," he said.

Maggie widened her eyes in surprise.

"Do not misunderstand. I am still very annoyed," he said with a frown.

"So if it wasn't the lie then why were you so angry?"

He touched her cheek and his expression softened.

"You are not the only one who fears losing someone you love."

Laurent kissed her and then pulled a tendril of hair from behind her ear.

"What did Sybil whisper to you tonight?" he asked.

Maggie settled in his arms.

"She said I had a friend for life in her. I've decided I need to do a better job of being a real friend to her. I'm pretty sure she needs one."

Laurent nodded. "That is a good idea, *chérie*. I have come to a similar belief about her husband. Although in my case perhaps less of a friend than a warden."

Maggie kissed him and cupped his cheek with her hand.

"I am so sorry, Laurent."

"No more apologies. We are both sorry. We will both do better and we will still both make mistakes. But I promise I will never turn away from you again. Not for a week. Not for an hour."

"Oh, Laurent," Maggie said, her heart swelling with love and relief.

He kissed her then, tenderly at first and she wrapped her arms around his neck again and for the first time in a very long time, felt the joy of all the important pieces of her world click firmly and perfectly into place.

To follow more of Maggie's sleuthing and adventures in Provence, order **Murder in Avignon,** *Book 17 of the Maggie Newberry Mysteries!*

RECIPE FOR LAURENT'S CHOCOLATE SOUFFLÉ

There's nothing overblown about Laurent's chocolate soufflé. A favorite with the kids and his hip pocket go-to for any dinner party, this recipe is easy to make and always elegant to serve. And the taste? Trust me, Laurent would never let you down with this standard classic.

You'll need:
    57 g (2 oz or 4 TB) butter
    31¼ g (1.1 oz 4TB) all-purpose flour
    360 g (12 fl oz or 1.5 cup) milk
    85 g (3 oz) unsweetened baking chocolate
    133 g (4.7 oz or 2/3 cup) sugar
    4 TB (2 fl oz) hot water
    6 eggs, separated
    1 tsp (.17 fl oz) vanilla

Preheat the oven to 325° F (163° C)
    1. Melt the butter, add the flour and then, while stirring constantly, gradually add the milk.
    Cook until boiling then turn heat off.

2. In a separate pot, melt the chocolate, then add sugar and the 4 TB of hot water and stir until smooth. Combine mixtures, add well-beaten egg yolks and let cool.

3. Stir in vanilla and fold in beaten egg whites. Pour mixture into soufflé dish or small ramekins.

4. Bake for 40 minutes. Serve with whipped cream.

ABOUT THE AUTHOR

USA TODAY Bestselling Author Susan Kiernan-Lewis is the author of *The Maggie Newberry Mysteries,* the post-apocalyptic thriller series *The Irish End Games, The Mia Kazmaroff Mysteries, The Stranded in Provence Mysteries,* and *An American in Paris Mysteries.*

Visit www.susankiernanlewis.com or follow Author Susan Kiernan-Lewis on Facebook.

Printed in Great Britain
by Amazon

14289095R00198